KEEP ME CLOSE

ALSO BY ELIZABETH COLE

Honor & Roses

Choose the Sky

Raven's Rise

A Heartless Design

A Reckless Soul

A Shameless Angel

The Lady Dauntless

Beneath Sleepless Stars

A Mad and Mindless Night

Regency Rhapsody:

The Complete Collection

KEEP ME CLOSE

ELIZABETH COLE

SKYSPARK BOOKS

PHILADELPHIA, PENNSYLVANIA

SkySpark Books
Philadelphia, Pennsylvania
skysparkbooks.com
inquiry@skysparkbooks.com

Publisher's Note: This is a work of fiction. Names, characters, places, and incidents are a product of the author's imagination. Locales and public names are sometimes used for atmospheric purposes. Any resemblance to actual people, living or dead, or to businesses, companies, events, institutions, or locales is completely coincidental.

Ordering Information:
Quantity sales. Special discounts are available on quantity purchases by corporations, associations, and others. For details, contact the "Special Sales Department" at the address above.

KEEP ME CLOSE / Cole, Elizabeth. – 1st ed.
ISBN-13: 978-1-942316-28-2

Chapter 1

"GET YOUR PAWS THE HELL off me!" Dom shouted as the demon grabbed for him.

He rolled away from the thing's gigantic claws with millimeters to spare. As he regained his footing, he felt a draft and looked at the brand new rips in his t-shirt. Nope. Make that one millimeter to spare.

"Get over here," the demon hissed. Its voice penetrated Dom's skull, going through not just his ears but the ether itself, slipping into his brain and setting off a thousand whispers that echoed the demon's command.

The worst memories of his life, the ones he tried to bury deepest, suddenly surfaced as if they'd all happened yesterday. When he broke his leg. When he thought he'd hurt his little brother Mal. When his parents left for the last time. When Rachel found him. Everything combined in a swirl of emotion—guilt and pain and misery.

Dom winced, trying to shake off the attack. Unlike most humans, he'd suffered this type of assault before. He knew how to deflect the worst feelings, how to shove the memories away to be dealt with later. He really wished demons would learn to fight fair.

The demon approached Dom, confident the mortal

was paralyzed by the psychic pain hurled into his brain. Hot breath, which stank like week-old garbage, blasted Dom's face. Just as the demon reached out for him, Dom moved. Gripping his favorite demon-fighting knife, he slashed sideways, aiming to sever the sinewy, oversized forearm.

The blade hit the flesh with a sizzle. The demon roared and pulled back. Dom could see the wound briefly drip dark blood. Then the flesh sealed up again, healing within moments.

The demon roared with laughter, a huge, dark sound that reverberated through the humid air. With narrowed eyes, it looked at Dom and the knife he held, then growled.

"You're a supernasty I don't need to run into again," Dom muttered, pulling something from his pocket.

He hurled a little, paper-wrapped object at the demon. It detonated at the thing's ugly feet, causing smoke to furl up.

Expecting something more than a smoke bomb, the demon sprang away and waved its arms to diffuse the grey cloud.

Using the few seconds of distraction, Dom reached into his pocket again and pulled out a vial of salt—a simple but very useful tool against many creatures from the otherworlds. He bit off the cap and spilled the salt into his palm.

He dragged the blade of his knife through the salt, coating the silver surface with tiny white crystals.

Just in time. The demon hurtled out of the smoke, its arms held out wide, claws splayed for maximum slashing—a pose that left its torso completely exposed.

Instead of running away, Dom lunged forward, knife

held steady. The blade connected, creating a deep slash in the middle of the thing's scaly hide. The blessed salt worked with the enchantments on the blade to form a bond that cut through even a creature from the roughest neighborhood in the otherworlds. The demon's shriek pierced Dom's skull. He knew the sound was mostly echoing in the otherworlds. Most folks in the real world wouldn't hear it at all, and if they did, they'd mistake it for a police siren.

But Dom couldn't ignore it, and he winced at the instant headache the unholy scream brought pulsing between his ears.

The monster regarded him in disbelief. These creatures assumed that all humans were easy prey. Dom was happy to prove them wrong, one by one.

"You are bound," Dom managed to gasp out past the pain in his head. "Bound by blood and salt. Flesh and earth." As he recovered his breath, his voice strengthened. Dom held up the bloody knife blade. He took a moment, picturing the spell he wanted to work in his mind. He needed to keep the demon from slipping away into the otherworlds. The binding of blood and salt would hold only so long. He needed a more permanent solution.

Solution.

He dumped the remaining salt into a water bottle and muttered in Latin, "Let the sea that gives life take life back. Let this be the sea inside."

The water in the bottle didn't change appearance, but a wave of intense force rolled over Dom, as if the power of a strong tide invaded the space they'd been fighting in.

The demon snarled, straining against the quick spell contained in Dom's knife cut. It writhed, the vicious claws flexing instinctively as it prepared to wrest itself free and pound on Dom.

"I'll cut your skin into slivers and make you watch while I eat them," it hissed. Flames dripped from its mouth as it spoke.

"Sure you will," said Dom.

"Watch me! I can—"

Perfect. A big mouth. Timing it right, Dom flung the contents of the water bottle directly into the demon's open gullet. The salt water hissed and steamed when it hit the hot flesh of the demon.

"Let the tide rise," Dom said in Latin.

The creature looked surprised, then sick. It started spitting a mixture of oily goo and salty water onto the ground, but something was happening inside of it, something it couldn't stop.

It clawed at its stomach, forming deep gauges. Pink, brackish water leaked out, and the monster began to gasp like a fish drowning in the air.

Dom kept his knife tight in his right hand, but he knew the final spell worked. The creature was drowning, trapped in an environment that was particularly nasty to its kind. The salt of the earth prevented it from escaping to its home in the infernal otherworlds, and the magically summoned water was the element opposite its own fire.

Dom watched as the demon kept fighting to breathe, to escape the ocean inside it. It wasn't strong enough, though, and finally succumbed to the lethal combination of salt and water. It seemed to crumple, looking like a piece of trash floating in a shifting mass of water.

"Carry the remains to the sea," Dom murmured, once again in Latin. "And then be free."

The elemental force he'd summoned immediately seeped lower, below the surface, into the earth itself.

Dom should have guessed that here in Florida, more of a swamp than a state, the fastest way to the ocean was just to sink into the lawn.

Finally, Dom stood up, his skin slick with sweat, demon ichor, and the salty water from the spell. His hands were covered in blood. Not his blood, but that didn't make him feel any better. He was dead tired. Fighting a demon tended to do that.

He muttered a prayer in Spanish, one his mother taught him years ago. "Santa Muerte, keep me close to you and on the side of the living so I can keep sending you the dead." The words helped center him, and after fighting a demon, Dom needed centering.

He pulled off his now destroyed t-shirt and used it to wipe away the blood. That's how his clients found him. Standing there in the sopping wet backyard, shirtless and bloody.

The husband, a big, tall white dude in a muscle tee, came up first, his expression awed.

The Cuban wife tried to hide a phone behind her back. She'd obviously filmed the whole thing. Dom didn't worry about it. Beings from the otherworlds had some innate ability to prevent their existence from being recorded. No one knew exactly why, but it had always been that way. Audio played back as static or garbled nonsense. Video either went black, blurry, or simply seemed to be from another scene altogether.

Dom's youngest brother, Lex, who was terrifyingly smart, theorized that demons warped space-time when they entered the real world, causing blips and strange effects. The woman could put anything she wanted up on social. No one would see the truth. And that was fine with the demon-hunters of the world. Mass panic was not a good situation.

The husband was saying, "We were watching through the window, but I'm still not sure what happened."

"I exterminated the demon that was harassing your family," Dom said. "Nasty bugger, too. Just say a sinkhole opened up in your backyard. Which is sort of what happened in the end."

The man looked fearfully out at the yard. "Where's the…"

"No body. The demon is gone," Dom reassured him. "Dead. Destroyed. You don't have to worry about it coming back."

"Are you all right?" the wife asked, gazing at Dom. He was very conscious of his sweatiness, his exposed upper body, his tattoos, and the fact that the wife didn't seem to mind at all.

"Yup. If you have some fresh water, I'll take it," he said. "Used mine up and I'm pretty thirsty."

"Sure thing," she said, apparently recovered from the demon in her home.

"Get him a shirt while you're in there," the man said pointedly.

She went off with a scowl.

"Thanks," Dom said. "If you have the money, I'll take that too."

A little while later, Dom was wearing a loose white t-shirt and had just polished off a bottle of water when his client handed over the payment in cash.

Dom counted it carefully. It looked like a lot, but he was already mentally deducting the many expenses he'd have to cover, from gas to sacred herbs harvested only when the full moon was in Scorpio. Demon hunting wasn't cheap.

The client said, "Um…how will this look to the IRS?"

"Mark the payment to Salem Associates. If anyone asks, the fee was for home improvement work."

"Home improvement?"

"Well, your home isn't inhabited by a demon now. That's an improvement, isn't it?"

"Good point."

"Thank you for your business," Dom said, sliding the folded money into his pocket.

"This won't happen again, will it?" the client asked nervously.

"Your home being plagued by a demon? Not unless you do something else that's either really unlucky or stupid. But you still live in Florida, so I can't guarantee something else bizarre won't happen to you."

"Yeah, well. Florida." The client shrugged. "Bizarre is fine. It was the way the demon kept leaving claw marks in the mirrors and walls that bothered me. That, and how it kept trying to kill us."

Dom picked up his backpack. "I'll get out of your way now."

His client trailed him to the front door. "So with a last name like Salem… Does that mean your family was around during…you know?"

"I don't really like to talk about that," Dom said with a smile. The standard line.

Her tone serious, the wife said in Spanish, "You've seen Santa Muerte's face."

"I don't really like to talk about that either," Dom said to her. He kept to English, having seen the husband's confusion when his wife spoke Spanish.

He reached for the door handle. "If you meet anybody with any other problems of a supernatural type, you've got the number. Take care."

Dom returned to the crappy motel he was staying in during the job. The window unit air conditioner pinged loudly, protesting the humid air outside. The Salems always traveled cheap. Less overhead meant more money. They needed money to make their home actually habitable.

He called his brother Malachy. "All done," he said. "And paid."

Mal said, "I knew you'd get that one taken care of fast."

"How's our house?" Dom could picture the old Victorian on the outskirts of the small midwestern town they made their home base. The brothers hadn't lived there long, and it was a dump, but Dom missed it more than he expected.

"Slowly collapsing," said Mal. "I think the roof over the back bedroom is being attacked by pigeons."

"Lily's room?"

"No, the other one with the green walls. Greenish," Mal amended.

"Oh, right. Well, lock Behemoth in there. That should sort it out." Behemoth preferred to hunt supernasties small enough to get his claws into, but he wouldn't pass up a pigeon.

"If I can lift him." His brother sighed. "How's Pie?"

Dom looked at Piewicket, the little calico cat sleeping on the motel bed. "She's fine."

"She made a big stink about going along with you. Did she help?"

"With killing the demon? No, she didn't even wake up for the appointment." Dom wasn't sure why Piewicket had been so insistent on joining him for the job. He was happy she was there. Piewicket was undeniably the sweeter cat in the Salem house. But she'd done nothing more than keep him company, just as she'd done for his whole life.

Piewicket and Behemoth were family pets…sort of. They were more family than pets. And though both cats seemed to be normal felines in every respect, they had been in the Salem family a very *long* time. Far longer than any self-respecting veterinarian would believe.

Behemoth had been a big, savage black cat when Dom was a little boy, and he was a big savage black cat now. Behemoth had been a big, savage black cat when his *grand*mother was a young girl. He just stuck around the Salems, occasionally killing, but mostly sleeping. Piewicket was more adventurous and frequently accompanied the brothers when they had to do a job, though not usually one this far from home.

"I miss Pie," Mal said. "Tell her that."

"Why? I'll be home in two days."

"Actually you won't," Mal said. "There's a new job, and it's time sensitive. A ghost is haunting a rich guy. So we need you to be a ghostbuster."

"It better not be in Florida."

"West coast, bro. You'll like it."

"I should come home anyway to resupply."

"Buy what you need out there. The client's loaded, Dom. He'll cover the costs, but he's serious about the timeline."

"Maybe he should have called earlier instead of waiting till the ghosts got out of hand."

"You know how some people need to work up the nerve to call. It takes a huge event for some to even admit this stuff is real."

"Yeah, yeah." Some people never seemed to get that until it was way too late. "Speaking of huge events, has anything happened across the street?"

The house they were now living in had previously been inhabited by an elderly relative, another Salem who fought the supernasties that plagued the world. Aunt Jo had been keeping watch on the neighboring property, because signs suggested the place was a hellhole—a magnet for demonic activity. But after her health declined last year, the brothers got the house for free when they agreed to take over watching duties. Aunt Jo had packed up for an assisted living facility, still grumbling about leaving such an important job to "the boys."

Mal snorted. "Not a thing. I don't know what the family was so worried about. This is the most boring surveillance job ever. No one goes in and no one goes out."

"You're sure?"

He could hear Mal's sigh of frustration as a crackle over the spotty connection. "Dom, I'm sure. I've been watching the place. When I'm not watching it, Lex is watching it. When neither of us can watch it, the cat watches it. We're *all* bored. Trust me, you can take this next job without peeking in on us. And we really need this paycheck."

"Okay," Dom said, still with some misgivings. Ever since their parents had died, Dom felt responsible for his younger brothers. But Mal was right. They did need the money. "Send me the details. I'll hit the road tomorrow."

"We have a new job," he told Piewicket after he hung up.

The little cat blinked slowly. *Yes, I know.*

Dom felt the cat's response form in his mind. The Salems always had a telepathic bond with their two family cats, and Dom had grown up thinking such conversations were totally normal. He asked, out loud, "Is this the job you really wanted to come along for? What's going to happen?"

We go to hunt, for love and justice and fresh meat.

"You mean I'm going to take out another supernasty and you're going to get a treat after I get paid for all my hard work." As he said that, Dom sat on the bed next to Pie, his shoulders slumped after a day of demon-smashing.

Such is the order of things.

"You weren't a lot of help today, you know." He scratched behind her ears, and Pie's eyes closed as she leaned into him. "Did you just want to get out of the house?"

The cat's tail twitched. True, this demon was no match for your power.

"It was just a quick spell."

Stop that. False modesty is an ugly human trait. Few others have the gift of a quick spell, as you put it. Glory in the power you have.

"It doesn't feel glorious." It *was* rare, though. Piewicket had him there. Most spells required extensive research and a lot of preparation to cast, and could only be done in alignment with the proper stars and seasons. But Dom had been born with the ability to sidestep some of the usual restrictions. He could reach into the well of magic he always felt close by, and speak a spell without more than a moment's notice.

And since he was a Salem, born and raised, he used that magic to fight the multitudes of evil, corrupt beings that plagued the world. That's what the Salem family had done for generations, no matter how dangerous it was and no matter how many people gave up their lives in the fight. Like his parents had.

"I'm pretty wiped out," he said, unwilling to chat about his gift or his calling.

Yes. Now you must sleep.

"Yeah, it'll be a long day tomorrow."

Perhaps. Mostly, I desire warmth, and that is paramount.

Dom shrugged and said the only thing he could be certain of. "You're such a cat."

As soon as he lay down, Pie nuzzled next to him, purring. He was drifting off before he could warn the cat not to use her favorite sleep-inducing spell. He dreamed of a real house, a home to hold his family, his whole family.

In the dream, his parents were still alive, his brothers were with him, and someone who he was sure was a sister. Lily, he thought, though in typical dream logic, sometimes she looked like Lily and sometimes not. It was summer, the smell of the grill in the air along with the bitter smoke of cheap fireworks and the heavy, sweet scent of twilight air before the night came on with its fireflies and stars. It was the perfect summer day, in the perfect house, with the perfect family. There was even a dog on the lawn, barking happily.

Dom fell deeper into the dream, aching for the simple joy of it. That's what he wanted, what he wanted his whole life, since that horrible, soul-shredding moment when he heard his parents weren't ever coming back, and that nothing would ever be safe or the same again.

There was a spot of wetness on his face. Tears? No, just Piewicket poking her little nose at him.

Sleep. The past is done and the future is free. Sleep.

Chapter 2

"GET YOUR PAWS THE HELL off me!"

Vinny shoved the guy away from where she sat in the passenger seat of the car plowing down the desert highway. The guy was six three and probably nearing three hundred pounds. She was five nine on tiptoes and less than half his weight. But she still would bet on herself in a fight.

The guy leaned back toward the driver's side, jerking the steering wheel as he went. A car was such a bad place to hit on a girl, especially when it was in motion. At least this stretch of highway was straight, and the scenery uncluttered by distraction—uncluttered by anything, really. The part of Texas they were crossing was filled with dusty, hot nothing.

Vinny had hitchhiked a lot in her life, often enough to know most of the crap that could happen and how to prevent it from happening. On this particular trip, she'd been lucky up till now. Leaving New Orleans, where she'd been living, she'd ridden with a nice trucker from South

Carolina who knew a lot about German shepherds and breeding them and was happy to share every bit of his knowledge. He'd apologized every time he'd referred to a female dog as a bitch, which made Vinny laugh.

Then she'd got in with a young band on their way to Chicago for a gig. But their van started having engine trouble, so they had to pull over. She gave them as much cash as she could out of her stash, because she remembered being in the situation when she toured. But repairs would take a while, so she was forced to find a new ride.

Enter Wade. Wade wore a bright red trucker hat and had loud opinions Vinny didn't agree with. But he was headed west and didn't blink when Vinny took a photo of him and his license plate to send to a friend. She warned Wade that if she didn't check in, that photo would get sent to the cops.

The warning usually worked pretty well. And Wade had behaved for the first couple of hours. Until now.

"Keep your eyes on the road, moron," she added, under her breath. She didn't want to get hit on, and she definitely didn't want to get killed.

"That's it, blondie." He hit the brakes, and the car screeched to a halt. Vinny lurched forward, held back only by the shoulder belt. The guy's head almost hit the windshield, but Vinny's luck wasn't so good that he got some sense knocked into him.

"What now?" she muttered, automatically glancing around. There was no one on the road behind them. Or ahead of them. This area was totally deserted.

Vinny felt for the little folded knife in her pocket. Still there. She hoped to hell she wouldn't have to use it.

Wade shook his head in disgust. "Stupid bitch."

"I'm not the one who tried to attack someone while

driving," she snapped. She unbuckled her seatbelt with one hand.

"Didn't attack you," he growled. "Just being friendly."

"We're not friends. And there's nothing friendly about groping a women without asking."

"What are you talkin' about? You wear those tight clothes and got that fake blonde hair and you ride with any stranger who says okay. You're asking, baby."

She glared at him. "What decade are you from?" She grabbed her backpack. "If you asked for gas money, no problem. But you don't get to feel me up."

"You're in *my* car. I get to do whatever I want."

"Then I'm out of here." Vinny reached for the door handle.

He leaned across her, grabbing her wrist. "Hold up, now."

Vinny twisted back and hissed at him. "Back off. You try anything with me and I'll cut you up."

He grinned, evidently not worried about her threat at all. "Tough little bitch, ain't you? Bet you're fun once you know who's in charge."

Vinny spat directly in his eye, then opened the door and launched herself out of the car. She hit the ground awkwardly, but she picked herself up fast, pulling her bag up from where it had dropped.

"Want to see how much fun I am?" she said. She flicked the knife open.

His face twisted into something ugly, but he just said, "Fuck this. You ain't worth the trouble."

He revved the engine and pulled the passenger door closed. "When you're begging for water out here with the snakes, you'll wish you were nice to me!"

"Go to hell!" Vinny screamed as he drove off.

The car became a speck in the distance. Vinny just stood there for a little while, half-fearing her scuzzy ride would come roaring back with a gun in his hand. But nothing happened. He didn't return.

She was alone in the middle of nowhere. Vinny looked around. There were no road signs, no houses, no hint of civilization. She didn't remember how long it had been since they passed a gas station or something, but it had been a while.

"Not good," she muttered.

The sun was high in the summer sky. Vinny, dressed in jeans, a thin t-shirt, and a leather jacket, was already feeling the heat. She wore a bunch of necklaces, too, and the metal of the chains already felt hot.

She dug in her pack for her umbrella. The tiny shadow it cast would help keep the direct sun from beating on her skull. But this was a desert. It would hit a hundred degrees today. She had one half-full bottle of water in the bag.

"Damn," she said. "That guy really left me here."

She pulled out her phone. She'd call 911. This must qualify as an emergency.

No reception. No bars. No nothing.

Was it her device acting up, or was it the total desolation? Vinny cursed out the phone and tried everything she could, but nothing changed. She couldn't even call for help.

She'd just have to start walking. She chose west—that's where she was headed anyway. There'd be something on the side of the road soon enough.

Vinny trudged along the road. She talked to herself while she walked, both to keep herself company and to keep her spirits up. She worked best when fueled by anger. Rage could keep her going for hours.

"This is nowhere near the worst situation you've been in, Vin," she said. "Remember that night in the Bronx after Malika's party. *That* was bad. This is nothing."

But the night she'd usually considered the worst of her life was a little different, if only because there'd been people around. Mostly bad people, sure. But it was in New York, not the middle of nowhere.

"Oh, get over it. This is a highway. People use highways. Someone else will come by. No decent person would just drive past a damsel in distress. Right?"

In fact, no fewer than six drivers were perfectly willing to drive past a damsel in distress. Every single car that passed by—four going east, two going west—ignored her stuck out thumb, her frantic handwaving, and her shouts for help. Most of them sped up. Was she that scary looking?

"Keep walking, Vin. Think about Emma. She'll flip when she sees you."

Emma would certainly do *some*thing when she saw Vinny, because she hadn't seen Vin in, what, three years? They hadn't parted on the best of terms, and though they exchanged texts and such, the rift was still there. Vinny had been afraid to bring it up, because maybe bringing it up again would torpedo their friendship completely.

But then Vinny had the nightmares.

As a kid, she had nightmares all the time. The usual stuff about monsters and getting lost in the dark, and being trapped in a huge spiderweb, which her therapist said was a 'metaphor for Vinny's difficulty with her parental relationships' or whatever.

As she got older, and stopped going to that stupid therapist, her nightmares lessened.

Then, last week, she suffered three nights in a row of vicious dreams. The same spiderweb showed up, but this time, the person stuck in the middle was Emma.

And every night, Vinny watched, screaming, as something horrible devoured Emma. The nightmares started differently each time—a club, in Vinny's old house, in the woods somewhere. But they ended up with Emma being caught up in sticky webs, one silvery strand at a time. Vinny could see them, one by one, but each time, she didn't quite realize what was happening until it was too late.

And then everything was darkness, and there was Emma, begging for help, and no matter what she tried, Vinny could never *reach* her. She tried and failed and watched as Emma died. Then she woke up, sweaty and tangled in bedsheets, telling herself it was just a dream.

Three nights in a row.

Vinny couldn't take it anymore. She had to get to Emma. This wasn't a phone call situation. Hey, what's up? Been a while. Listen, I think you're maybe going to be devoured by a massive spider. And even if it's a metaphorical one, it's still going to eat you.

Nope. Vinny couldn't text that. This required a face-to-face.

Trouble was, Emma's place was all the way across the country from Vinny. And Vinny was nearly broke. But what else could she do? Ignoring this wasn't going to work. Vinny didn't believe in dreams or magic or anything other than pure rationality. But when a paralyzing nightmare occurred out of the blue and kept repeating, it meant something. The spider wasn't important. What was important was the horrible certainty that her friend was in danger.

The nightmares faded to a manageable level as soon as she started traveling, which Vinny took as a good sign.

Besides, it wasn't like she had any other obligations. She was between jobs, having quit her last gig as a cocktail waitress in the French Quarter. The money she made was barely enough to scrape by. She made a bit more playing in bands, but that was never steady work.

Vinny worried about money. She knew what it was like to have a lot of it, and what it was like to have none of it. Having none of it sucked. At almost twenty-eight years old, it was time to stop coasting and start thinking about the future. She couldn't survive on short-term, part-time gigs forever. And she'd die before asking her family to help with anything.

"Think about helping Emma," Vin said. "Think about *staying* with Emma. Those damp cool days. The mist. The rain. Oh, Lord, the rain."

Vinny would practically sell her soul for a good thunderstorm about now. But the sky remained stubbornly clear.

The sun crawled westward, hotter every minute. Vinny kept walking. A low, pulsing headache began in the back of her neck and slowly spread upward. Sweat trickled down her face and the back of her neck in a steady stream. Her jeans were plastered to her skin. She wanted water. She needed water. She waited as long as she could to drink the last drop from her bottle, but it was mid-afternoon now, and things were starting to look pretty bad.

She automatically looked behind her every five minutes or so, hoping, praying that some speck in the distance would turn out to be a good Samaritan in an air conditioned SUV filled with lemonade.

Nothing. She must not be damsel-ly enough.

Then she did a double take. Something glinted in the distance, the flash of sunlight on chrome.

She turned toward it and waited. Through the shimmering heat, a shape appeared. It was a motorcycle, not a car.

She moved to the very edge of the baking-hot asphalt and held up one hand, waving to it.

A miracle occurred.

The bike started to slow down.

She watched as the motorcycle slowed further, then stopped. The guy driving it put one foot on the ground, steadying the bike. He pulled his helmet off and pushed his black hair away from his face.

Wow.

Vinny was glad she had her sunglasses on, because she knew she was ogling him. He was hot. Smoking hot. All bad boy in faded jeans and a shiny black leather jacket.

Are you kidding me? Vinny thought. The one person to stop looks like more of a threat than the guy who left me here?

The guy looked her over, too, though she couldn't tell what he was thinking behind those very pretty eyes.

"You need a ride," he said. Said, not asked.

"Not from you, thanks all the same." Even in this situation, Vinny knew better than to get near anyone who looked like him. Good thing she didn't believe in luck. Because her luck seemed to be tanking.

He raised an eyebrow. "You waiting for your limo?"

"I'm not actually hitching," she said, ignoring the fact that she had flagged him down. "I'm just walking to the next…whatever."

"Are you serious?"

No, Vinny was not serious. She had no idea how far the next whatever was. "No offense, but I left my last ride because he was a creeper. Not making that mistake again."

"Look, I don't really want to give you a ride," the guy responded. "But it's too hot. You'll get heat sickness if you stay out here. Or dehydration. Or worse."

She wiggled the umbrella. "I've got shade."

"How's that working out for you? Feel ready to run a few laps? Stand out here for another two hours with the sun in your face the whole time?"

Vinny closed her eyes. That sounded like hell.

"You could call the cops," the guy suggested. "State troopers pick up stranded travelers all the time."

She laughed at that. She hadn't seen a single bar on her phone for hours. But she did notice the battery draining away. "Tried that. No signal."

He pulled out his own phone and checked it. "Yeah, you're right."

Then he reached into a side pack and produced the holy grail—a bottle of water. He held it out to her.

Vinny snatched it and guzzled half of it down before she thought about all the awful stuff a person could slip into a bottle of water.

"Whoa, slow down," the guy said, looking alarmed.

She couldn't. She was too thirsty. She drained the bottle and wiped her mouth. "Thanks."

At that moment, Vinny's gaze caught a movement at the side of the guy's bike, the same place where the magic bottle of water came from. She blinked to make sure she wasn't hallucinating. Was this what heat exhaustion did? She'd never hallucinated a calico cat before. "Is that a cat?"

He glanced back. "Yup." After a long second, he added, grudgingly, "Her name's Piewicket."

Fascinated, Vinny watched the little creature, which had crawled out of a sort of side pannier saddlebag thing. It stretched out, first front paws, then back paws. Then she looked at Vinny with big eyes, blinking slowly.

"You own a cat. A cat who likes motorcycle rides?"

"Own's not really the right word," he said, now with a hint of a smile. "Pie wanted to come along for the ride, and she's kinda in charge."

She looked at the cat for another long moment, trying to figure out what the scam was, then back at the guy. No one who rode with an adorable calico cat in his saddlebag could be evil. Right?

Vinny made a decision. She said, "I'll take a ride, just to the next stop. Gas station. Restaurant. Whatever. I just need to crash somewhere, and I'll call my friends to bail me out."

The cat surveyed Vinny, then yawned and crawled back into the saddlebag.

"Fine by me," the guy said. "Normally I wouldn't even let you on without a helmet, but leaving you out here in the sun wouldn't be much better."

She bit her lip. "I'm not good on motorcycles. I've only ridden one once before in my life."

"Just get on," he said. "I'll go easy on the speed."

Vinny nodded. But first, she walked to the front of the bike and held out her phone to take a picture.

"What are you doing?" he asked.

"Standard hitchhiking procedure," she said. "I send pics of the plate and the driver to a friend. If I don't check in, she'll send this to the cops."

She held up the phone to get him in frame. "Say

cheese."

"No."

She clicked anyway, then pocketed the phone again and collapsed the umbrella. She adjusted the backpack and got on. "I suppose I've got to hold onto you."

"No one else around."

He waited until she was settled, then put his helmet back on. Vinny found herself in the awkward position of needing to essentially hug a stranger for an extended period of time.

Vinny was terrified she'd fall off the bike once it got going, but the guy didn't drive like a maniac, so that was good. He probably just wanted to protect his cat.

The road got even more desolate than she imagined possible. The sun was well on its way below a mountain ridge when they finally saw a lighted sign in the distance.

Vinny dreamed of bathrooms and cold water and cell phone signals, but once they got closer, she had to readjust her expectations.

The place was a dive. A creepy gas station backed up to a creepy garage, populated by creepy, leather-faced, bearded bikers.

It was the unfriendliest place Vinny had ever seen.

The guy pulled in, but stopped well short of the gas pumps.

He pulled his helmet off, then turned his head enough to say, "Not to go all white knight, but there is no way in hell I'm dropping you off here."

Vin breathed a sigh of relief she didn't realize she'd been holding. "Good," she said quietly, "because this place makes my skin crawl."

"Yeah, mine too." Nevertheless, he got off the bike. "Stay right here. I'm not kidding."

"Where are you going?" she asked, feeling very anxious.

"Creepy or not, they're bikers. They'll have a spare helmet to sell."

"Um. Can you get some more water too?" she asked. "I'm still thirsty."

"There's a full thermos in the righthand saddlebag," he said. "Drink that. Water around here is probably poisoned."

"Be careful," Vin said.

"You too. Don't wander off."

Then the guy—whose name she didn't even know—proceeded to wander off, straight toward the bikers.

Chapter 3

Dom hated the place. He wasn't naturally gifted at sensing auras, but the vibes around the whole location were so aggressive a blind person could see them. It was bad. Purple black, like a thundercloud or a bruise. The people who called this place home were only human in the literal sense.

But they were definitely bikers, with a line of shiny chrome bikes in the large garage. Big beasts of bikes. Mostly Harleys or hacked-together choppers, all heavily accessorized with black leather and more bad vibes. The men standing around talking near the huge garage door had the bruise-colored auras he sensed around the rest of the place. Even their laughter had a tinge of meanness, like bullies on a playground.

Just buy a helmet and leave.

He stepped into the office of the gas station.

A stocky man with a huge greying beard looked him over. "If you want to gas up, amigo, you need to get the bike a little closer to the pump." He cast a non-casual look outside to where Dom's bike was parked, with the woman still near it.

A couple of other gang members laughed, non-casually moving to flank Dom. One said, "Maybe he needs a little help getting the pump in the tank."

Dom resisted the impulse to roll his eyes. "I'm looking to buy a helmet. We're one short."

"Ladies like to feel the wind in their hair," the guy said.

"Not this one," Dom disagreed. "You got one to sell or not?"

"Sure, I got one. Almost new."

The way the other guys laughed at the last words made Dom cringe inside. He did not want to know how they got the helmet in the first place.

Bearded guy turned and pulled out a helmet from a shelf in the booth. He plunked it on the counter.

Dom picked it up, examining it for cracks. It was black, plain but unbroken. "Looks okay," he said. "How much?"

"Four hundred."

"I don't want to buy everything here, just the helmet," Dom said. "How much?"

"Four hundred dollars. American. What's the matter? Don't think your lady's skull is worth that much?"

"I don't think this helmet is worth that much. I could buy a brand new one for that."

"Yeah, if you were somewhere else. But you ain't. You're here. And the only helmet for sale is four hundred dollars American." The bearded guy slapped a hand on the counter, as if he just got a great idea. "If you don't got the cash, how about a trade. Ten minutes alone with your lady sounds good."

Dom went still. "Say again?"

"You heard me."

"Not interested." Dom took a slow breath.

The bearded guy put both hands on the counter, leaning forward slightly. "Worried she'll like it?"

That was the last thing Dom was worried about. Her being alive at the end, that was something to worry about. He pulled out some cash from his right pocket, counting out the bills carefully. "Three hundred in exchange for the helmet and an apology for insulting a lady." He held the folded bills up.

The guy laughed, but his eyes were locked on the cash. "Sorry," he said, not sounding sorry at all. "Sure she's a real angel."

Dom wouldn't know, but he nodded, reaching for the helmet. He dropped the cash on the counter. He didn't bother to say goodbye.

He went outside with the helmet, feeling a target on his back the whole time. Though the conversation didn't take more than a few minutes, it felt like an hour. If anything had happened to his bike, his cat, or his passenger while he was distracted, he'd do something permanent to this place.

But as soon as he sighted his bike, he got sidetracked by something he didn't usually see with his bike—a gorgeous woman.

"Wow," Dom breathed. He'd seen her before, obviously, but not like this, leaning casually against the machine, as if she belonged to it.

For a girl who said she didn't have much to do with motorcycles, she sure looked good with one. The worn, cropped black leather jacket fit her frame perfectly. Underneath the jacket he could see the mess of silver necklaces she wore around her neck, easily a couple dozen. She was leaning against the side of the seat so that her legs were straight out, crossed at the ankles. The skinny jeans she wore outlined every contour of sleekly muscled legs.

Her black leather boots didn't come up much above those crossed ankles, and the leather was dusty with long wear, the toes all scuffed up. Shitkicker boots, his brother Mal always called them, in contrast to the ones designed for a fancy night out. These looked like they kicked plenty of shit.

But that actually wasn't the main event. She had her phone out in one hand and a tube of lipstick in the other. Using the phone as a mirror, she swiped an intense red across her lips.

Dom hated lipstick. But it was still sexy as hell to watch her put it on.

She took her time, pursing her mouth in the mimic of a kiss, though she smiled only at the phone, not even glancing around. Her disdain for her surroundings was louder than any insult she might have screamed. It was defiant. It was unnecessarily provoking. And it looked great.

He was not the only man watching. Two other bikers had strolled up while he was inside. Dom wasn't sure why they weren't getting too close. Then he saw Piewicket pacing in a tight figure eight pattern between the new guys and the bike.

One guy took a step forward and earned a hiss from the cat, who arched her back in the classic Halloween pose. They laughed, but didn't try to move any more.

"Pussycat's got claws," one said.

"Which pussycat you looking at?" the other said, and laughed again.

Dom did not like that sound. He'd had enough of this place.

He moved faster. Not running, but not wasting time.

"What's the rush, pal?" the first biker asked, seeing him pass.

Dom didn't answer.

His passenger must have been more alert to the situation than she seemed, because she somehow put her phone and lipstick away and swung one long leg over the seat by the time he reached the bike.

Like hell you don't ride, he thought. But all he said was, "Put this on."

She took the helmet dubiously. "Will it fit? How's it supposed to feel?"

"I honestly don't care," he muttered. "Just put it on. And hold onto me, because when I drive out of here, I'll be doing it fast. Got it?"

He glanced at the side pannier where Piewicket already nestled. The cat knew what was about to happen.

Dom tore out of the gas station like he was outrunning the apocalypse. His danger sense had been screaming at him the whole time, and he wouldn't feel better until he was out of range.

She listened to him at least, to judge by how tight her arms were around him. If he wasn't thinking about evasive maneuvers and getaway plans, it would have been a nice ride. He couldn't remember the last time a beautiful woman was pressed this close to him.

Well, yes he did. But he'd gotten good at shutting that train of thought down fast.

Don't think about Rachel. Think about getting gone.

In the deepening twilight, it was getting hard to see the road in front of them. Dom was driving way too fast for conditions. On any other bike but his, this speed would be suicidal. But his bike had so many enchantments worked into it that he could take a risk.

He tore straight down the highway for a few minutes, concentrating purely on speed. But once he rounded a curve—one sharp enough that the bike flattened out nearly horizontal to take it—he started looking for side roads or something to get him off the main route.

He took a sudden turn, heading down the narrow road toward a distant ridge. The girl behind him didn't say a word—not that he'd hear it, with the helmets and the wind. She molded herself even more tightly to him, basically banking on sharing his fate.

Dom kept following the road as it climbed. Once he hit the crest of the ridge, he slowed the bike considerably. Then he rolled to a halt, killing the engine and the lights.

She had her helmet off as soon as he did, then grabbed his forearm, stopping him getting off the bike.

"You trying to kill us both?" she hissed, sounding more scared than angry.

"Nope." He kept his eyes on the main highway in the valley below them. "Just wait for a minute."

"What are we waiting for?"

He pointed to a collection of motorcycle headlights in the distance. "They're following us. I could see them getting ready to ride when we left. They wanted to chase us down."

"What a bunch of assholes," she said. Despite her defiant words, her voice was really shaky.

"That was pretty much my impression," Dom said. "Don't worry. They won't know where I turned off the road."

"What makes you so sure?" she asked.

Because magic, he thought. But now was not the time to explain things like that to a civilian.

They watched silently as the group went by down below. None of the bikers took the side road or saw them up in the darkness.

"Not much imagination," she said in relief, once it looked like the immediate danger was past.

"Nope," said Dom. "All right. Mind if we take this road for a while? Not crazy about running into them tonight—at least not out here."

"Agreed," she said. "Do you know where you're going, by the way?"

"I usually figure it out." Dom looked over at her. "I, uh, need my arm back."

She let go as if he were on fire. "Sorry. Did I cut off your circulation?"

He shook his head. "I'm fine. Sorry I couldn't give you more warning. It wasn't as dangerous as it seemed. My driving, I mean."

"If you say so. Anyway, it beats getting caught by that crowd." She shivered, probably thinking of what that gang had planned for entertainment.

He gestured to the helmet. "Get that back on. We'll keep moving."

"Wait. What's your name? You never told me."

"Dominic Salem. Dom's fine. You never told me yours either."

She paused, then said, "It's Vinny."

Dom gave her a very long look, letting her know he didn't believe her for a second. "Okay, then."

"Thanks for giving me a ride…Dom." She fiddled with the helmet. "Hey, how much did this cost?"

"Don't worry about it."

"Come on."

"I said don't worry about it."

"Well, I worry. I don't like anyone but me paying my way."

"It was overpriced. I paid it cause I wanted to get out of there, but you are not paying me what I paid them. It's a gift."

"It's my birthday next week," she said, looking at the helmet. Her voice was quiet. She was talking more to herself than to him. Then she looked up. "I don't do gifts, though. Especially not from some guy I just met." She bit her lip, once again looking uncertain. "Though I also like having a functional skull."

Dom almost laughed. She seemed to have a brain as well as attitude. He wanted that brain to stay intact. "Get the skull protector on, and we can argue about it later."

"Count on it." She put the helmet on, the visor obscuring her face completely.

Chapter 4

DOM DROVE ALONG THE NEW route for about an hour, hoping to get out of Texas before the end of the day. Eventually, the twilight got deep enough to make driving dangerous. The mule deer numbered in the thousands around this part of the country, and they could leap onto the road at any moment.

Just as he saw a sign marked Private Land—No Trespassing, he heard Pie's voice in his mind. *This area is safe. Nothing beyond the usual dangers.* Meaning that while there might be coyotes or bears, there shouldn't be any ghosts or demons.

He headed into the marked land, which had a few clumps of pine trees, but mostly dirt and rocks. It was deserted, and there were plenty of spots that would make a good place to sleep. In the deepening night time, Dom selected a spot he liked. He killed the motor and pulled off his helmet.

"Welcome to the great outdoors," he announced in the sudden silence after the bike's roar vanished.

"Very fancy." Vinny—or whatever her name actually

was—got her helmet off and swung off the bike in less than five seconds.

Jesus, Dom thought. *Am I toxic?*

She looked at him consideringly. "That wasn't so bad. The motorcycle, I mean."

"That's good news for tomorrow," Dom said. "Or however long you stick around. Where you headed, by the way?" He expected her to avoid the question, or lie, just as she'd obviously lied about her name. *Vinny*. Like she was some Brooklyn bartender.

He released Piewicket from her confinement, and the cat meowed before dashing off into the darkness.

She said, "I'm headed to my best friend's place in Seattle. You?"

"Uh, pretty near there, actually," he said, surprised at her words. "Though I'll drop you anywhere before that, if you want."

"Am I cramping your style?"

He shook his head. "You said you don't like bikes." *Or gifts.*

"I'm getting used to it," she said. "For some reason, I feel like I won't fall off. I've always been scared of falling off a motorcycle."

"You won't fall off mine."

She rolled her eyes, apparently chalking up his comment to cockiness. Whatever. Dom couldn't exactly explain that he cast a lot of magic to make his ride as safe as supernaturally possible. It was self-preservation, but it worked for anyone who happened to be riding it.

Then he squinted at her. "Your lipstick's gone." Even in the faint light, her whole face looked softer, her lips no longer contrasting sharply against the skin.

"What? Oh, yeah." Vinny shrugged. "I wanted to take

some pics of the gas station just in case something happened, and the subtle way to do it with the phone is to pretend I'm a vain bitch who needs to touch up in the middle of the desert."

"It worked. You sure didn't look like you were photographing. The red was, um, distracting."

She grinned knowingly, showing a flash of white teeth. "That's what it's for. I don't wear it in real life."

"Good. I mean…" He trailed off. "Never mind what I mean. You should drink more water. If you were out in the sun half the day, you need it more than you think."

Hoping to distract himself, Dom spent several minutes studying a paper map in the light of his phone's flashlight. There was no reliable signal for an internet search. Finally he looked up. "Good news is that I know where we are."

She offered a golf clap, then said, "And the bad news?"

"Where we are is pretty far from everything. So you'll have to wait till tomorrow to get rid of me. And we've got to camp out." He gestured to encompass the surroundings.

He expected her to recoil. She surprised him. Again.

"Wouldn't be the first time," she said easily. "You'd be amazed at the places I slept when I was in a band. This is a lot better than some of them."

"Well, I've got some gear," he said. "It'll be reasonably comfortable."

"For you," she said.

"What?"

"Don't tell me you've got spare bedding."

"I'm willing to share."

She angled her chin up in a defiant, proud pose. "And what exactly do you think I'm sharing?"

"Hey, hold on. I didn't ask for *any*thing," Dom said,

his voice heating up despite his efforts to keep cool. Did he hit on her? No. He saved her from heatstroke, and a possible biker gang, and his reward was getting categorized with the creeps?

"Look," she said, taking a step back. He could tell she was nervous despite her outwardly tough look. "Don't take it the wrong way."

"You just took me the wrong way," he said. "I'm supposed to be delighted? And anyway, it's all practical. Sleeping next to me is still better than letting the hypothermia get you. Deserts get cold at night, *Vinny*. So yes, we'll share the blanket and yes, I'll behave myself," he added, before she could bring it up again.

"Oh. Good," she said, looking apologetic. Then her eyes narrowed. "If you don't, you will so regret it. I have a knife, and I will use it if I have to."

"What are you like when you're not going out of your way to be charming?" he asked sarcastically.

"I'm a peach normally," she said. "This isn't normal."

"Whatever," said Dom. "Besides, I don't believe you really have a knife."

"You think I'm lying?"

"You were lying about sending that picture to your friends. There was no signal to send it."

Vinny looked a tiny bit chagrined. "You got me on that. But I do have a knife." She slipped a folding knife from her pocket for a second, flipped it open and closed, then slid it back.

"Well, now I'd better behave." He thought it best not to mention he had a couple knives of his own. She'd be running into the hills at that news.

Vinny looked around at the emptiness. "Don't suppose you got firewood packed away on that bike."

"Nope, sorry. You afraid of the dark?" he asked, starting to pull his gear from the bike.

"No. And I'm not afraid of things that go bump in the night, either."

He stopped what he was doing and gave her his full attention.

"Why not?" he asked, wondering if this woman knew the truth about the world, the truth Dom and his family lived with every day, but couldn't ever talk about with ordinary people.

"Because I don't believe in monsters," she said.

Dom sighed. So much for that notion.

Vinny went on, "I don't need to blame monsters for bad stuff when I know humans who are real monsters."

He kept watching her for a moment longer. Then he shrugged, accepting her answer. "Good enough."

"What's the matter?" Vinny asked, her eyes on him. "You believe in ghosts?"

That's just the beginning of what I believe. "Doesn't matter if I do or not. We're still stuck out here tonight." After Dom got the blankets arranged and wadded up his sweatshirt as a pillow, he laid down. Vinny still sat on a rock near the bike.

"It's safe, you know," he said. "I won't bite."

"Oh, really." She arched an eyebrow at that. The expression was sexier than she probably intended it to be.

"Well, to be totally honest…" he said, then trailed off.

"Go on," Vinny said, eyes narrow.

"…if the mood's right…"

"What."

"Piewicket might bite. Fair warning," Dom finished. He pointed to the cat, who'd returned from wherever she'd been.

Vinny's laugh was sudden and electric as a lightning strike. With a smile on her face, she looked like a different person. "Oh, that's fine. She can do whatever she wants."

Of course I can, Piewicket thought in Dom's mind. *I am a cat.*

Evidently willing to risk it, Vinny walked over to the blankets and sat down, kicking off her boots and sliding out of the jacket. The metal chains of her multitude of necklaces jangled softly.

"You won't choke on all that jewelry?" Dom asked, genuinely curious.

"Nah. I wear these twenty-four seven. Hasn't killed me yet." Vinny stretched out, pulling the top blanket over her. "I've made myself really, really clear about what's allowed, right?"

"My impression was that nothing is allowed."

"Damn straight."

"You don't know a lot of decent guys, do you?"

"I know a few," Vinny said. "But the point is that I don't know you, Dom."

"Fair enough."

Dom closed his eyes, trying to get the message through this girl's head that he wasn't a danger to her. He was pretty tired, actually, but he was hyperaware of the woman next to him. She slept fitfully at first, waking up at every sound and twitch.

Then a soft, furred shape slinked onto the blankets. Piewicket nuzzled into the space between Vinny and Dom. The cat stretched, filling the gap as only a cat can. Vinny made a sleepy, murmuring sound—an entirely too intriguing sound to Dom—and then her restlessness subsided. Dom drifted off to sleep himself, Piewicket's subtle purring in his ears.

He woke up once, very abruptly, in the middle of the night. The temperature had dropped a lot. The night sky was clear, with a bright half moon high in the sky, and a rich scattering of stars visible overhead. By habit, Dom picked out several of the constellations, all useful for those who did magic for a living.

He glanced over at Vinny. She was lying on her side, facing toward him, completely lost to the world.

Piewicket lay cuddled next to her. The cat's eyes gleamed in the darkness.

"Thought she'd never stop tossing," he said softly to Pie.

I made her sleep, Piewicket told him. Or she would be awake still. She doesn't trust you.

"Because I'm a guy."

And because you're human.

"Smart girl," Dom said, curious about the woman sleeping at his side.

He leaned over. Being very careful to avoid touching Vinny, he examined a few of the necklaces now half-lying on the blanket. Most of the charms were cheap—silver-colored but not silver. But there was a beautiful real silver cross that had a certain power in it. It made Dom's fingers tingle when he touched it.

Blessed, he thought, feeling the threads of an old spell inside the metal. There was also a tiny glass bottle filled with salt, which vibrated with a different sort of power—protection. Not very strong, but definitely real. He wondered where Vinny picked it up, and if she knew that it was actually magic. He suspected that each necklace she wore held a story, and he was interested in hearing every single one.

His gaze drifted from the necklaces back to her. She

was pretty. Sexy was one thing, and she *was* sexy, even when she was going out of her way to run for mayor of Icetown. Dom felt bad for any guy who ever thought she was just playing hard to get. Vinny acted very comfortable with that pocketknife.

But now, when she wasn't threatening to kill him, she was simply pretty. Straight blonde hair covered part of her face. He had to stop himself from pushing it off her cheek —he didn't want to lose any fingers. Sleep made her features softer, less tense and wary. Her mouth was slightly open, and her breathing came soft and even. Dom could imagine that mouth on him.

Shit. He shouldn't have done that, because he had a good imagination and his body immediately reacted to the idea of her all over him. Going by her attitude so far, she was probably a handful in bed, which was a really interesting line of thought.

"Ugh, stop that," he told himself under his breath.

You should sleep, Piewicket told him suddenly. I will watch. The night belongs to my kind.

"Wake me up if there's trouble."

I will wake you if it pleases me to do so.

"Typical."

Dom slid back into sleep, wondering what Vinny would do if a cat ever started talking to her.

Chapter 5

Vinny woke up just before dawn to find a dead chipmunk two feet away from her head. "Oh, Miss Piewicket," she groaned. "You shouldn't have."

The cat bounded into view and then got in her face, purring madly.

"Yes, thank you for the gift," she said, scratching behind Pie's ears. One was white and one was muted orange. "It was super sweet and you're a vicious killer."

Piewicket looked proud, accepting that praise. She also seemed to really like the ear scratching. Vinny smiled at the cat. "You kept me warm last night, and you're kind of a purr machine."

"That she is."

Still petting Piewicket, Vinny looked over to Dom, who was already up, moving around by his bike. "Is that why you take her with you? To keep you company? Seems like this isn't her first rodeo."

"She's very well-traveled," Dom said. "But mostly I keep her around to look less intimidating."

Vinny laughed, having noticed how Dom was trying

not to smile as he spoke. And this morning, he looked much more approachable than he had yesterday. Maybe that was just because he wasn't a complete stranger now. In fact, he'd gone a full night without losing his nice guy status. Vinny wanted to pretend she wasn't impressed, but she was.

"I'm sorry I was mean to you last night," she said suddenly. "I was kind of on edge. I had a bad day until you picked me up. And I should have been grateful…and I *was*, but…"

"I get it," Dom said, reaching into one of the bike's packs. "If I had a sister, I'd freak out if I heard she hitch-hiked. Oh, here it is." He moved back toward her, dropping an energy bar by her head. "Last one."

Vinny grabbed it. She was ravenous. "Thanks. Dead rodent's not my first choice."

"Too bad. Pie doesn't go hunting for just anybody, you know." He gave her a half-smile and turned away again, offering a bit of privacy for Vinny to sit up and get herself together. Pie mewed and ambled after Dom.

She devoured the bar and rolled out of the blankets. She had them both bundled up within minutes.

"You're a pro," he said, taking the packed blankets to stow.

"Told you. I was in a band. We toured for years. No frills. No fucking around."

"Yeah, I got that."

"I didn't mean…oh, never mind."

"I don't mind," Dom said. She got another half-smile she couldn't decipher.

Dom was a little too good-looking for comfort. Why couldn't Vinny have been rescued by a family in a mini-van? Oh, right. They would have driven right past someone who looked like her.

"Hey," Vinny said then. "I didn't wake you up at all, did I?" She didn't remember having a nightmare, but it was possible she did and he heard something.

But Dom was shaking his head. "You're a sound sleeper." He gestured to the bike. "Let's get moving. Real breakfast in a couple hours if we're lucky."

It was full on morning when they pulled up at a diner on the side of the highway. A large neon sign proclaimed it served the best coffee in the West, and Vinny was very willing to test that claim personally.

Dom ordered the biggest breakfast on the menu, and after a second Vinny echoed him. She should have stuck with coffee—cheap fuel. But she was so hungry she almost attacked the sugar packets on the table.

The coffee came fast, and was very good. Vinny felt much more human after the first cup. Sitting across from Dom, she surveyed him as subtly as she could. He still looked good. He needed a shave, and his t-shirt was totally wrinkled, but neither of those things looked bad.

"Where were you coming from when you drove by me?" she asked.

"When I stopped for you, you mean?"

"Yeah."

Dom took a sip of coffee, then said, "Florida, but only because of a job. I'm not from there."

"Where are you from?"

His brow furrowed. "Um, that's not an easy question. Sort of all over. My family moved around a lot. Now I live with my brothers in a big house just outside a small town in Ohio. Flyover country. I'd tell you the name, but it wouldn't mean anything."

"Probably not," Vinny agreed. "I've been living the

last few months in New Orleans, but I spent most of my life in New York City. Lots of traveling when my bands were on tour, but always through big cities or college towns."

"Bands, plural? How many were you in?"

"Twenty-two."

Dom put his coffee down. "Seriously? What do you play?"

"Bass guitar, mostly. Guitar if I need to."

"And you're good enough to be in bands that tour."

"You don't have to be good to tour," Vinny explained. "Just crazy. And the reason I was in so many bands is because the half-life of a punk band is about six months."

"When did you *start*?" he said, looking more surprised. "That's over eleven years."

"Longer than that. Some of the bands didn't suck as much. Which is not to say they were stellar, or that I was."

"Yeah, but still. People wouldn't keep asking you to be in a band if you were no good."

Vinny smiled. "Having a girl boosts a band's, um, stage presence." She paused. "I suppose I did get one skill out of all those gigs. I'm good at wrangling packs of immature dudes."

"Is that what you put on your resume?" he asked, with a smile.

"Do I look like I have a resume?" she asked, feeling a surge of cheerfulness. Must be the coffee. "Resumes are not punk rock."

"You got that look," he agreed. "All the metal and necklaces and such. How many of those are you wearing?"

"About thirty?" she guessed, looking down at the collection. "I don't keep track."

"Don't the chains get tangled?"

"Sorting them out gives me something to do on long trips."

"Like hitching to Seattle," he said, his expression becoming more curious.

"Yeah," said Vin quickly. She did not want to get into her reasons for heading there. "Tell me something. How much did the helmet set you back? I know you said it was gift, but it's not. I want to make it up to you."

He made a face. "Three hundred."

"Are you kidding? You paid three hundred dollars for that?"

"You don't want to know what the other option was."

She raised an eyebrow. "I do now."

Dom shifted uncomfortably, but he said, "If I didn't feel like paying cash, the guy offered an alternative form of payment. Ten minutes alone with you. I nearly knocked his jaw off."

"What an asshole. Him, not you," Vinny said, her flesh crawling at the thought of being alone with those guys. Lucky Dom was there. Oh, wait. She didn't believe in luck. "Why would you do that? Hit him, I mean? You barely know me."

"General principle," Dom said, his expression tight. He pressed his hands on the table, palms down, as if they'd ball up into fists otherwise. "And I didn't hit him. I just really, really wanted to. But I didn't like the odds."

"Cheese and crackers. Okay, I owe you."

"I said it was a gift."

"It was literal highway robbery, and I'll make it up to you. Let's not argue about this."

"Did you just say cheese and crackers?" he asked suddenly.

"Yeah. Instead of Jesus Christ, you know? I went to Catholic school for a while," she said, hoping that explained it.

He was clearly trying not to laugh. "That's fair. I actually did a few years in a Catholic school too. My dad was half Irish, and my mom was Mexican. You can do the math."

"Hold on. Your dad *was* Irish and your mom *was* Mexican?"

Dom's smile slid off his face. "Uh. Yeah. My parents died when I was ten."

"Oh, my God," she said, picturing a car accident. Without thinking about it, she reached over to take his hand. His fingers curled around hers, gripping tightly.

Vinny wasn't exactly a nurturer, but she hoped she could make him feel a little better by being there. "That sucks. I mean, I'm sorry."

"It does suck," he agreed, taking a deeper breath. "It's been twenty years, but it hurts every day still. But I have my brothers—two of them. And our extended family, which is, um, extensive. And friends. It could be worse."

"That's why you were so insistent about the helmet," she guessed. "Why it couldn't wait."

"Partly. Life is so much more fragile than most people think. And you usually don't get much warning when things are about to change." Dom looked directly at her, his gaze intense. "Not to mention that you just don't know what's in your hands and what's up to fate or chance or whatever you want to call it. If I'd picked you up to stop you from dying in a desert and then you died because you didn't have a helmet on the bike…"

"That'd mess anyone up," she said, feeling shaken.

"Thinking you saved someone but really you…"

"Condemned them." Dom looked bleak when he said that, as if something was eating him up inside.

"Not condemned," Vinny said quickly. "I was going to say that you couldn't avert fate. I mean, I don't believe in fate, but maybe some things happen a certain way no matter how hard we try to fix them or change them or stop them."

Dom looked at her, right in her eyes. "Yeah. And when that happens, it haunts you. It makes you realize how little power you have."

Vinny had no idea what to say to that.

It was Dom who broke the silence. "At least the conversation didn't get all heavy." He laughed, and it made Vinny smile. She was relieved he could laugh after that. Sad Dom wasn't something she liked seeing, and she barely knew him.

"We sure dodged that bullet," she said.

She tilted her head, trying to fit Dom's revelation of his parentage with what he looked like. His skin was darker then hers, sure, but she never would have guessed he was part Hispanic.

"Maybe there is no part-Hispanic," she said, not realizing she was musing out loud.

"What?" Dom asked.

"Sorry. You said your mom was Mexican, and I guess I was trying to see it."

Dom raised one eyebrow and said something in rapid Spanish.

"What did you say?" she asked.

"I asked if I looked more Hispanic when I speak Spanish." He took a sip of coffee, then looked out the window. "Funny. When I say I'm part Irish, no one asks if I speak

Gaelic."

"Do you?" Somehow, she wouldn't be surprised if he did. Dom seemed to know a lot.

"I know a couple of prayers from my dad's dad."

"I really didn't mean to offend you," she said quickly, worried that she'd hurt his feelings when he'd just told her something incredibly personal. *Nice move, Vinny.* "I was just surprised. I mean, your name is…pretty…"

"Pretty white, yes. Mom and Dad thought it would be easier for us to have names Americans are used to. She pushed for Dominic, even though *her* grandfather was Dominico. Malachy is as Irish as you can get, so I assume Dad pushed for that. And Lex is short for Alexander, though visit the relatives on her side and he's Alejandro the second he steps into the yard." Dom was smiling by the end of this, and she guessed it was brought on by the thought of all his relatives, a perspective utterly unreal to Vinny.

"You sound like you have a big family," she said. "Sometimes I wish I did. Then I remember that more family members means more people to disappoint. I'm better off on my own."

"Are you?" he asked, a challenge in his tone.

She forgot what she was going to reply when Dom took the check from the waitress.

"I got it," he said, before Vinny could protest. "Just add it to your tab."

"I will," Vinny said, though she was secretly relieved that she wouldn't have to tap into her cash. Her supply was getting dangerously low.

They were outside the diner when Vinny remembered a question she wanted to ask. "So why are you headed to Seattle?"

Dom was messing around with the side panniers on the bike, adjusting straps. "I have a job there."

"Like you're moving there?"

"No. It's a short term gig." Piewicket's paw emerged for a second and took a swipe at him. "Damn, Pie! Stop that. I didn't mean to wake you up."

Vinny liked the way he talked to the cat, as if she were a roommate instead of a pet. "Who hires a guy from fifteen hundred miles away for a contractor position?" she asked.

He gave her an odd smile. "I'm kind of a specialist."

"At what?"

"Does it matter?"

"All right, don't tell me." She paused. "You're not an assassin, are you?"

"A *what*?" he asked.

"Hey, look at you. You travel light, you accept short term gigs from across the country, and you don't say what your job is. You could totally be a hit man."

He frowned, evidently taking her words seriously. "I'm not. And I hate guns."

"Just what a hit man would say."

Dom straightened up. "I don't talk about my job because I respect my clients' privacy. Also, I don't like to talk about my job. But I don't kill people."

Vinny relented on her teasing. "Okay. I guess you do have the cat."

He looked at the spot where Piewicket lay in wait. "Exactly. If you're looking for a killer, she's the one you got to watch out for."

They drove the rest of the day, taking a few pit stops. Dom kept a sharp eye on his gas tank, their water supply, and the time.

When evening fell, Dom pulled off the highway and into the lot of a two-story motel, the kind where all the doors opened straight to the outside.

"I don't like to drive at night if I don't have to," he said. "You okay with staying at the..." he squinted up at the flashing sign, "...the Starlight?"

"After camping? You bet. Well, depends on how many mice are in the rooms."

"With Piewicket around, any mouse population will drop sharply. Trust me."

In the motel office, the woman behind the counter blinked in surprise when Dom insisted on two double beds instead of a king. Vinny breathed a sigh of relief—then realized she was getting even more in debt to Dom, since he was paying for the room.

In fact, Dom had been doing a number of rather nice things for her in the past twenty-four hours, and Vinny was starting to feel the weight of obligation. She loathed the idea of owing anyone for anything. She knew it was a hang-up, but that didn't make it better.

"Hold tight," Dom told her once they reached their room, which was on the second story of the motel. "I'm going to chase down something to eat. And drink. You and Pie get settled, all right?"

She nodded, and Dom left.

Vinny went to Dom's leather bag on the bed, lifting up the main flap to release Piewicket. The calico stretched before she left the bag, leaving Vinny plenty of time to view the contents. Most of it was expected. Shirts, spare jeans, a pair of faded orange swim trunks. Then she saw a little cache of some strange stuff.

Glass bottles, sealed test tubes, a few odd rocks, several candle stubs, and a little leather bound notebook wrapped with a cord to keep it closed. "That's weird."

There were several saints' medals mixed in among a few quartz crystals, and Vinny frowned as she tried to make sense of a couple metal discs inscribed with what looked like hieroglyphics. It looked sort of religious but not a religion she'd ever heard of. The saints' medals, at least, were familiar. She saw Catherine, Anthony, Benedict, Mary, Paul, and Nicholas on her first glance.

She shifted her attention to the bottles. Some were empty, some were filled. One held what looked like salt, and another held some dried, faintly green herbs. She opened one and inhaled a scent teasingly like sage, but not. She capped it, and put it back with the rest.

Vinny touched the leather notebook, but Pie batted at her hand with one paw.

"All right, all right," she told the cat. So snooping wasn't polite. It wasn't like Vinny was going to rob him. She closed the bag again. Maybe Dom just liked a lot of salt and oregano on his meals while he was on the road. Whatever. Not her business.

Piewicket nuzzled her hand, and then leapt down from the bed and began to prowl around the room, sniffing intently at the corners and near the heat register.

"You got mice on the brain, don't you?" she asked.

Pie looked over at her with an expression that was a pleased *yes*. Then she focused on the hunt.

"Good luck, sweetie." Vinny sighed. If only mice were the biggest trouble she had. She looked around the dated but decent motel room, trying to decide how to get out of the hole she dug for herself the second she got on Dom's bike.

The problem was simple. She was broke. She couldn't afford to pay Dom for anything. Not now, and not for the foreseeable future. She owed him for the ride, for the meals, for the hotel room, for the bike helmet. And she simply didn't have the dough to pay him back.

An alternative form of payment.

The phrase had been Dom's.

Vinny thought about it as she freshened up in the bathroom. Who said she had to pay him back in money? Vinny always thought sex was secretly currency, anyway. Women spent it, men took it. And sometimes it was fun.

She could do it that way. She had noticed a few signs of interest from Dom, and anyway, he was a guy. When did a guy ever turn down sex?

Not to mention that she actually really liked him, from what she'd seen so far. If she was going to do this to get over her twitchy need to give *something* back, shouldn't she do it with a guy who was nice? That way, it would be less transactional, and more like friends with benefits.

Back when she'd had a therapist, she was told she was extremely good at rationalizing her emotional needs. Vinny sneered at the memory of those sessions. She hated it when other people told her what she was thinking.

And she was sick of thinking now. Now she just wanted to *feel* something.

She brushed her teeth, made some strategic changes to her outfit, and combed all the tangles out of her hair so it almost looked polished. She was about to put on the red lipstick, but then she remembered Dom's comment after the first time he saw her wearing it. He obviously preferred women without a lot of makeup.

"Just be normal, Vin," she told her reflection. "It's just sex. He'll like it, you'll stop feeling like you owe him so much, and the world will go on."

She hoped that was true. As a general rule, Vinny

didn't do casual. Hook-ups might be fun, but to her the aftermath felt like leaving a hallway full of open doors in her wake. Vinny had some very personal beliefs about relationships, and one of them was that every single relationship—from the hi/goodbye with a waitress to the emotional bond with a lifelong partner—caused a sort of thread to grow between those two people. Sometimes, the thread was no thicker than a spider's silk, easily broken and not particularly bothersome. Others grew into heavy chains that could hold back the *Titanic*.

And who knew what sort of thread a random hook-up would create until it was too late to take it back?

Still, she knew she was going to make the offer.

A little while later, she heard the rumble of his bike, and then Dom walked into the room with two bags of fast food, and a four pack of bottled beer. "Success!"

"Hey there. Glad you're back." She smiled at him, in what she hoped was a sexy way. She was a little out of practice.

"What's going on?" he asked, looking at her warily.

Vinny shifted, putting her weight on one leg, sticking her hip out.

"I was thinking that I still owe you for the helmet, and the food, and the everything. If one guy thought it was worth ten minutes with me, why not you? Maybe we can start in on a little repayment plan."

"I've…got some ethical issues with that," he said, though he looked extremely interested.

"Oh." She shrugged out of her jacket, having adjusted her wardrobe slightly. She wasn't wearing anything beneath it but her necklaces. No shirt, no bra. Just the tangle of silver chains and charms. "What issues?"

Dom put the beers down, nearly missing the table,

since his gaze was locked on her. "Um."

"That's your objection?" she teased.

He was still staring at her. "Not good with words right now."

Vinny stepped forward and wrapped her arms around his neck. "We don't have to talk much. Ten minutes isn't that long. You don't want to waste it."

"What happens at the end of the ten minutes?"

"We'll worry about that in ten minutes." Vinny looked him in the eye. "What are you waiting for? Kiss me."

He kissed her, hard.

Vinny almost pulled back, not ready for that level of aggression. But after a second, she leaned into it, tightening her grip on him. What else did she expect when she just propositioned him in a motel room?

It probably wasn't the first time he got propositioned in a motel room, to judge by how fast he had her up against the wall by the bed. Vinny didn't even register that they'd moved, because Dom's mouth was burning across her bare skin, and physical reactions she always assumed she was in charge of were happening without her oversight.

For one thing, she was sweating. *Sweating.* Hot beads of sweat made her skin slick, so Dom's hands glided right over her body. He reached for the tangle of necklaces and moved the whole mass so they hung down her back instead. The weight of the chains against her throat made her strangely excited.

When he slid one hand over her left breast, the shape of her fitting almost perfectly into his palm, she knew she was not going to walk away from this encounter without some brain-searing memories.

"Keep going," Vin moaned when she realized his other hand was working the button of her jeans. Not that he'd be able to get them off her. Not the way Vinny's legs were wrapped around him. God, when did that happen?

Before she could think about it, she leaned in to kiss him again, her hands digging into his shoulders. "Keep going," she ordered, against his mouth.

He hadn't said anything yet, not since he first kissed her. Vinny felt a twinge of fear. What if he wasn't that impressed with her?

"You like it?" she asked. "I skipped the lipstick for you."

"Good." His response was a growl that got her even hotter. "You don't need it. You don't need anything."

She worked her hand between their bodies to gauge just how interested he was in continuing. When she felt the bulge under his jeans, Dom groaned and pressed her harder against the wall, keeping her pinned where she was.

Which Vinny decided was just fine with her. She ran her fingers over his tattooed biceps. She hadn't seen his skin up close before. One arm was covered from shoulder to elbow with a color-saturated image of that skeletal but beautiful woman Vinny associated with the Day of the Dead. The other arm was a full sleeve of abstract swirls that looked more Celtic in design.

"Ask about the ink later," he hissed, his eyes intent on her.

She grinned, then bent her head to lick his skin, tasting salt.

Then she realized that he'd got her jeans unzipped. He worked his hand under the thin fabric of her panties, making his way to right between her legs. Vinny closed her eyes when she felt him slide one finger into her. The edges of the necklace charms bit into her back, but she didn't care at all. "Oh, yeah," she whispered. That felt perfect.

"Look at me," Dom said, his voice rough.

When she didn't respond, he repeated it. "Look at me." He started to withdraw his hand.

She opened her eyes to find Dom staring straight back. "What do you want?"

Dom eased his finger back into her. "I want you to look at me."

Vinny kept her gaze on him, even though it felt painfully intimate to let him see her face while he was touching her like that. She gasped when he rubbed her just the right way, and closed her eyes by instinct.

"Look at me."

She opened her eyes, but looked off to the side. "I can't."

"Why not?"

Because gazing into someone's eyes is what people in love do. "It's just not my thing."

"Maybe it's my thing." He withdrew his hand, making Vinny moan at the lost sensation. Lord, she hadn't been this hot for a guy in years. At least he still had her pinned to the wall, wrapped around him.

"Dom, tell me what I have to do," she begged.

He touched one breast, his thumb circling just around her nipple. Holy hell, that felt good. Vinny sighed. "That's fine, too."

"I'll keep doing it," he said. "But first I need you to tell me something."

"What is it?" Vinny asked, stretching in response to his touch. Anything to feel this for a little longer.

"What's your name?"

She stilled. "It's Vinny." *Watch out for attachment*, she warned herself.

"I don't believe you." His voice was flat.

"What's my name matter anyway?"

"Call me old fashioned. I like to know who I'm fucking."

"That's not part of the deal."

Dom took a deep breath, his eyes virtually black in the dim light of the room. "Then no deal."

"Are you serious?"

He let go of her abruptly, leaving her to nearly lose her balance as her feet hit the floor again.

"Yeah, I'm serious."

Then he turned and stalked to the bathroom, slamming the door closed. She heard the click of the lock a second later, and then the rush of water as he turned on the shower.

Just like that. Turned on the shower. Turned off her.

Vinny leaned against the wall, shaking from the soured rush of adrenaline in her system, the ache to get off still rushing through her body. What did her name matter to him?

Chapter 6

THE WATER COULD NOT GET cold enough. Dom needed a glacier to cool down after seeing Vinny like that. After feeling her like that. The memory of her wearing nothing but those tight jeans and her three dozen necklaces was going to *haunt* him. And the last thing he needed was another girl haunting him.

Why couldn't she have just told him her name?

Eventually, he got back to normal and turned the water off. Thank God there was no such thing as running out of cold water. He took the precaution of pulling his clothes back on before he left the bathroom, even though he was one hundred percent sure that he'd find an empty motel room. No way would Vinny stick around after what he just did to her. Or didn't do to her. Or didn't do *with* her.

"Fuck," he muttered, meaning it every way he could think of.

The room was empty. Vinny's bag was gone. A weird feeling ripped through him. Loss.

Barely knew her, he told himself.

The door to the outside was open a few inches. Vinny

couldn't even be bothered to slam it properly. He moved to close it, but caught sight of something that stopped him in his tracks.

Vinny was sitting in the metal chair on the long balcony outside the room. Piewicket sat on her lap.

Dom edged the door open a bit. "You're still here." A surge of hope shot through him, along with an uncomfortable return of the lust he thought he froze out of his body.

"Pie dug her claws in and wouldn't let me go. Besides," Vinny bit off the next words, clearly mortified that she had to confess, "I'm broke."

Dom leaned against the doorway. "So that's why you came up with your alternative payment plan?" Well, that was a letdown. Whatever desire had been lingering in his system evaporated when he understood why she'd acted like she wanted him.

"Most guys would have taken it."

"Guess I'm not most guys."

"Yeah." Vinny stared at the sodium-lit parking lot. Her eyes were suspiciously glassy.

"Look, come back inside," he said.

She got up reluctantly, reaching to snag the strap of her bag by her feet.

Pie jumped from her lap and meowed loudly as she passed the threshold. Vinny, however, stopped right at the edge. "I should just go."

"Go where?" Dom asked. "It's getting late. Just get in here."

She stepped inside, and Dom secretly exhaled with relief.

"You have a bed to yourself," he went on. Was he babbling? "Just... Sleep here and figure it out in the morning."

He needed to keep himself calm. Cold, even. Mostly because he still felt Vinny's skin under his fingers. She was amazingly soft. Smooth, clean, sleek skin. Warm mouth. Long legs that wrapped perfectly around him…

"I need a beer," he muttered. He grabbed one, not even caring that it wasn't cold.

"Be happy that's all you need," Vinny said, not looking at him. She was wearing her t-shirt again, but otherwise looked far too similar to before. Dom kept his eyes on the ceiling.

"You say you need help getting out to Seattle. You could call your friend any time," he pointed out, involuntarily looking over at her again.

Her face went pink. "She…uh, she doesn't know I'm on my way."

"What do you mean?"

"I was going to surprise her. It's hard to explain."

"Friends are friends, though. She'd help you out, right?"

"Yeah. Of course." But Vinny didn't look convinced of that. "I'm going to have a beer."

She took one from the table. Before he could hand her the bottle opener attached to his key ring, Vinny angled the cap against the edge of the table, gave the bottle a confident whack so the cap flew off, and took a swig with the assurance of someone who lived half her life in bars.

"Your friend," he said. "Is she in trouble?"

"What do you care?"

"Just trying to have a conversation."

Vinny shook her head. "You wouldn't believe me if I told you."

"Try me."

Then Vinny sighed. "The reason I wanted to surprise

Em is that we kind of had a big fight the last time we saw each other. And I don't know if she'll be happy to see me. But I have to be there. I *have* to."

"Why?"

She sighed, looking frustrated and fearful, an expression Dom had seen on clients pretty often. "I think she is in trouble," Vinny said, her voice low, confessional. "I had a dream where…where she died."

"Okay." Dom took another sip of beer. This was something he could focus on. "Go on."

"I know how it sounds," she said, sitting on her bed and turning partly away. Hiding. "But it was vivid. Way too vivid. And I kept having the nightmare, night after night."

"What exactly happened in the nightmare?" he asked.

Vinny's free hand clenched into a fist. "She gets eaten by spider. And before you say anything, no, I don't believe that she's actually going to get bitten by an actual spider and die of its venom. It's more how the dream felt."

"How did it feel?" he asked. He didn't know if there was a supernatural element to Vinny's dream—there were plenty of other possibilities—but Dom knew fear when he saw it, and Vinny was scared when she thought about this dream.

"Desperate," she said quietly. The beer was forgotten in her hand. "Emma was desperate for help, and I felt desperate to get to her, and when I woke up, the only thing I could think was that I *needed* to be there. To see her. That maybe the only thing that could stop Emma from dying was me being there."

"I can see why you're in a hurry, then," Dom said.

She looked over her shoulder, her eyes big. Her whole

attitude was vulnerable, the exact opposite of earlier, when she'd been totally in charge of herself, despite being half-dressed. "You don't think I'm nuts?" she asked.

"I've heard weirder," he said with perfect honesty. "And obviously I don't know what the nightmare means, if anything. But I bet a visit from her best friend would cheer her up."

"I hope so." Vinny gave a little shrug, and then smiled tentatively at him. "It had better. I don't have a lot of friends I'd hitch cross country for."

Good, Dom thought. The idea of Vinny hitching on the regular did not sound safe to him.

"If you can't call her, could you call someone else for help? Friend or family, someone on the West Coast?" Who would Vinny actually take a loan from?

She was still for a moment, her hand toying with a few of her silver necklaces. Then she said, very quietly, "No. No one who could help without going out of their way. And I don't like to owe people."

"Yeah, I got that."

She looked over to him, her cheeks going red. "I *will* pay you back. In money."

"Whatever." Dom wasn't rich, but the last thing he cared about was settling up with Vinny. God, he was stupid. He never should have kissed her.

Sure, it had been a while since he had a girlfriend, and yes, it had even been a while since he'd had a date that led to post-sex breakfast talk. But Vinny did a number on him just by standing there, and they were still technically at the pre-sex beer talk stage.

What was happening? Vinny wasn't exactly his preferred type of girl. He didn't even know what type of girl she was, other than tough as hell and way too self-sufficient to tolerate him for longer than she needed to. And anyway, she was going to be out of his life soon. Maybe tomorrow, if she found a more direct route to her friend. Which he should be happy about. The faster he got her out of his system, the better.

Problem was, he wasn't sure how to do that.

They each took a bed. The space between them felt achingly wide to Dom. He couldn't possibly have gotten used to sleeping next to Vin after a night. But sleeping alone suddenly felt…lonely.

When she'd muttered a goodnight at him, Vinny warned him that she might have the nightmare again. However, Piewicket cuddled close to Vinny all night, and in the morning, she seemed rested and reluctant to part… with the cat.

"I was going to say bye when we checked out of the room," Vinny told him. "But this little bugger here is so sweet."

"Well, if you're hitching again, I am going in the right direction," Dom said, sure that Piewicket was up to *something*. "You can ride with me a while longer."

She bit her lip. "You sure?"

"I wouldn't have offered otherwise." Like he would leave Vin stranded at this point. And her story about the repeated nightmare was sort of up his alley, professionally speaking. Maybe he could help her out with some information before they had to part ways.

He drove all morning, but his low gas tank finally forced him to stop. He picked a small, isolated place to gas up, primarily so Vinny wouldn't bolt. Judging by the look she gave him, she knew exactly what he was doing.

A few hours later, they stopped again to grab some lunch. Vinny ordered black coffee and fries, then stared at the menu like she was deciphering cuneiform.

Okay, so she wasn't feeling chatty. Dom fidgeted with the toothpick dispenser, popping little sticks out one after the other. He started forming some sacred symbols with them, realized what he was doing, then stopped abruptly. He put the toothpicks in his jacket pocket.

"When we get to Seattle—" he began to say.

"We are not going to Seattle," Vinny interrupted. "Not together. Look, thanks for driving me as far as you did. But I'll get a new ride at the next stop."

"And maybe end up with the sort of ride that left you on the side of the road where I found you."

"That was a fluke. I'll be fine."

"You'd be fine with me too."

"No offense, Dom, but there is no way I'm going through yet another awkward night with you. It was one thing the first time, because circumstances. But after last night…" Vinny shook her head quickly, her hair partially obscuring her face. "It's for the best. And I am the one in charge of my life. Not you."

"Hitchhiking with some new person is not safe."

"Not any more dangerous than getting on your bike in the middle of nowhere. I can really take care of myself." Vinny rustled around in her bag. She didn't meet his gaze. Was she embarrassed? Or maybe she regretted starting something with him, because she thought he'd push for more tonight.

Dom tried another tactic. "Just stick it out till the next city, okay? I will pay your ticket on whatever. I'll drive you to an airport. You can fly the rest of the way."

She frowned. "Run up my bill even more? No thank you."

"Vin, I just want to know you're safe. You can pay me

back, whenever you want. I'll let you know where to send it. But let me help you."

"I don't know." She chewed on her lower lip, obviously unhappy with her choices.

After the meal, they went back outside. Piewicket was awake, though mostly hidden from the average person.

"Hey, Pie," he said dully. "More driving. Enjoy it, 'cause Vinny's leaving us for real when we reach civilization."

Pie reacted to that news by turning big, innocent eyes on Vinny, mewing piteously.

Vinny smiled, the first time she'd done so all day. "Oh, Pie, you charmer. Don't think you're fooling me." She picked the cat up and nuzzled her.

Dom watched, feeling Pie's words in his mind.

She is strongminded.

He sighed, not able to answer her out loud. Vinny was strongminded, and her mind seemed totally focused on getting away from him.

Chapter 7

THEY RODE ON.

Vinny kept an eye on the needle of the gas tank, so she knew Dom didn't have forever. She didn't want to find a new ride. Hitchhiking was dicey, and Dom would certainly be better than some stranger. But then Vinny would have to stay near him, with all the weirdness of a failed seduction and her own less than clear motives. She really should extract herself, if only to save her sanity.

Just after sunset, Dom was forced to pull into a gas station at a rest stop. This was one of the new ones—bright and shiny and busy with truckers and travelers.

Vinny got off the bike as soon as it stopped. "I'm going to stretch my legs."

Dom hadn't even gotten to the pump yet. "By running away?"

"I didn't say anything about running away."

"No, which makes me suspicious. Besides, Piewicket's in your bag. So please don't take off with her."

Vinny was about to call him on trying such a blatant lie, but then felt her bag shift. "Damn it, Pie. You are in there. How'd you *do* that?"

Dom pointed to a few picnic tables nestled under a massive tree. "Wait over there while I gas up. You can coax her out and we can both take a rest before we move on."

After walking briskly over to the picnic tables, she sat on top of the nearest one, her feet on the bench. Pie was already wiggling out as she put the bag down. The calico stretched luxuriously, cast an inscrutable look at Vinny, and then leapt down to the ground, dashing off for a stand of tall grass. She wasn't worried about the cat at all—Pie seemed pretty wily. But part of her wanted to say good-bye.

But she didn't believe in goodbyes. They tended to get schmaltzy, or tense, or awkward, and who needed that? She liked to get out before things got weird. Her dad was a master of the Irish goodbye. When it came to ducking out, he was unparalleled.

Vinny shook her head, pulling herself back to the present. She had to decide if she was really going to stick with Dom until Seattle, or if she should just take off. It might be better if she left now, without a scene. She actually liked Dom, and to Vinny, that was a danger sign. Liking people led to connections, and connections led to broken connections. It was just a fact...

"Excuse me, miss."

Vinny swiveled. A slight, middle-aged man stood near her table. She didn't even hear him walk up. "Can I help you?"

He scratched nervously at his short beard. "I really hate to ask, miss, but you look like a smart young lady, and I'm in a bit of a crisis."

Vinny looked him over more carefully. He didn't set

off any obvious red flags. He was shorter than her by an inch or so, and thin in a wiry sort of way. He had sad eyes, like someone who'd been through one heartbreak after another. He seemed agitated, and she felt bad for him. "What's your crisis?"

"My daughter is in a state, and I can't talk to her... She's just thirteen, and she says she can't tell me..." He paused.

Vinny instantly pictured a poor teen having some emotional meltdown, the image of an awkward, blond-haired girl swirling into her mind as if it had always been there. She'd been that girl at one point in her life. She knew how awful it was. "What's wrong?"

"If you could just talk with her. For a minute. I know it's so much to ask..."

"No, it's fine," Vinny said, already sliding off the table. She wanted to help this poor girl. Why not? Vinny wished someone had done the same for her so many years ago.

"I'm parked that way," he said, gesturing vaguely. "It'd mean a lot to me. I just don't know..."

"It'll be okay," she reassured him, despite not being entirely sure what was wrong in the first place. A little niggling unease told her that she should be doing something else right now, but what? She couldn't remember. Her mind actually felt a little fuzzy, like she'd been awake for too long. "It'll be okay," she repeated

"Yes, ma'am. I'm Mike, by the way."

"Vinny," she said.

"Funny name for a girl," he said. "Not that it's any of my business. This way."

Vinny looked over her shoulder toward Dom, who was facing away from her, hunched over the bike as he checked something. She felt a qualm. Was she supposed to tell him something? She glanced toward the grass where the cat disappeared. Piewicket would find Dom all on her own.

And the girl needed her. The girl who looked like Vinny when she was younger.

They walked toward the other end of the parking lot.

"That red truck down at the end," he said, pointing. "I don't like parking close. Bad drivers ding the paint every time."

Vinny nodded, not really listening, her thoughts lost in when she was thirteen and everything felt so rough. The red truck was all the way at the end, and no one else was around here. The night felt darker than before, far away from the main hub of the rest stop.

As she got close to the truck, she heard a weird yowling that interrupted her mental trip back to her own past. "What's that sound?" she asked.

Mike was looking around for the source too.

The yowl came again. Vinny saw a familiar streak moving toward her. "Pie!" she called out. She felt a jolt, as if she'd been sleeping and the cat woke her up.

"Damn cats," Mike growled.

Vinny glanced over at him. "It's not a feral cat. I know her."

Piewicket hissed at the man.

"Pie," Vinny chided. She reached to scoop the cat up. "It's okay, sweetie. Did you want to say goodbye?"

"Might as well," Mike said, still in that growl.

Vinny frowned. "Hey, dude…"

She trailed off, confused as she looked at the man who called himself Mike. The guy no longer looked…nice. His face was paler, for one. Bloodless. Dead. And his teeth were longer. Vinny blinked, trying to clear her vision.

Piewicket jumped free from her arms, hissing again as she stood between Vinny and the guy. Oddly, Mike looked at the cat as if it was an actual threat. And Pie spat at the guy like he was a monster. Which maybe he was.

"Okay." Vinny found her voice. She stood up, her legs feeling way too shaky all of a sudden. "I'm going to leave now."

"No, you ain't, cause you're my dinner tonight," Mike said, his words sounding odd past the *fangs*. "Gotta love a girl who hitches."

Vinny stepped back, and hit something solid.

She started to scream, but then heard Dom's voice over her shoulder. "It's me, Vin."

"Dom," she gasped as she turned to face him. "This dude…"

"Get on the bike," Dom said. He didn't meet her eyes. His attention was locked on the *thing* that called himself Mike. "I'll deal with this."

"Deal with this? He's…" Vinny looked back at Mike, hoping that she'd been wrong and there was a really good reason why he looked so scary before. Trick of the light. Some perfectly rational explanation.

When she saw the fangs again, Vinny froze up.

"Two for one deal?" Mike laughed, then lunged toward Vinny.

Dom seized her by the shoulder, pushed her behind him, and literally put himself on the front line, just as the thing was rushing forward with its mouth wide open, fangs gleaming in the cold light of the parking lot lamps.

But before the thing reached them, a streak of cat crossed its path, yowling in fury. Piewicket—sweet, tiny Piewicket—had launched herself at the thing, and slashed at it with her claws.

Vinny stared in astonishment as whatever the thing was hissed in pain. Thin streaks of red appeared on his face and arms…then almost instantly faded.

"Oh, shit," Vinny breathed.

Dom used the second of distraction caused by Pie's unexpected attack to push Vinny firmly toward the bike, and out of range of the thing.

"Dom…" she mumbled, not sure what to even ask. Her brain was short-circuiting.

"I'll deal with this," he repeated. "Vinny, please get on the bike."

"Why?" She hadn't even heard him drive it up.

"Listen," he said. "Get on the bike and say *there's no place like home*. Don't argue, don't ask why. Just do it. *Now*."

Propelled by a hard shove from Dom, Vinny half-ran, half-stumbled to the bike. Dom would be running just behind her. Right?

She swung herself onto the seat. What did he want her to do? Oh, right.

"There's no place like home." As she spoke the words, Vinny could feel something happening in the air around her. A bending of light, or something like the waves of heat that caused a desert mirage. It was strange but somehow reassuring. She exhaled.

Looking back, she saw Dom standing exactly where he'd been before, blocking the thing's path to her.

"Pie! Get over by her!" Dom ordered harshly. Amazingly, despite being a cat, Pie did so, bounding to the bike. She stopped at the rear wheel, looking quite calm as she sat facing the two men. She lifted one paw and began to wash her face.

Mike peered past, eyes narrow. "What the hell, man? What's happening?" The monster looked very put out that his dinner was suddenly not being delivered.

"Basic home security spell," Dom said. "So you won't be able to pass the threshold uninvited."

What? Vinny thought. Did he just say spell?

The thing's eyes narrowed further, shifting back to Dom. "What threshold? That's a fucking bike."

"It's also my home, at the moment. And it's protected."

"Not from me." Mike growled. His face twitched, and the little remaining humanity in it faded away. The thing's —the *vampire's*—eyes glittered with a cold, shrewd intelligence. "I'm going to suck your girlfriend dry."

Dom said, "She's not my girlfriend."

"Still gonna kill her."

Vinny felt sick. A cold, clammy sensation crept up her legs and into the pit of her stomach. She fumbled in her jacket pocket for her knife.

Just as she got her fingers around it, she noticed that Dom also had a serious-looking knife in his hand.

The vampire moved into a fighting stance.

"No," Vinny gasped. She did not want Dom, or anyone, to get hurt because some crazy dude thought he was a vampire and wanted to suck her blood. "Dom, don't do this. We can leave. Please."

Dom barely glanced at her, and just said, "It's too late for that."

Chapter 8

DOM HAD GOTTEN THE CREEPING feeling that something was wrong when he'd looked up from the bike and Vinny was nowhere around. Then he heard Piewicket's warning in his mind—*lurker near*—and he immediately gunned the engine, driving toward where Piewicket was. He kept the headlight off, but he was still startled by the paleness of the vampire that had somehow found Vinny and tricked her into following it away from everyone else at the rest stop. What were the odds? Even when he was minding his own business, he met monsters.

Dom's fingers tightened around the handle of his knife. The blade was custom-made and featured a silver coating laced with spells.

The lurker's grin widened, becoming unsettling to look at.

"Oh, look," it said. "A knife. That's not going to be enough."

Dom glanced at the side pannier on the bike. That's where his gear was, and that's where the wooden stake was. The lurker was right. Dom's knife would hurt it more than a normal blade. But to kill a vampire, you needed a weapon made of wood, enchanted to defeat the undead.

The stake was there, less than twenty steps away. Unfortunately, Dom doubted the lurker would give him a time-out to go grab it. And he wasn't about to disturb the shell of protection around the bike, since that was the last line of defense for Vinny if Dom and Piewicket went down.

So, armed with only the knife, Dom went to work.

The lurker was hungry. It pounced toward him, moving unnaturally fast. Any regular person who made it this far would be shocked at the speed and reflexes of the vampire. But Dom had experience with this particular kind of monster, and he knew what he was up against.

He kept the blade up and moved fast, relying on years of fight training with his brother to keep from becoming an instant vampire snack.

Almost by accident, he managed to get a good swipe at the vampire's chest. The silver-coated blade cut into the dead flesh of the monster, causing pain and blood and a bit of surprise.

It retreated a few steps, just out of range of another hit. "What sort of toy you got there?" it asked conversationally. Vampires didn't breathe, and barely tired.

As Dom watched, the gash healed up, just like Pie's earlier claw marks. "Shit."

"That's what you're in, kid," the lurker said. "I haven't lost a fight with a meal in…ever."

Dom needed to think fast. He needed his stake. But turning his back on the thing was suicide.

He was a hunter who practically specialized in vampires, and now he was stuck fighting one without the one weapon that would work.

Audame. He cast the thought out the way he used to yell for his parents when he got in trouble.

But it was Piewicket who answered.

You are a hunter. Stay calm. Assess. Panic is surrender.

Dom took a breath, just in time for the vampire to attack again. He barely got out of range of the fangs in time, but he did jab hard with the knife while the vampire was close. Dom was rewarded with a little grunt of pain. The vampire jumped back, un-kabobing itself.

So Dom had a few precious seconds of time. Think. How can you get a stake in two seconds?

What did he have on him? Nothing. Just his knife, his wallet, and some gum and toothpicks from the diner.

Toothpicks.

"Holy shit." Dom reached into his pocket for the toothpicks he'd absentmindedly shoved in there earlier. The tiny sticks stabbed at him. Perfect.

He closed his hand around them, still watching the lurker. Its eyes were darting between Dom and the bike.

"Not your girlfriend, huh? Maybe I'll take her off your hands."

Dom knew it was thinking about leaving him for easier prey. It would rather risk dealing with the circle of protection than getting needlessly stabbed with the enspelled knife.

Calm. That was Pie again.

Dom took another breath. He needed to work a spell, fast. He summoned up the need—binding the proper magic into the little wooden vessels. He spoke the words under his breath, a mash of Latin and Spanish. The language mattered less than holding a crystal-clear intention in his mind, and these words were ones he knew very,

very well.

"Send life into this weapon, so that it may kill what is already dead."

The lurker couldn't hear his words, and might not have known what was going on. Usually, such magic was cast long before any encounter with a vampire, because those bastards didn't let most people live long enough to do anything to hurt them.

"That's the story you'll tell your brood, huh?" Dom asked, louder and in English again. "You wimped out on me to get the girl? Cause you're that tough?"

The vampire glared at him. Most lurkers considered themselves solitary creatures, beholden to no other. But they were inveterate socialites, hungry for fame and standing within their strange hierarchy. This one would hate to be called a weakling.

It rushed him, using the utmost of its unnatural abilities to practically blur through the space between it and Dom.

Dom allowed it to grab him, and even let his own center of gravity get pushed too far. Dom intentionally fell backwards, pulling the lurker with him. The thing's mouth touched his skin, and Dom had to fight off a desperate urge to push the monster away with all his strength. Once the fangs penetrated flesh, it was over for the victim. The saliva contained a venom which caused paralysis and lassitude. A victim would literally lie there helpless until the vampire took every drop it wanted.

The lurker was so intent on getting to Dom's vein that it didn't quite realize what happened when Dom rolled, forcing the vampire to lie flat on the ground, with Dom straddled on top. It was trying to grab Dom's shoulders, pulling him down to fang level.

Dom didn't want to die, so he plunged his knife direct-ly into the heart of the vampire.

The magic within the blade made it cringe horribly, but it only laughed, even as it tried to direct its energy to getting the blade out. Its cold hands curled around Dom's fist, which gripped the blade.

"Not enough, kid," the lurker hissed. "You need a stake, or flame. You have neither. Sucks for you."

Dom sat up, holding his other hand in a tight fist, the tiny bundle of toothpicks sticking out past his curled pinky.

"Surprise. I do have a stake. So sucks for you."

Dom was feeling mean. He shoved the first sliver of wood into the gap made by the knife, right up in the vam-pire's heart. The monster barely squeaked when Dom knifed it. But this tiny sliver was a whole other thing.

Dom told him, "Might take a few minutes for the ac-tual dying, but trust me, you're dead. For good this time."

The vampire's eyes widened in pain, but it still hissed, "My brood will come after you."

"God, yes, send them along." Dom withdrew the knife, then jammed the remaining toothpicks, all six of them, into the narrow gash.

The spell Dom spoke worked fast, and the toothpicks acted like needles in the vampire's dead heart. Though it wasn't alive, it needed blood to flow through its body, and the spell within the slivers of living wood prevented the blood from moving. The lurker couldn't heal up its wounds. Soon it wouldn't even be able to move the limbs of the body it used as a vessel.

Dom stood up, stepping to one side of the prone mon-ster. It tried to grab his leg and failed. The arm fell back to the ground, like a heavy weight. With each passing second, the monster grew closer to a corpse.

Seconds later, the vampire died, forever. Dom's spell separated the grip of the malevolent force and the body it occupied. The spirit of the vampire wailed, a sound heard only in the otherworlds. Then the sound withered away, leaving just the body.

Mike had been a vampire for a while, judging by how fast the body turned. The whole mass sort of collapsed and shrank, then crumbled into dust, mixed with scraps of cloth and bone fragments.

Dom sighed in relief. "Senora de Santa Muerte, take the dead and find peace for their soul." Then he switched to English "…even though they haven't had a soul in years."

After scattering the small pile of dust and crumbled bone with a swift kick, Dom sheathed the knife in its holster, concealed in a specially designed rig under his motorcycle jacket.

Dom glanced around. Luckily, no one else around the rest stop seemed to have noticed the tussle. The lurker chose its spot well, keeping as far as possible from human eyes and cameras. Still, it would be good to get moving.

He turned back to the bike where Vinny was waiting, her eyes big and her expression frozen. She looked so fragile right then, just like a little girl losing her innocence about the world. Which was essentially what just happened.

"You all right?" he asked once he reached her. There was no way she was all right.

"I don't know." Her voice came out in a whisper. She clutched Piewicket in her arms. Cats could cross borders without disturbing the delicate balance of magic, and Pie must have decided she'd be more useful to Vinny inside the circle than out. "How about you?"

"Fine. We should leave now," he said. "Together."

She nodded, accepting that with no hint of an argument. Piewicket jumped to the side pannier and readied herself for the highway. Dom got on the bike, and Vinny's arms slipped around his waist.

Dom drove away from the rest stop at a reasonable speed. This stretch of highway was straight, and he didn't have to worry about keeping it on the road.

He was sore, but not sleepy. He was too wired, just as he always got after a fight. Actual combat just wasn't something that most people got used to, even if they did it over and over. Dom was in more than his share of fights, and he still didn't feel easy after one, even if he won. He much preferred to use magic to resolve a situation before things got violent. But vampires never asked what he wanted.

He was clear headed, and intent on the road. Vinny's grasp around his body slowly loosened as the miles passed. At least she was relaxing a bit.

Dom looked for a place to pull off—Vinny needed to decompress. And honestly, so did he. He found a likely road a few miles later, following signs to a national forest. Sure enough, there was a wayside a mile or so up. No electric or water, and no one else around. But it would be fine for them.

He parked the bike and got off.

Vinny followed, looking shaky as she took her first few steps.

"You okay?" he asked.

"I don't know. I'm going to sit down." She sank onto the ground, legs crossed. She looked lost. Pie bounded out of her hiding spot and joined Vinny.

Dom got their little campsite ready. He felt the chill in the air and decided a fire was a worthwhile risk. He had a system down, and Vinny helped get the fire going, apparently grateful to have something to focus on.

Dom moved the bike so it would help block the light wind coming from the west. Then he sat beside her, careful not to touch her. He didn't know how Vinny would react to any unexpected contact just now.

Vinny barely said a word since she got off the bike, but her face was a parade of emotions. Dom waited for her to start.

"What the hell kind of specialist are you?" she asked finally. She looked at him, her face pink from the heat of the fire.

He returned her gaze. "Demon hunting, mostly," he said honestly. "But any occult weirdness or supernasties can be handled for a fee. Kind of a family trade."

"Supernasties?"

"Our fun slang for monsters," he said.

"Which ones?" Vinny asked. "Vampires, obviously. You said demons?"

"Yes."

"Zombies?"

"Oh, yeah," Dom said, wrinkling his nose in memory of the smell. "Raised dead can be a problem."

"Werewolves?"

He leaned back, relaxing at that one. "They exist, but I don't hunt them. They're generally not evil. Our great aunt Silver married one. Still dangerous, though. Werewolves, I mean. Not Auntie Silver."

"Is that true?"

"Yes. Wait. She might be a great great aunt. I'd have to look it up. Definitely married a werewolf, though."

She shook her head, not able to process that bit of information. "How about ghosts? Do you believe in ghosts?"

"Yes."

"How about angels?" she asked then, hopefully.

"Never seen one, but I keep an open mind."

"I'm gonna need a minute." Vinny took a few breaths, then closed her eyes. "Nope. I think I might still freak out. You said family trade?"

"Yup. Whole family. Our parents did it, their parents did it. We've got a bunch of aunts and uncles and cousins in it too."

"Sounds like you got more hunters than monsters."

"Sadly, no. We're outnumbered."

Vinny put her head on her knees. "I can't deal with this. I nearly got eaten by a freaking vampire. And I just wandered off with him…it….whatever. What the hell was I thinking?"

"You weren't thinking," Dom told her. "Vampires exert a sort of hypnosis over their victims. It's powerful, especially if you're not prepared for it. Trust me, the most skeptical, street smart people in the world can't think right when a vampire has them. You're compelled to do what it suggests."

She shivered. "My mind was so…fogged up. It had some sob story, about a daughter. In trouble? I don't even remember if it made sense."

"They use your own humanity against you. It's natural to want to help someone. The vampire has a little story, and uses its hypnosis to make you fill in the blanks." Dom added, "It's *not* your fault."

"What if you hadn't been there?" she asked. "Wait, back up. What was a vampire doing at a highway rest stop?"

"It's a prime hunting ground for the modern lurker. Lots of in and out, everyone focused on their own journeys. Transient population, sketchy jurisdiction. So people disappear, and who really knows where they last were?"

"Their cars would be left there," Vinny objected. That amount of logic proved that she was actually taking this surprisingly well. Dom was impressed.

"The lurkers steal the cars and resell them," he explained. "They're scavengers."

"And you beat that one." Vinny looked over at him. "Thanks. Seriously."

"Just doing my job." Dom paused. "Can I ask you something?"

She laughed, at last sounding more like herself. "Ah, the old *I just saved your life so now I get a free question* maneuver. Shoot."

"What's your real name?"

Chapter 9

OF COURSE THAT WOULD BE Dom's question. He seemed to know everything else.

"Vinny *is* my real name," she insisted. "Well, my real nickname."

"Tell me your whole first name."

"Okay, but don't laugh," she warned.

"Promise."

She took a breath, then said, "It's Lavinia."

"That's very old fashioned," he said. "But pretty."

"It's silly." Vinny had never liked her name. It was so prissy. "Worse with the middle name. Lavinia Rose. Is there any wonder that I became a punk rocker? Lavinia Rose Wellington Wake."

Dom closed his eyes for a second, as if absorbing the sound of the name. "I like it."

"What's your name, since we're sharing here?" she asked.

He pulled out his license. "Otherwise you might not trust me," he said, handing it to her.

She took it and read out, "Dominic B Salem. What's

the B stand for?"

"Benno. And, full disclosure, I have a few more names in my name, but they didn't make it onto official records. My family plans ahead."

"What does that mean?" she asked, confused.

"Names hold power," he said, leaning toward her, his expression serious. "It's smart to not let people know your whole name, unless you trust them. I'm really glad you told me, but you're right to keep it close. Don't tell people if you don't have to."

"That's a magic rule?"

"It is."

"Nice of you to tell me after I gave my full name to you."

"I only asked for your first name," he reminded her. "You did the rest on your own."

"Whoops," Vinny said absently. She was thinking on the *Benno*. "Saint's name."

"Not many people know that one," he said.

Vinny handed the license back. "Well, I was good at Catholic school."

"Thanks. Now I've got that to think about too."

"Not in a dirty way," she said, laughing again. "Dom? I'm sorry I got you into a fight. Cheese and crackers, I thought I was being nice to a stranger, and I nearly got eaten by a freaking vampire."

"Yeah, they're not super respectful of ethics," Dom said. "I know that from experience. Trust me, I don't feel bad about nixing that one."

"So I was half-right before," she said triumphantly. "You, Dominic Benno Salem, are a hit man. Just not for humans."

"Yeah, you got me." He paused. "Vin?"

"Yeah?"

"Are you okay? I mean, mentally?"

"Yeah, but I have lots of questions," she said. "Are vampires, um, common? Like, is it safe to sleep outside?"

"You didn't get killed the other night, did you?"

"No, but I know more now."

He said, "We're safe. I've got a couple of…let's just say insurance policies."

"Like that knife." She remembered only that it looked scary, and that Dom was very comfortable with it.

Now, Dom produced it from somewhere under his jacket and handed it to her, hilt first.

She took it, feeling the silky grain of ebony wood under her fingers. There was some design etched on the hilt, but she couldn't tell quite what it was supposed to be—some abstract pattern, very intricate and a little spooky. Then she looked at the blade itself.

It was gorgeous. A work of art. A very sharp, deadly work of art. It was a double-edged blade with a wicked pointed tip. The blade itself gleamed silvery blue, ripples seeming to cascade over the surface like water on a windy day. Vinny had never seen anything so beautiful and badass at once.

"Does it glow blue when orcs draw near?" she asked. She didn't mean to be flippant, but there was a lot of serious going on right now.

"When I meet an orc, I'll tell you," Dom said. "But in fact, I use it on demons and other supernasties. Sorry I didn't mention it before, but I didn't want to scare you."

Yes, that would have caused a lot of questions in Vinny's pre-vampire world. "Is it magic?"

"Yup."

She handed it back, because she had no business holding a magic anything. "You'd better keep it then. In case more vamps show up."

"Not likely. Honestly, vampires are urban predators. There's other things out here that are way scarier to a vampire than I am."

"That vamp seemed pretty scared of you. And you did, you know, kill it."

"I really, really hate vampires."

"I have more questions." Vinny paused. "Do you mind?"

"Not at all. Go."

"Are you special?"

He tipped his head to the side, puzzled. "In what sense?"

"Do you have superpowers?"

"Nope."

"You're not magically strong or fast or whatever? You said you cast a spell."

"Well, yes," said Dom. "But technically, anyone can do that if they study up and commit to it. I can cast a little…more, um, spontaneously than most people. That's the only gift I have."

"But…sorry, I keep coming back to the fact that you killed a *vampire*. How can you do that? Aren't they super hard to kill?"

"I have motivation."

"Why? What makes them worse than any other monster? You got a history with one, or something?

"Actually, yes."

Vinny thought he'd shut down after that. He looked so fierce just then, and so distant.

But then he took a breath and said, "There was a girl."

Oh, no. Vinny steeled herself. No way was this story

going to have a good ending.

"Her name was Rachel," Dom said. His voice was quieter than before. "I met her on my twenty-first birthday. First legal drink, so my friends took me out to celebrate. I don't remember much about that night after I met her. She was gorgeous, and smart, and sweet. And for some reason she liked me. By the end of the night, I was stupid drunk. But I got her number. After I got over the hangover, which hand to God took three days to recover from, I called her. We started dating." Dom fell silent, tracing patterns in the dirt with his finger. He wouldn't meet Vinny's eyes.

"Tell me she wasn't a vampire."

He regained a little composure. "No, she was human. Very human. A great human. I loved her. I totally thought she was the person I was going to spend the rest of my life with."

Vinny didn't like the desolation in his tone. "I'm guessing it didn't work out. Did she not like your demon hunting?"

"She didn't know about it, not at first anyway. We don't tell most people the truth about the world, at least not until it's necessary. So I didn't tell Rachel until we'd been together for a while. Until I trusted her with it. She took it fine. She had a spiritual streak, and hearing that monsters and the otherworlds are real didn't faze her. But no matter what I said, she didn't take the dangers seriously. She started asking questions and getting involved with some pretty dark stuff. I didn't realize what was happening until it was too late."

"She ran into a vampire?"

He nodded. "Either that, or one heard about her asking questions and sought her out. That's exactly the way lurkers play with their food. Stalk them, reel them in, trick them into being vulnerable. Vampires love mind games."

Vinny nodded, having gotten a glimpse of that.

He went on, "They love to draw out sympathy or to get people to believe they're lost, tortured souls who just need a hug. They're not. Vampires have no soul and no conscience. They're pure killers."

"And one killed your Rachel."

"I wish that's all it did to her." Dom paused, and Vinny saw that his hands had clenched into fists.

"What it did was get close to her. They're wily little fuckers. I think this one played on her curiosity about the otherworlds. She probably didn't know it was a vampire at all—they can hide it well if they want to. But that one stuck around and learned everything about Rachel, and that meant it learned about my family, and about me."

"Such as the fact that you actually hunted vampires."

"Exactly. So it kept Rachel in its power, probably drawing off a little blood here and there, but also seducing her into believing whatever it said. Then it decided it was time for round two. It took Rachel to its lair and let me know it had her. At that point, all I knew was that Rachel had been kidnapped by a vamp. I didn't know it had been playing a game for weeks already. I went after Rachel to get her back before she got turned into dinner."

"What happened?"

"I succeeded, mostly. The vampire got away, but I was able to get Rachel free. I took her home. I was ready to quit hunting, do whatever I had to so Rachel would never be in that sort of danger again."

"And?"

"I was telling her all that, and she just kept telling me that she was sorry she'd taken the risk and that she loved me and that she just wanted us to be together. And then we got to the door of my apartment."

Vinny had to remind herself to breathe. "And?"

"I had a lot of wards up around my home. Same thing I did with the bike earlier. Spells of protection and binding, and general anti-evil stuff. The second Rachel's foot touched the border, she started hissing, and I found out I hadn't saved her at all. She'd been turned already. She *was* a vampire."

Vinny saw the emotion he was trying to keep below the surface. Don't give him a hug. He's a demon hunter and demon hunters probably don't do hugs.

"Did she try to kill you?" Vinny asked instead.

"Not right then. She laughed at me, then got away before I could bind her. And then she spent the next few months tormenting me. For fun. Because that's what vampires do."

"How did she do that?" Vinny asked, not sure she wanted to know the answer.

Dom sat up, his attitude shifting to something angrier. "Sending me little messages. Letting me know she knew where my youngest brother was at all hours. Or she'd leave her victims for me to find. But the worst was that she'd play mind games, pretending that she still remembered her humanity. She begged me to help her find a way to unvamp her, to get her soul back. Even just to kill her…which was the one thing I couldn't do, because despite everything, I still loved her."

"But…" Vinny said slowly, aware that she was treading into waters she didn't know, "if you loved her, you'd kill her. Especially if she was just an evil husk, right? I'd want you to kill me in that situation. Or I would before I got made into an evil husk, I guess."

"I tried to save her first," Dom said. "I worked with my family and people they knew to discover if there was any possible way to change what happened. But there's no cure, and no way to actually end a curse like that. All you can do is destroy the thing that looks like the person you want to save. So in the end that's what I did."

"All alone?"

"I had some help. My family is deeply weird, but proactive when it comes to destroying evil. We tracked Rachel the vampire, trapped it, and killed it. *I* killed it," he added. "And afterward, I had to live with the consequences of everything I'd done to put her in that situation."

"It wasn't your fault a vampire found her."

Dom shook his head. "It was my fault for not preparing her better, or warning her. Or even protecting her more, which I could have done if I'd known her full name. Which, turns out, I actually didn't."

"Oh." That explained his saltiness about the name thing.

"Yeah. So that's the long version of why I hate vampires." Dom looked away, out into the darkness beyond.

Vinny wished she could do something to pull him back from the memories he was lost in. "I'm sorry. I shouldn't have made you talk about something like that."

"You didn't make me do anything, Vin. I wanted you to know what happened. What could have happened to you too."

"I'm really glad you were there tonight."

He gave her a little smile. "Me too."

They both fell silent. Vinny stared into the flames, her mind unsettled. Piewicket climbed into her lap after a while, and curled up, purring. Vinny slowly calmed down.

She wasn't calm, exactly, but something about the fire and the cat helped to knock the edge off the weirdness she'd just learned about.

Something cracked in the darkness behind her, and Vin looked back in alarm.

"Just a mule deer," Dom said, his attitude unperturbed. "Actually, two. I can see their outlines."

She nodded, trusting him. Vampires probably didn't sound like deer, and Dom could probably tell the difference.

A little while later, despite her newfound knowledge and the return of the dread she'd managed to bury up till now, she was having trouble keeping her eyes open. Sleep didn't seem compatible with the idea that the supernatural was real, but she yawned anyway.

"I guess it's time for bed," she said, half hoping he'd say it wasn't.

"Good idea. Blankets are out."

She removed Piewicket from her lap and crawled to the blankets, which Dom had arranged to be separate, probably because the fire would be enough to keep them both warm, unlike the first night they'd been forced to sleep outside.

She took a nervous breath, then asked, "Dom? Can I sleep by you? Not in a sexy way. Just…" Because she was suddenly scared of the dark, and this guy could kill monsters.

"Sure."

"Because I know I did that thing last night, which I shouldn't have and…"

"Vin. I said sure. No strings attached."

"Oh. Thanks." Vinny brought her blanket close to his and laid down. He shrugged out of his leather jacket, then did the same.

She wriggled her body to be next to his. To get comfortable, she had to put her arm over his chest, which was a little awkward. "This all right?" she asked.

"I'm not complaining, am I?"

"Do you always answer questions with questions?"

"What do you think?"

She smacked him gently in the chest. "You're a smart ass."

"Thank you." He paused. "I'm not going to try anything. Unless you ask nicely."

"Don't hold your breath. Sexytimes is the last thing on my mind."

"You're safe, Vin," he promised.

Vinny tucked her head on his chest, trying not to think of how well she fit next to him. That thought would lead her dangerous places, and the world was already way more dangerous than it seemed just a few hours ago. "What makes you so sure it's safe?" she asked.

"I got a sense about these things. Like when we met those bikers, or even when I stopped to pick you up."

"You thought I was dangerous?"

She felt rather than heard him laugh, a low rumble in his chest. "Let's say I thought you looked like trouble."

"But you picked me up anyway."

"I knew I could handle you."

Vinny wanted to roll her eyes…but she also wanted to think about exactly how he could handle her, and whether it would be like in the motel room, or something else. But before she could decide, her body finally gave in to post-panic exhaustion, and she fell asleep.

Chapter 10

THE MORNING SKY WAS LIGHT, but the sun had not quite risen when Vinny woke up. The air was downright chilly, even with the blanket. She huddled closer to Dom, seeking heat.

"See? A vampire-free night," he said, his voice rolling over her like warm honey.

"You're awake," Vinny said.

"Getting there. Not much incentive to get up, so I've just been thinking."

"Thinking of what?"

Dom shifted slightly, and Vinny found herself face to face with him.

"I'm thinking I'm going to kiss you," he said.

He kissed her, gently enough that she could pull away if she wanted. She did not want to at all. She leaned into the kiss, seeking not just the warmth of him, but something else too. Connection.

And the connection she felt was like an electric current. Dom needed a shave, but she didn't care. She just wanted to melt into him. She opened her mouth, because why stop now? He wasn't shy about slipping her some tongue, and she wasn't shy about taking it, because she practically glued herself to him to get more.

She pushed the blanket aside to get better access to him and in the morning light, she saw his tattooed arms clearly. Reaching out to trace the lines of the Celtic-style sleeve, she said, "You told me I should ask about these later, and it's later."

Dom glanced to where she was touching the ink, at the center of a complex spiral design. "It's not that long a story. My dad's side of the family has some Irish roots. So I wanted to represent that, I guess."

"These spirals look like the stones at Newgrange," Vinny said, idly following the curve of one of them.

"That's exactly what it comes from," Dom said. "How do you know about Newgrange?"

"I've been there. It was one of the stops on my European tour."

"Your band went on a European tour?"

She wrinkled her nose, annoyed at herself. "No. Not any of the bands. I meant I traveled Europe—the British Isles and some of the continent, mostly the Western part. It was a while ago."

"I could see you backpacking that," Dom said.

Actually, Vinny hadn't backpacked at all. Her mother had paid for the trip, which included stays at exclusive guest houses and five-star hotels. It had been her last bid to get Vinny to come back to school and be a good, respectable daughter.

It didn't work.

"It doesn't matter," she said. "Point is, I hit a lot of the landmarks. Newgrange was one of them. I thought it was really cool. Kind of like being in a church. I'm not churchy, but it felt sacred."

Dom nodded seriously.

She pointed to the other tattoo, the Mexican Lady Death. "You probably had some church-going in your life."

He grinned. "More than I wanted. I was an altar boy."

Vinny laughed out loud. "I'd pay to see a picture of that."

"Pictures exist. My abuela would show you them for free."

"But you didn't get this ink when you were an altar boy," she said.

"Much later," he agreed. His eyes darkened. "Let's change the subject."

"To what?"

He kissed her again. Vinny was content to let him pull her beneath him. She liked the warmth of being surrounded by the blankets, and then him. It blocked out the world, and left only them.

God, this was bliss. It was so different than before, when Dom had been aggressive, and even harsh. Now he put no pressure on her, he just was there, diligently making her turn to liquid with every touch of his mouth. She could stay like this for hours, just kiss after kiss after kiss. An all-day make out session.

The jangle of a cell phone ring spoiled the mood.

Dom sighed, and rolled away for a second. He got his phone out of a pocket and mashed the button to stop the call. Then he looked back at Vin with an apologetic smile.

"So" she said finally. "That was good until the interruption, anyway."

He lay back, staring up at the sky. "I've been wanting to do that since, well, almost since I met you."

"You hid it well. Especially when you flat out turned me down in the motel room."

"The timing was bad," he said.

Vinny's reasons were bad, is what he meant, but Vinny knew he was too polite to put it like that. "And it's better now?"

"I don't know. But before, it felt wrong." He shifted again, seeking another kiss, this one a little more searching. "Feel that?" he asked after he pulled away.

Vinny felt a little lightheaded. Kisses weren't actually supposed to taste sweet, were they? That was a metaphor. But that last kiss, she could eat that up with a spoon.

"Feel what?" she asked.

"It's want," he said seriously. "Before, you didn't want me."

"Um, no offense, but you're an idiot."

"I don't mean you weren't turned on, Vin. Hell knows I was. But you didn't put on that little show because you liked me. You were trying to pay for something. It was all wrong, especially because I didn't want to get paid."

"But it's different this morning?"

"Yes." He kissed her again. "Now we know each other's names."

"That's not the same thing at all."

"I'm not good with words right now." He slid a hand down to her waist, then her hip. "Vin, how would you—"

The phone rang again. Dom closed his eyes, and growled, "For fuck's sake, Mal." He grabbed the phone. "*What?*"

Vinny couldn't hear the person on the other end, but after a moment, Dom said, "Today. Swear it. I lost a little time. Killed a lurker. No, just happened to cross paths with one. No client. Yeah, okay. Don't call again."

He put his phone back into his pocket. "Damn it."

"Who's Mal?"

"My brother. Helpfully reminding me that I have somewhere to be."

"I really wish we both didn't have somewhere to be."

"But we do," Dom said. "The timing's still bad. Sorry."

"Uh, it's probably for the best. Not that you'd know it, but I swear I don't do casual."

"Neither do I. All evidence to the contrary." He briefly touched her cheek, then said, "Things don't always work out."

"Story of my life," Vinny agreed. She sat up before she could change her mind. "If we hit the road, we can get some breakfast. I'll even pretend to try to pay before you beat me to the check."

They stopped at a roadside restaurant not long afterward. Breakfast was quiet. The diner was pretty empty, but more than that, Vinny and Dom didn't know what to talk about.

Her mind still on the insane events of last night, Vinny muttered, "When the magic flies away and the shadows dry next day…"

"…all that's left is dust," Dom finished.

"You know *Dark Carnival*?" she asked. Not many people did.

"You kidding? It's one of my default movies. My brothers and I watched it practically every weekend for a year. I can recite all the lines."

"Isn't Gene Kelly *so* good in it? He's terrifying in that one scene with the funhouse mirror. The ways he *moves*… Good on one side, evil on the other. I love it."

Dom nodded, but didn't add anything.

They fell silent again. Vinny had to tell herself that trading obscure movie quotes was not the way to disentangle herself from a guy.

Vinny drank too much coffee, trying to make her brain behave. It kept jumping back to Dom's kisses that morning, replaying, offering a hundred potential futures if they'd done things a little differently.

"Vin?" Dom was looking at her.

"What?" she asked, realizing he'd asked her something. "What did you say?"

"I asked if you were okay."

"Yeah. I'm…thinking. Sort of. Overthinking."

"I do that a lot," he said. "Let me know if you want pointers." Then he showed her the map he'd been looking at on his phone.

"We'll reach Seattle by the end of today, no problem. Late afternoon, if we're lucky," he said.

"Great," Vinny said. She didn't feel great. As much as she wanted to get to Emma, she wasn't looking forward to saying goodbye to Dom. She knew chances were very slim that they'd see each other after that. Maybe they'd stay in touch online, but how often did that work, really? And what did they have in common, really?

"Guess we should get on the road for real now." Dom turned to her. "I kind of want to drive slow. But I won't. I don't want to keep you from your friend."

"Thanks," Vinny whispered. Damn. Why did this demon hunting bad boy have to be so nice?

She held onto him the whole day, wishing life wasn't complicated.

He gassed up a few miles before they hit Seattle. "Getting close. You should give me your friend's address so I know where I'm going."

"Oh, no. You don't have to do that. Just drop me anywhere near transit and I'll do the rest myself. You're not a chauffeur."

He said, "You think I'm only going to go ninety-nine percent of the way, Vin? Be serious."

"Look, it's fine. You've got your job to get to. I'll call now that I'm close…"

"Vin." He shut her down. "Give. Me. The address."

She gave it to him—she knew it by heart.

He paused, entered it into his phone, and frowned.

"It's out of the way," she said hurriedly. "It's not quite in town, so…"

"I'm taking you, Vin. No argument."

"But it's *far*."

"Nope," he said. "Let's roll."

Chapter 11

DOM HAD GIVEN HER A funny look when he heard the address, but he had insisted on taking her, so Vinny decided to just roll with it. She wanted to get the most out of the last part of their time together, so she held onto him way tighter than she had to.

Emma lived well outside the city, where the ground rose rapidly to take the bike into hills swathed in lush evergreens. A little fog hovered in the tops of the branches because this area was so close to the sound. There were a ton of bays and little waterways around here. They drove across a bridge over a fast-running river, high from rains and snowmelt. The very few houses that could be glimpsed from the road tended to be big and expensive.

At last a familiar gate appeared. Vinny tapped Dom on the shoulder and pointed to it. He slowed the bike, stopping directly by the gate. It was heavy metal, and locked in a serious way. An electrified fence ran along the property.

Dom edged the bike up next to the security intercom positioned so people could press the button without getting out of a vehicle. He pulled his helmet off, and Vinny did the same.

"Time to let her know you're here," he said, looking back at Vin.

Feeling more nervous than she would ever admit, Vin learned over and pressed the buzzer. "Hope someone's home."

After a few seconds, a woman's voice answered, the sound crackling a bit. "Hello? Who is it?"

"Hey! It's Vinny. You should open your gate."

There was a pause. "Vinny? Vin?"

"How many girls named Vinny do you know?" she asked.

A shriek burst out of the speaker. "Oh, my God! Vin? Is that really you? Like right outside?"

"Open your damn gate and find out," Vinny responded with a huge grin. A huge weight around her heart lifted, and she took a breath. Had she really thought Emma wouldn't let her in? Was she that messed up about friendships?

"Opening! Get in here, you little snot!" Emma's voice cut off as the gate buzzed and started to swing inward.

"Okay if I keep the helmet off for the rest of the trip?" she asked Dom.

"Just this once." He smiled back at her. Then he said, more seriously, "Hey, Vin. Don't mention what I do. If anyone asks, I'm your ride."

She hadn't planned on mentioning it. How do you explain a demon hunter to your friends?

He drove up a very long, twisting driveway to the top of a ridge. A huge, modern house sat up there, flanked by a forest of tall pines on one side. On the other, the ridge fell away to offer a view of a sparkling bay. Behind that, another line of mountains hid the Pacific. The sunsets here were spectacular.

"This is nice," Dom said in a neutral tone, taking in the mansion and the view. What he thought about it all, Vinny couldn't say. Maybe he found it pretentious. But after all, this house was built on rock and roll.

Emma was already running out the front door, hopping ridiculously after one of her shoes fell off on the steps. Vinny just got off the bike in time to be tackled by her friend.

Emma crushed her in an embrace. Vinny returned it, so happy to see her. Why had she stayed away so long?

"Hey, there," she gasped out when she could get a breath.

"Ohmygod…ohmygod…ohmygod…," Emma kept saying. "You're here. This is the best. I can't believe you're here. And why'd you sneak up on me? I would have flown you out, you jerk."

"Surprise." Vin couldn't stop from laughing, not from the expression on Emma's face, but from the sheer joy of being with her best friend again. And more importantly, seeing Emma perfectly healthy and happy. Not in danger at all.

"Holy shit, you're such a sneaky little…I'm so glad you're here!"

Vinny laughed again, prying herself out of Emma's arms.

Emma finally noticed Dom. Her eyes widened. "Um, hi."

"Hi," Dom said, looking exactly as cool and distant—and hot—as he had when Vinny first saw him.

"Oh, hey," Vinny said awkwardly. "Emma, this is Dom. Dom, my best friend Emma. She lives here." *Duh, Vinny. Of course she lives here. It's her house.*

Dom nodded, then offered a hand to shake. Emma took it, but obviously wanted nothing more than to corner Vinny and ask her a million questions.

Just then, Dom's eyes shifted to someone else coming out of the house. Emma turned and yelled, "Jonas! Vinny's here!"

"Yeah, I got that," the man said. His tone was deliberately cooler-than-thou. If he was surprised, he didn't show it. But then, Jonas was always like that.

Vinny waved to him. "Hey! Surprise!"

Jonas gave her the smile that had been plastered on albums and posters and magazine articles for years. "I am shocked, *shocked* to discover Vinny in this establishment." His smile faded a bit as he took in Dom.

"Hey. Jonas Belling, but you probably knew that," Jonas said, offering a hand.

Dom shook it politely. "Call me Dom."

"Jonas, how about you show Dom around real quick? We girls have to catch up." Emma immediately pulled Vinny over to another spot of the yard. The men walked toward the gigantic garage, presumably so Jonas could show off all his fancy cars, which he tended to collect. Vinny waved at Dom when he was dragged off.

"You look great!" Emma said.

"Ha," Vinny retorted. "You look better than me...as usual."

It was true. Not only was Emma gorgeous, with pale, clear skin and dark brown hair that fell in waves down her back, she was also curvy like Vinny wasn't. Ever since Vinny met her, Emma was always the one men looked at when they walked into a room. Vinny was never jealous of that. In fact, she felt relieved when attention went to Emma.

Years later, she was still gorgeous. Only her eyes were a little strained, with shadows underneath. But she was smiling, and she did look fantastic.

Emma looked over at Dom, then grinned conspiratorially at Vinny. "I see you showing up wasn't the only surprise. Nice arm candy you've got there. Bad boy comes complete with bad boy bike. How come you never mentioned him?"

Vinny shrugged, playing it down. "Nothing to mention. He was my ride. Most of the way. He picked me up on the side of the road in Texas. It was hot."

Emma's eyes widened. "Picked up? As in, literally? You hitched a ride with him?"

"Yup."

"But he's not just a ride anymore, right? He drove you all the way from Texas, which means you got to know him. I hope you did, anyway."

Vin knew what Emma meant by getting *to know him*, and she got a rush of shyness. "Uh, no. Not really."

"You didn't?" Em sounded so disappointed.

"No," said Vin. "But we did, um, make out a bit once. Maybe twice."

"Oh, that's better. I guess any more would be fast for you. That hasn't changed, right?"

"Of course not," Vinny said, feeling defensive. But then she glanced over at Dom, and he smiled back at her. It was a smile with *voltage*, and not only did she forget what she was going to say to Emma, she almost forgot to breathe.

"Uh-huh," Emma murmured, having noticed Vinny's

reaction. "Even if he's just a ride, this guy is interesting. If you let him go without at least trying him on for size, I will never let you forget it."

"Let's see if you still approve after you actually, you know, talk to him," said Vinny. She knew Emma would approve. Dom got more charming every second he was around. Even when Vinny was mad at him, she still liked him.

Then Emma looked over Vinny's shoulder, an odd expression on her face. "Is that a cat?"

"Oh! Piewicket!" Vinny spun and saw Pie standing near Dom's bike, looking around the place as though it *might* be good enough for her. Or not. "Yes, Dom's got a cat."

"He has a cat? You should totally snag him!"

"A pet is a terrible reason to hook up with someone." Vinny wasn't a relationship expert, but she was pretty sure of that one.

"I've hooked up with people for way worse reasons," Emma said. Then she zipped toward the cat. "Oh, you're so cute!"

After seeing the cat claw a vampire, Vinny didn't think cute was the best word to describe Pie, but that would be hard to explain. So all she said was, "She's an extremely good kitty."

"I love her! Does she like being petted?"

Pie nuzzled Emma's hand and purred loudly.

Emma's expression slid into the blissful zone. "Oh, you poor thing. We need to get you some food and treats, stat. Do you like milk?"

Pie's purring volume increased.

"Using your looks to get what you want, huh, Pie? Typical."

The men had rejoined them, and it was Dom who commented on the cat's opportunism.

Jonas bent down to pet the cat, but Pie flattened her ears at him and scooted away.

"Oh, look at that," Emma teased. "Guess she likes me better!"

"That's fine," Jonas said, straightening up. "I'm allergic to cats anyway."

"Since when?" asked Emma, with one eyebrow up.

"Maybe this cat is allergic to me."

"Well, hope she's okay in the house."

Jonas looked alarmed. "They're not staying here!"

"Oh, we can't push Dom out now," Emma said with a conspiratorial smile toward Vin. "He just drove Vinny all the way here. He's got to stay for dinner at least. You need to eat, right?" she asked Dom.

He nodded. "Sure do."

"And your kitty needs downtime. Let's get you guys comfortable."

Emma and a reluctant Jonas led them into the house. Jonas said Vinny had to have the blue bedroom—that being a nice big one that looked out over the bay. He then pointed Dom to a much smaller room across the hall and down at the end—away from Vinny's.

"You can chill there, and the cat doesn't need a ton of room, right? You can keep her in the closet."

"Jesus Christ, Jonas," Emma snapped. "Show some class. Dom, let the cat do whatever she needs to do. She doesn't have to be locked up."

"Say that again after she claws the hell out of the furniture," Jonas muttered.

"She's good," Vinny said, in defense of Pie.

"We'll let you guys get settled," Emma interjected.

She put her hand on Jonas's arm, virtually dragging him away. "Come on downstairs for drinks when you're ready! We have so much to talk about!"

Once Emma and Jonas disappeared, she turned to Dom. "So."

He dropped his leather bag on the bed. "So. Who exactly are these friends of yours? What do they do?"

"They're musicians."

"I didn't know musicians were millionaires."

"Well, one of Jonas's bands made it big. You heard of Mercury Thief?"

Dom looked puzzled, as if mentally going through playlists. "Maybe?"

"Do you live under rocks? Anyway, the band had some great timing, and their songs got on the soundtracks for those movies with the car racing and the robots…shit movies, but people liked the music. There were tours and a lot of ticket sales. Then Jonas got a gig to actually write the score for the next movie in the franchise. He banked a ton of the money. That's how they were able to build this place. There's a recording studio downstairs and practice space and everything. Jonas planned it all out."

"What about Emma?" Dom asked.

"She was in another band when they married, but she's more of a writer. Music journalism and profiles and stuff. She knows a ton of people in the industry."

"But the money is Jonas's?"

"Why?" Vinny asked.

"Just curious. Did you two used to date?"

"Me and Jonas? Hell no." Vinny laughed. "Why?"

"He was very…not pleased at the idea of me. I got the impression he was jealous."

"That's crazy. He's got Emma, who's way hotter than

me."

Dom looked skeptical. "He's got something for you."

She shifted, uncomfortable with the idea. "That's his rock star persona. He's just real flirty."

"Huh. He wasn't being flirty when he was warning me off you."

"What did he say?"

"He said I'm not your type."

Vinny bristled immediately. "I don't have a type."

"That's what he said next. He said you do have standards, implying that I'm not up to them. Or that nobody is…including him."

"You read him wrong," she said. "And anyway, why do you care what he thinks?" Vinny grabbed his hand. "New subject. If I forget to say it later, thanks for everything."

"Hmm. Well, don't thank me yet."

"Why not?"

"Save it till the end, is all," Dom said cryptically. "We should probably go downstairs. Emma is expecting us… mostly you."

"Oh, she's curious about you too. Prepare for a lot of questions."

Since Emma had declared, loudly, that Dom had to stay for dinner, that meant he stayed. And dinner was very nice. Emma, now wearing a long, casual dress that made her look like a boho princess, served it outside on the deck so they could watch the sunset as they ate.

Dom took it all in stride, apparently perfectly comfortable with these new people. Emma warmed up to him instantly. She kept nudging Vinny's foot with hers every time Dom said something that made her laugh.

Partly to save her poor foot, Vinny volunteered to

clear the plates, and Jonas stood up to help.

"Wow, look at you being all domestic," Emma said to Jonas, a bite to her comment.

Vinny could tell that the couple was not having the best time, but she tried to smooth it over. "Always nice to have help. We'll be back in a bit."

In the house, after they got the plates to the kitchen, Jonas pulled Vinny along into a side room and closed the door. "Hey, sweetheart. It's really good to see you. Honestly. But also I wanted to talk to you."

"What's up?" Vinny asked. "Are we having a secret meeting?"

"Sort of. What's the word on this guy you're dragging around?"

Vinny remembered Dom's comment that Jonas seemed jealous. She hadn't really believed it, but there was something in Jonas's voice now. Maybe big brother protectiveness?

"You heard the story at dinner," she said. "I got into a bad spot while hitchhiking and Dom helped me out. That's it, really."

"Then why did he drive you all the way here? This guy could be some kind of stalker."

"I don't think it counts as stalking if I say it's all right," Vinny pointed out.

"Is it all right with you?" Jonas asked. "Did he suggest it? Or pressure you?"

Vinny made a face. "What's your problem? You don't like him."

Jonas sighed. "Look, sweetheart. I've got some experience with this. When random people appear out of nowhere and hang around, it's because they want something from you."

"Well, then I'm good, because I don't have anything. I'm flat broke. Seriously, Dom paid for most of my meals on the way."

"You let him do that?" Jonas was surprised. He knew as well as anyone that Vinny didn't like to owe people.

"I'm going to pay him back. But seriously, you're getting worked up over nothing. Dom doesn't want anything from me. It's not like I'm rich or famous. Not like you, superstar."

"You're pretty cute," Jonas said, giving her a grin. "He might want a piece of you, baby."

Vinny blushed. "Maybe." *Definitely.*

"Just be careful," Jonas said. "You come running to me if that guy tries anything you don't like."

"Since when do I come running to anyone for protection?" Vinny asked. *Other than when a vampire attacks.*

"There's always a first time. Anyway, I'm here for you. Me and Emma."

"Thanks." She stepped toward the door.

"Hey, we're not done. I've got something for you."

"You do?"

"Birthday present."

"You didn't know I was coming!"

"I got it a while ago. Never knew where to mail it. You move around so much." He pulled a little jewelry box from a pocket and held it out to her. His hand shook a little, and Vinny wondered if he was feeling all right. "Here."

Vinny took the box and opened the lid, revealing a rather delicate looking gold charm on a long, thin gold chain. The charm was all metal—no stones—and it was an odd, geometric style, with a triangle overlaying a circle and some other bars laid across those. Art Deco. Or something.

The necklace was not exactly her style, but there was something compelling about it. Vinny touched the charm gently. "This looks old. Like an actual antique." The golden color was very soft, almost matte. Nothing like the bright, gleamy gold jewelry in all the stores.

"Yeah, I think so." He paused. "Actually, Emma found it in some junk shop when we were traveling through Europe a while back and she just…thought of you. You and all your crazy jewelry. So we bought it. You can add it to your collection, hey?"

Vinny put it on, mostly to make Jonas happy. Once added to her many other necklaces, it blended in surprisingly well.

He smiled. "Looking classy, Vin. Just like you. Happy birthday. Few days early, but what the hell."

"Thanks," she said. "Let's go find the others."

They returned to the table, and Vinny forgot the necklace as soon as she looked at the sky. The sunset had moved to the red and purple phase, and Vinny wanted to stop the colors from changing more, because every second that passed brought them closer to the time Dom would have to move on.

Emma offered a chocolate cake as dessert. It was crazy good and Vinny practically inhaled hers. Dom seemed to be more into the coffee, which was much fancier than the diner coffee they'd lived on for the road trip. Vinny wondered if Dom was drinking coffee to stay awake once he left the house.

"More coffee?" Emma asked him. "We have it roasted special. I know it's insufferably coastal elite of us, but it really is good."

"Amazing. As a non-elite midwesterner, I approve."

Dom gave Emma a smile that nearly made Vinny's stomach flip.

Jonas put down his fork. He'd barely touched the cake. "Hey, look here, Dom. I know you have to get on the road again. Vinny's all pay-as-you-go, but that's not my style. And since you brought Vinny to me—us, I insist on paying you for your trouble."

"No trouble," Dom said.

"In any case, this should cover expenses." Jonas casually dropped a wad of hundred dollar bills onto the table.

Vinny raised an eyebrow. That amount would cover a charming vacation in the Caribbean. Jonas was showing off, in the most blatant way possible.

"Well, thanks for that," Dom said, without making a move toward the cash, "but I'm not leaving."

Both Vinny and Emma leaned in, saying simultaneously, "You're not?"

"Nope."

Jonas frowned. "Why not?"

"Because I haven't even heard about your problem yet, Jonas." Dom sat back in his chair, totally at ease.

"*My* problem?" Jonas asked.

"Yeah. You did get the message that I'd be the one to show up, right? You, Jonas Belling, called my family business, Salem Associates, to take care of some supernatural trouble. I'm Dominic Salem. But yeah, call me Dom." Now he reached for the cash. "Let's get down to business. What's haunting you?"

Chapter 12

DOM DIDN'T BELIEVE IN COINCIDENCES, so when Vinny gave him an address matching the one he'd been given by his brother, Dom knew something strange was going on. Strange didn't faze him. But it did make him extremely curious. There was a reason why he ran into Vinny a few days ago, and it was linked to whatever was happening here, with his client. The very time-conscious Jonas Belling.

And his client was definitely not spilling everything he knew. Not even to his wife.

"*Haunted*? What the hell do you mean by haunted?" Emma demanded. She looked outraged. "I live here, and this house is not haunted! Jonas, explain."

"Uh, I didn't want to scare you, babe."

"Let me ask again." Emma leaned on the table and gave Jonas a look that Dom definitely would call scary. "What exactly has been happening in the house that you'd say means it's haunted?"

"Well." Jonas glanced at Dom, but didn't say more. He looked incredibly uncomfortable.

"I'm fairly difficult to surprise when it comes to para-normal things," Dom said. "Why don't we start with what you told my brother when you first contacted him?"

Jonas nodded. "I got a hold of your number through a friend who said you were legit. Cody Hodge?"

"Oh, yeah," Dom said. "I remember that. We stopped a poltergeist from tormenting his daughter."

"He said he didn't think it would do a damn thing, but whatever you did really worked. So I was hoping you could do the same thing here. A sort of full-house de-haunting? Or general demon decontamination. Whatever you call it."

"It doesn't quite work that way. I need to know exactly what's causing the problem so I know exactly how to fix it. So describe what's going on."

"Well. I haven't been able to sleep for a while. Weeks. Few months really."

"That's true," said Emma.

"And I hear a voice sometimes, at night. More than that. Almost every night. Nothing that could come from a real person in the house. Mostly it's just the two of us here anyway. And I hear music in my head."

"You're a musician," Emma said. "You're supposed to hear music in your head."

"Not like this," Jonas said with a shudder. "It's creepy as hell. Anyway, I honestly believe that there's some-thing…otherworldly…causing it. And I want it to stop."

"I'm going to need a lot more detail than that," Dom said. "Why don't you start at the beginning? When did you first notice something wrong?"

Jonas's eyes flitted to the women, then out to the spec-tacular view. "Maybe…a year ago."

"A *year*?" Emma burst out.

"About that. I came home after a trip to LA, and the house was freezing, then hot, then cold again. I thought it was the HVAC on the fritz, but it wasn't. I began to realize that the hot and cold was…in a pattern. If Emma and I got into an argument, the temperature dropped right after. The cold would follow me. And I started to hear whispering."

"Words?" Dom asked sharply.

Jonas shook his head. "No. Not exactly. It's really hard to describe. It was like eavesdropping on another language. Weird hissing and sounds that were almost words, but not quite. I heard the whispering in my dreams, and I kept waking up. Emma, you remember."

"You did get insomnia," she said slowly. "But you told me it was anxiety over that movie score gig. Rewrites."

"What else could I say? I didn't want to tell anyone, because that would mean I had to prove it was real. I didn't know who'd believe me."

Dom considered, then said, "I'll need to spend some time checking the house out. And the property. And asking questions."

"How much time?" Jonas asked anxiously.

"It depends."

"You gotta solve this by the end of the week."

"There's a deadline?" Dom asked.

"I'm making it a deadline," Jonas said. "I'm paying for whatever voodoo you're doing."

"It's not voodoo," said Dom. "Voodoo is a very specific type of magic, and I doubt it's relevant here. Unless you've previously worked with a voodoo practitioner for any reason?"

"No! I haven't worked with anyone because I've got an *image* to maintain, and I don't want to sound like a crazy person."

Dom was used to clients who hated the fact that they had to take the supernatural seriously.

But Emma said, rather frostily, "Believing in spirits isn't going to push the needle on the celebrity crazy meter. I can't believe you didn't tell me about this. Not that we talk anymore." The last words came out like razors. Dom glanced at Vinny to see how she took her friend's statement.

Vinny looked right back at him, but the only thing he saw in her eyes was anger. Whoops. She was pissed.

Jonas glared at Emma, but then said to Dom, "You can do whatever you got to do. Start tomorrow."

"I'll start right now," Dom said. "It's getting dark, and that's when stuff usually gets interesting. I'll just look around. Let you know if I have questions."

He excused himself. Partly, he really did want to get the lay of the land, and partly he wanted to get away from the cold war between Jonas and Emma. But he also didn't like the way Vinny was glaring at him. That was going to be a fun talk…assuming she ever talked to him again. After all, Vinny was exactly where she wanted to end up when he first met her. She didn't need Dom anymore. She could easily avoid him in this mansion. And once he wrapped up the job, he would be gone. Without her.

Dom used a favorite meditation technique to push thoughts of Vinny out of his mind, along with the awareness that he was not at all looking forward to leaving her. After a couple of minutes, his head was clear. Mostly. Anyway, he had work to do.

Chapter 13

AFTER DOM LEFT, VINNY LET out a huge breath. "What. The. Hell."

"Seems to be the question we're all asking." A very put-out Emma looked first at her, then Jonas.

He stood up from the table, wobbling on his feet. "Um, I gotta take care of something. You girls can catch up."

"You're not getting out of explaining *anything*," Emma shouted after him as he fled the scene. Then she took a big drink of red wine and looked back at Vinny. "So. What the hell?"

"I didn't know. I swear."

"You didn't know what? That your bad boy was an exorcist?"

"He's not my anything, and I meant I didn't know he was coming here already. Or that Jonas asked him here. I promise."

"This is nuts," Emma said, rubbing her temples. "I have no idea what I'm supposed to take seriously right now. A haunted house? *Our* house? And this random guy is supposed to be able to fix it?"

"I don't know about any haunting," Vinny said, slowly. "But Dom is for real."

"How do you know that? You've never been into any of this woo-woo stuff."

"Understatement. But I know he's not a faker."

"Again, how?"

Vinny didn't see any way to avoid it. She told Emma the whole story, from getting picked up on the side of the road, to her running into another guy who turned out to be a vampire, and how Dom had handled that little situation in a terrifying and terrifyingly competent way.

Emma's eyes got wider and wider as Vinny told the story, making Vin glad she decided to leave out the part where Piewicket also joined the battle against the vampire. For some reason, she knew that asking Emma to believe a *cat* fought monsters would be over the line.

"So whatever is happening with the house or with Jonas, I'm pretty sure Dom will know what to do," Vinny concluded. "Even if his only answer is to move out."

"I don't want to move out," Emma said, looking out over the scenery. "I love it here. I'll do anything I have to to stay here."

Something in her tone made Vinny a little nervous. What did Emma mean by *anything*? "It's just real estate," she reminded her friend.

"You don't get it, Vin. You don't care about this sort of stuff. You drift like…a drifter."

"Nice analogy, lady."

Emma stifled a laugh. "Give me a break. You know what I mean. You've never cared about having a home. You go from place to place to place. You're always ready to move on. I can't live like that."

Vinny nodded. Emma was way more of a nester than

she was, though most of Vinny's moves were involuntary. She ran out of rent money, or lost a roommate, or just had to squeak out of the way of her parents, who tended to try to find out where she was living despite Vinny telling them several times that she never wanted to see either of them again.

But that didn't mean part of her didn't long for a home base. A place bigger than her backpack. Maybe a place where she could stash a few books, and have a bed, and know that she could always stay there.

"You can always hang out here," Emma said. She often had the best friend gift of reading Vinny's mind.

"Too fancy for me," Vinny joked.

Emma snorted. "This house isn't half as fancy as what you're used to. Speaking of which…"

"What?"

"I got to tell you," Emma said. "Your dad called me. Maybe three weeks ago."

A wash of cold rushed over Vinny, a visceral reaction to the unwelcome news. "He did?" Her father wouldn't have known that Vin and Emma had a bit of a falling out a few years ago. It was pretty natural for him to think Emma would know where Vinny was at all times.

"Yup. He wants to see you."

"Did you tell him how to reach me?"

"Of course not." Emma looked offended at the notion. "I just told him your last phone number stopped working like a month before. A totally believable explanation, by the way, you vagabond."

"Good." Vinny sighed. The idea of her dad popping up out of nowhere made her furious. As if he could just walk back into her life after what he'd put her through.

"If you just talked with him, or your mom, maybe you

could…"

"Nope." There would be no reconciliation. No making nice. Vinny was her own person, and she didn't need her parents for anything. "They had their chance with me. They both blew it, in their own special ways. I don't know what my dad wants, but you can bet it's got nothing to do with making *my* life better. Let's change the subject. What's going on in your life now? Tell me something good."

Emma smiled at last. "Oh, I got something. You know who I've been working for? You'll never guess."

"Then you better tell me."

"Remember Brennan?"

"You mean Nitro Bombs Brennan?" The Nitro Bombs were a surprisingly long-lasting punk band and Brennan was the one original member left when it finally dissolved.

"Yup. We started talking online a while back, after I did an interview on women in the music industry. A sort of then and now thing for a TV special. Brennan saw it and got in touch. He sparked so many ideas, I just wanted to write again!"

"That's fantastic," Vinny said sincerely. Emma had really dropped out of writing for a while, and Vinny thought she was unhappy about it. It was one of the subjects that got them into their fight.

"He's been so great," Emma went on. "Always willing to work through my messy ideas. Got me back into writing and the scene. God, I feel like I've been asleep for the past few years. He's got a lot of connections with magazines, of course. He's working with me on a long-form project for his magazine. And he's been helping me pitch some other articles, even if he's not the one publishing them. He's so supportive."

"Sounds just like him." Secretly, Vinny wasn't surprised at all. Bren had the worst crush on Emma back in the day. Apparently, he still carried a torch for her. Possibly fueled with atomic energy.

"I thought maybe I would come out to New York and hang out with him in person…" Emma trailed off.

"You're a wife, not a prisoner," Vinny said firmly. "It's fine for you to have friends who are guys. Jonas has plenty of friends who are women."

"I know," Emma said, her voice tightening.

"Or is one of them more than a friend? Tell me." Vinny was certain Jonas had cheated on Emma more than once, though he never admitted it. He blamed all his bad behavior on addiction, and always said he was going to do better. But Vinny thought Emma made a mistake by giving in. Jonas didn't exactly have a strong moral code when it came to fun. He liked girls, and he liked drugs, and he liked having a good time. Emma was the one person who kept him from the worst of his vices. But that also meant Emma saw a lot of shit no one else ever did.

"It's not that," Emma said reluctantly. "Not cheating. But…he's getting back into the harder stuff. I've never been able to stop him drinking. But he's doing more than that again."

"Ugh. Sorry. I thought he looked a little shaky earlier. Have you talked to him about it?"

"Not directly. He's been really stressed out and weird for like the last six months. More than that. Nine? I guess because he thinks the house is haunted? But maybe it's simpler than that. He could be hallucinating it all."

"You want me to mention that possibility to Dom? In a subtle way."

"I know I can't talk about it to some stranger." Emma sighed. "I really thought that once Jonas and I got married and got this house, things would settle down. He'd grow up. We'd have a pretty normal life, with…kids and all that."

"He's still against the having children thing?"

"Yeah. He keeps saying we should wait. But I'm going to be thirty in a couple years. I don't want to wait forever."

"It'll work out," Vinny said, trying to sound convincing. "Let's sort this haunting thing first. Then you can rip him a new one for getting back on the drugs. He promised you he'd stop that. And you deserve to be happy. With or without Jonas."

"We'll be fine. It's just a rough patch," Emma said, with the ease of someone who'd said that many times before.

Vinny leaned back in her chair, taking a sip of beer. An idea came to her. She was going to prove to Emma that she didn't have to stay with Jonas. The news about the drug use was interesting, but clearly even that wasn't enough to make Emma rethink her marriage. But if Vinny could get some solid evidence of Jonas's cheating… She knew he'd done it. She knew it in her gut, but she never had any facts. Jonas's behavior was just a thing that everybody knew about and never mentioned to Emma. Some BS "politeness" that kept them from telling her the truth because they didn't want to hurt her feelings.

Vinny was one of the few people who did actually try to tell Emma. She brought it up a couple of times in the past. But Emma wasn't having any of it, and in fact, their most recent conversation was what put their friendship on ice for the past couple of years.

Still, friends were friends, and Vinny had messed up enough in her life. Now that she was here, and saw that Emma was unhappy, she could do this one thing right.

"Vin," Emma said, her tone shifting. "What really made you come out here? What the hell made you *hitchhike* all the way here?"

"Lack of money," Vinny said quickly.

"Don't be cute. You know I would have covered you. Give me the real reason, 'cause I know there is one. Don't forget, sweetheart, I *know* you."

Emma did know her. And Vinny did need to tell her about the nightmare. No time like the present.

"I'll tell you, but you have to not interrupt. And you can't laugh it off."

"Oh, wow." Emma leaned forward. "I'm listening."

So Vinny told her about the recurring nightmares, how intense they'd been, and the underlying sense of danger she'd felt Emma was in.

"Oh, my God," Emma said finally. "That would scare the shit out of me."

"Yeah, well. Me too. So I came. Because I had to see you, and know you're okay."

"I'm fine," Emma said, spreading her arms out helplessly. "I mean, I guess my house is haunted, but…wait." Her forehead wrinkled up. "Am I in danger from a ghost? A ghost that's been around for a year?"

"I don't know," Vin said. "I'm honestly not sure about anything right now. Maybe it's nothing. Maybe I just need to go into therapy again. But I needed to get to you." She looked down at her necklaces, thinking she ought to thank Emma for the new one Jonas just gave her. But the light was failing, and the new necklace seemed to have gotten buried under several others, so Vinny couldn't pick it out.

Well, it would wait. She finished, with conviction, "I had to get here."

"And now you are here," Emma said with grin. "Whatever ghost is dumb enough to haunt this place is going to be so sad. Nothing's a match for a couple of ex-riot grrrls."

"Amen." Vinny finished the beer and rose from the table. "All right, enough of this talk. I got no answers and I'm beat."

"Sleep tight, pumpkin," Emma said. "I'll see you to-morrow. Glad you're here."

"Me too." Vinny gave her a smile and turned to go back into the house.

Once inside, a sense of quiet surrounded her. It was such a gigantic place, with so few people in it. Funny how she never thought of Emma and Jonas's house being like the ones she grew up in until now. She'd always lived in grand old houses and penthouses with pedigree, as her parents put it. Neither of them liked new construction—new construction was too easy to obtain. They liked ex-pensive estates with impressive addresses. And that meant old.

So Vinny never compared Emma's place to the cav-ernous spaces of her childhood. Right now, though, she felt a lot like she had so many years ago. Lonely, lost in a big, cold space with no friends or family she could run to for comfort.

Vinny took a breath, trying to shake off the feeling. It was the mention of her father earlier. That had thrown her out of whack, especially on top of everything else. She got a hold of herself and kept going. She didn't head for her bedroom, as she'd told Emma. Instead, she was going to poke around the house and see if she could figure out how to prove Jonas's years of misbehaving.

It would be tough. Emma would forgive nearly anything, and Jonas was a sweet-talker. That's how he kept Emma from going ballistic when she caught him doing stupid stuff. But even the drugs and the self-indulgent shopping—did anyone *need* a Jaguar E-type? No. Toyotas worked fine—didn't open Emma's eyes.

Vinny entered a room on the first floor that looked like an office. There was a big desk with trays of papers. Mail was piled up, some opened, some not. In a mood to snoop, Vinny spread the papers out with a swipe of her hand. She noticed several envelopes from Hollywood addresses. Those would be contracts and offers for work. Smaller envelopes looked like checks, or stubs indicating payment. She picked a few up and examined them. Holy shit. Jonas was getting royalty payments from a fifteen-second long "song" used in a commercial, and it was more than Vinny made all last month at her service job, with tips.

Well, she'd made her choice.

She looked through a few more papers, but what she wanted wasn't here. This was all official stuff, boring financial and legal exchanges. She needed to find out how Jonas was talking to people…especially women. She was going to take a look at his online life.

Just as she reassembled the papers on the desk so it wouldn't be totally obvious she was snooping, Vinny felt someone step into the room behind her.

She whirled around—but no one was there.

What the hell. She walked to the doorway and leaned out, looking both ways. No one.

But was that a laugh?

Vinny frowned. She was certain she hadn't been alone

in the room. She could have sworn there was a sound, and a presence.

A little chill ran down her spine. She shook it off angrily. Vinny was not going to turn into some sort of fraidy-cat just because the house had a draft.

Then all the lights went out.

Chapter 14

After leaving the dinner table, Dom had retrieved some of his tools and gone ghosthunting. In most cases, ghosts were relatively easy to hunt, because they were either consistent or obnoxious, or obnoxiously consistent. Such as when a ghost of a murdered spirit always manifested in the spot they were killed at the moment of the day they were killed. Easy.

Sometimes ghosts were less predictable, but even then, once you knew they were around, you could track them down without a lot of trouble.

Tracking a ghost was an art, not a science. Some of it was basic spellcasting, some of it was common sense, and a little bit of it was snooping. But mostly, he tried to relax his conscious mind and let the otherworlds near.

"Santa Muerte, show me where the dead are awake," he muttered. His connection to that particular spiritual practice usually helped him when looking for ghosts. Not this time.

Not only did he fail to uncover any hint of a ghost or restless spirit, he got the distinct feeling that something was actually blocking him from seeing clearly. He could see just fine in the real world, but the moment he tried to move beyond, to shift his consciousness to the other-worlds, he got pushed back.

There was something *wrong* in this place. Dom got a bad feeling. Less directly threatening than the biker's hangout, and not as sharp as the vampire. The feeling persisted no matter where he went in the house, from the first floor kitchen to the upper level with the guest bedrooms, even to the other wing that held the master suite. He only peeked in—the area was almost as large as the entire Salem house.

Dom wandered on, going up a staircase that led to a third floor consisting only of a room whose walls were one hundred percent glass. It was dark out now, so he couldn't see anything but a few sparkling lights from distant neighbors and more distant towns. Even that was spectacular. The daytime view would probably justify the house's selling price. Probably.

He should talk to Piewicket. The little cat was off scouting on her own, though, and Dom would just have to wait until she chose to rejoin him. Or he could go looking for her.

He walked down the stairs to the second floor. Just as he reached the bottom, the lights all flickered once, and then went out.

Dom stopped short. Partly, he was unfamiliar with the house's layout, and didn't want to trip. The other part was fear that the bad energy in the house suddenly chose to get active.

Muttering a few words in Latin, he drew himself down so he could crouch against the wall. He waited a minute, keeping his breath even as he listened for sounds in any world.

He heard a shuffling, a bump, then a low "Cheese and

crackers!"

Dom actually smiled. "Vinny. Over here."

He stood up and toggled the flashlight on his phone, creating a pool of light directed at the floor.

Seconds later, booted feet entered the lit circle.

"You can't magically make light?" Vinny asked.

"You're confusing me with a wizard named Potter," he said.

"No one would confuse you with him. Are you responsible for the blackout?"

"Nope." Dom angled the light up to catch a little of Vinny's face. "Are you?"

"Why would I kill the power?" She sounded annoyed. "I nearly tripped on the stairs just now."

"You survived. Where were you headed?" He reached out to take her arm, but she shrugged away from him. The pale light of the phone revealed her furious expression. "Whoa. What's wrong?"

* * * *

"What's wrong?" Vinny was happy that she'd run into Dom and not a monster while she was wandering around in the dark, but she suddenly remembered she was pissed at him. "Let's talk about that."

"About what?" he asked, too casually. She couldn't see his face, due to the crappy light. That only made her madder.

"Today. You knew we were going to the same place." she said. "And you didn't say anything. What's the deal?"

"Vin," he said. "I didn't know we were going to the same place until we were practically here. When you gave me the actual address. Remember? You never said which friends you were going to. I sure as hell didn't know that when I first gave you a ride."

She wrinkled her nose, realizing that part was right. Still, pissed. "But you could have told me when you did realize it! You let me get all the way here without a hint that it was your jobsite. They spent the whole dinner thinking you were my boyfriend."

"Is that a problem?"

"Not if you *were* my boyfriend, but you're not, and you used me for…whatever it is you're up to!"

"Hey, I barely used you." Dom's calm tone was insufferable. "There's a value in getting to see a place and people…unbiased. Both Jonas and Emma acted a lot more naturally because they didn't know why I was here. I got to sense the vibes without anyone getting in the way."

"Sense the vibes? Is that a technical term?" she asked, laying on the scorn.

"Sort of."

In spite of herself, she was curious. "What vibes did you sense?"

"You want to know?"

"They're my friends who are getting haunted. Of course I want to know."

The phone's light angled further down the hall. Dom said, "Let's walk to your room. I don't want to have this conversation in a pitch black hallway."

She nodded, though he couldn't see it, and turned to the end of the hallway where her bedroom was, keeping her footsteps just on the edge of the pool of light. Dom fell in step beside her, and she felt the touch of his hand at her back, a vaguely protective move that was both annoying and really comforting.

Then the touch was gone. Dom took her anger seriously, at least.

Her room was pitch black too. She kept her right hand on the wall, walking toward the dresser. "Hold on. There's a few candles over here. Emma's a nut for candles."

Dom lifted the phone up to help her find a lighter. Vinny lit three candles—mercifully unscented—and turned around to face Dom.

Her first thought was that he looked great by candle-light. The flickering glow of the three little flames cast a warm light, which did amazing things to his skin. She wanted to reach out and touch him, and see if the candle-light improved his looks below the neck too. Probably.

"Vin?" he asked, one eyebrow raised. Did he know what she was thinking?

"I'm still angry at you," she said quickly, to cover her sudden attack of lust. "And I still want to know what the deal is. With the haunting."

Dom shrugged one shoulder. "Hard to say. With only an hour or so of looking around, I can't tell exactly what's going on. Clearly, something is…odd." He gestured, referring to the blackout. "It doesn't feel haunted, though."

"According to your vibe sense?"

"Yeah. But Piewicket says she doesn't like the place either. Told me after dinner that it reeks of malevolence. Then she dashed outside."

"Malevolence?"

"Her word, not mine."

She paused, registering the weirder part of his comment. "Wait. You can talk with cats?"

"Piewicket can be very communicative when she wants to be."

"That's not what I asked," Vinny said, stepping up to him.

"Nope." Dom smiled at her. "I can't tell you all my secrets."

"Have you told me any?"

He reached out to her, then dropped his hand. His smile vanished.

Oh, no. Rachel.

He'd told her probably the worst, darkest story of his life. And she just acted like it was nothing. Jesus, she was a horrible person.

She sighed. "God, I'm sorry. That's not...I shouldn't have said that. I just felt like a dummy when you made your little announcement. Emma just gave me this look, as if I tricked her. And she's been through so much shit lately, I felt bad about it. I shouldn't have snapped at you."

"And I should have told you right off," he said. "Truce?"

"Yeah. Don't mind me. Everything's just so weird now."

"What do you mean by that?" Dom asked. "What's wrong?"

Vinny wanted to tell him about the creepy feeling she'd gotten just before the lights went out, but she also didn't want to look like a wuss.

"It's probably nothing, but I got...I got this feeling like I was being watched earlier."

Dom looked at her intently. "That's not nothing. Where did you feel it?"

"My spine?"

"I meant where in the house," he corrected, though he smiled at her words.

"Oh. Down in the office. First floor, that little room off the side of the hallway to the stairs."

"Were you alone?"

"Yes." She didn't want to explain why she was alone in the office, but thankfully, Dom wasn't focused on that.

"Did you feel it come on fast, or was it more like a build up?"

"Fast. I didn't notice anything, and then felt it all at once. And I thought I heard a laugh. Not a nice laugh. More like…evil clown laugh. Have you and your brothers ever had to take out a clown?"

Dom shook his head. "Not yet. And can we stick to today's problem, please? Did you hear the laugh before or after the lights went out?"

"A few seconds before," she said, then added, "If it happened after, I probably would have screamed."

"Yeah, no one likes evil clown laughter in the dark," Dom said. He sounded so *normal* about it that Vinny wanted to hug him.

So she did, her arms going tight around his chest, her hands interlocking on the other side.

After a second, Dom's arms circled her shoulders, and Vinny felt better right away. "Thanks for believing me," she mumbled.

"Vin, of course I believe you."

"It just sounds so nuts."

"Not to me." He gave her a final squeeze, then shifted back so he could look at her. "Better?"

"Yeah." She gave him her best *I'm not scared of ghosts* smile.

"Anything else going on?" he asked.

"In this house, you mean? Just family squabbles," she said. "I don't want to bore you with that."

"You have never bored me," he said, inviting her to share.

"It's just Emma. Not Emma. Emma and Jonas. They're, um, having some difficulties."

"Beside getting haunted?"

"Yeah, way beside. Obviously, Emma didn't even hear about this haunting thing till you showed up and Jonas admitted he hired you. She's got more typical marriage issues. I don't want to get into details."

"I don't think you have to," Dom said. "He still lives like a rock star. It's not super obvious, but he's skinny in a way that doesn't look healthy. I don't know what drugs are trendy right now, but I'm guessing he sure does. That's the short version, right?"

"Basically." Vinny thought of all the things Emma told her about, and her heart ached for her friend. "It's been rough on Emma."

"I'm sorry to hear that. Hopefully, I can at least take care of whatever supernatural thing is making life rough for them. But she'll have to do the rest on her own."

Vinny put her hands on her hips. "No. She won't. I'm going to do something about it. And I need you to not get in my way."

* * * *

Dom took in the sight of Vinny in her defiant, full fury mode, and liked what he saw. He said carefully, "I don't know what mysterious mission you've given yourself, but I promise to not step on your toes."

"Good." Vinny's shoulders slumped a little. She was exhausted, he realized. And so was he.

"I'm going to hit the sack," he said, moving toward the door. "You should, too."

"No kidding. Jonas wants me to do a backing track on

a song he's working on, which means I'll have to be, like, awake to do it."

"Sure you'll be great."

"You've never actually heard me perform."

"I'll hear you tomorrow, if you want."

She gave him a hesitant smile. "Studio is in the basement. Don't expect much—a single raw track can sound really boring."

"I'll risk it." He told her good night and left. Part of him hoped she'd ask him to stay, but she didn't. Guess the previous nights really had been because she had no better option.

The lights came on again just as Dom closed Vinny's door, reinforcing the impression that he'd been shoved out of some special bubble into the ordinary, Vin-less world again.

He desperately wanted sleep, but he should check to see if the others were okay after the unexplained blackout.

Downstairs, he found Emma in the kitchen, peering into the fridge.

"Sorry about that," she said. "It's so damp and rainy around here that the electric goes wonky fast, even in new houses."

"This happens a lot?"

"Sure. Well, enough that we've got a backup generator in case the power stays out for more than thirty minutes." She tapped the fridge door to make her point. "Wouldn't want to lose the ice cream."

"The blackout didn't take you by surprise?"

"Believe me, losing electricity was the least surprising thing today." She narrowed her eyes at him.

"I'll try to keep a low profile," he said. "Pretend I'm an exterminator. In any case, I should only be here a few days."

"Until you find some other problem, and then you want more money." Emma's voice turned sharp.

Dom didn't get offended; he'd had this sort of conversation before. "If I can't solve the problem in a few days, more money won't help. I'll do my best, and tell you what's what at the end. After that, you do what you want."

"Vinny said you were for real."

"Did she?" He was a little surprised Vin would vouch for him, when he knew she was angry before. But Vin never seemed like she'd be spiteful, and she never lied.

"Yeah." Emma still looked skeptical. "Guess we'll find out."

"Did you see Jonas after the lights came back on? He's fine?"

"Yeah, don't worry about him. Good night. See you tomorrow. I make pancakes at nine. Any other time, you can forage on your own. Mi casa, su casa."

Dom slept hard, but not well. He woke up with the sense that he'd had lots of dreams, most of them bad. Probably Rachel dreams. He hadn't had those in a while. But there were no details, just the vague sense of despair.

He looked to the foot of the bed, where Piewicket was curled into a tight circle. He breathed in relief. If Pie was asleep, things were all right.

Thumbing his phone, he saw that it was only six. He pulled the pillow back over his head for a while.

When he woke again, it was ten.

He got up without disturbing Pie. He shaved and dressed, then grabbed some cold pancakes that had been left on the counter, accompanied by a post it note with a D on it. There was still coffee in the carafe, and Dom drank it down gratefully.

Remembering Vinny's words from the night before, he went down to the studio. He heard music, played loudly and then cut off, replaced by voices discussing some detail of the song, presumably. Dom didn't know anything about how a song got written and recorded.

Following the noise to an open door, Dom peeked into the room. It was divided into a few smaller spaces, including the one that now held the practicing musicians. The walls were painted bright, loud colors, and each wall had a gigantic poster on it, all Mercury Thief album covers. Each album cover had Jonas's face on it somehow.

There were also shelves with awards, from fake crystal-looking pyramids to silver and gold colored things. Dom recognized a Grammy, and a gold-plated record in a glass frame. Dom wasn't a fan of Mercury Thief, but obviously a lot of people were.

Nothing, not the awards, not the art, not the style of the space, referred to Emma. Just Jonas.

Jonas was sitting on a tall stool, directing Vinny, who stood in front of a very expensive looking microphone.

"Try that opening again, Vin," Jonas was saying. "Go all growly."

Vinny retorted, "Let Tom Waits do Tom Waits."

"Come on. It's hot when you growl."

"Oh, really?"

"I meant when chicks growl."

Vinny put her hands on her hips. "You just called me a chick?"

Jonas laughed. "Am I pissing you off?"

"Damn right."

"How much more do I need to piss you off to get you to growl the damn lyrics?"

Dom did not like the way this conversation was going.

Jonas might be teasing Vinny, but it was clear that Vinny turned him on. Then again, it wasn't up to Dom who she turned on or not. And she was certainly capable of telling a guy to get lost, if that's what she wanted to say.

Then she started singing, and Dom forgot his whole train of thought. Holy shit, Jonas had a point. Dom couldn't say what the lyrics were. He didn't care. He just wanted Vin's voice in his ears, all the time.

"Wow," he said, when Vinny stopped to take a drink of water. It was literally the most intelligent critique he could manage at that point.

"She's great," Jonas said proudly. "Can you imagine someone wasting her at a piano keyboard?"

"Thought she played bass in her bands."

"Still a waste." Jonas turned to Vinny. "Second opinion confirms, Vin. You should absolutely be on this track."

"Wait, I didn't say that." Dom didn't want to get drawn into anything. "What track?"

"Jonas's doing some work for a movie coming out next year," Vinny said.

"You're perfect for it, Vin. You'll get a nice paycheck, and we can doll you up for some events."

"Doll me up?"

Vinny's eyes narrowed, and Dom instinctively stepped away from the blast radius.

Then a loud crackling filled the air.

"Fucking feedback!" Jonas yelled, rushing to a sound board to fiddle with some knobs. "I swear I'm going to get my money back on this equipment. Spent a fortune, and it behaves like some third-rate set-up in a community college."

Dom left the room before the awful sound repeated.

He also wasn't sure he could hear Vinny singing again without something very awkward happening. He already felt an urge to find a quiet spot to take care of the physical reaction her singing voice had caused.

The promise to stay out of her way might be harder to keep than he thought.

Chapter 15

DOM RAN INTO VINNY AGAIN an hour later. After coming up from the studio, she must have taken a quick shower, because her hair was wet and shiny. Her t-shirt was a white one he'd never seen before, because he would have remembered. It hugged her body so close that anyone could tell she was wearing a lace bra underneath.

Dom had a backpack slung over his shoulder and a few things in his hands, including several candles and his knife.

"What are you doing with all that?" she asked.

"Um. Magic." He went on, "Whatever the exact details of the haunting, some basic spellwork should help clear the air, and confer some protection on everyone here."

"So you're doing a protection spell? That's nice of you. Need help?"

"No. Not to be rude. But it's a solo assignment."

"Would my presence break your concentration?" she teased.

"Maybe." He was *not* going to stare at her very tight white shirt. Holy Christ, she would murder his concentration.

His gaze slid over her shoulder, grateful to have something else to focus on. "I should probably go. Don't want to waste my client's hard-earned cash."

Vinny glanced around and saw Emma watching them with amusement and something else in her expression. She looked back to Dom. "Yeah. You go bust some ghosts. And be careful with the knife. I don't want to have to come rescue you if you stab yourself."

"I know what I'm doing."

"Hey, I never doubted that. I've seen you in action." Vinny bit her lip. "Um. With the vampire fight, I mean."

Sure that's what you mean.

Dom smiled at last, thinking of her growly singing voice in his ears. "And I'd do it again. Save you from monsters, I mean."

Vinny's cheeks flushed with pink, which was adorable. She said, "Okay. Gotta go. Good luck. I'd give you a lucky charm," she added, plucking at her necklaces, "but something tells me you don't need it."

"I wouldn't want to take your luck, Vin. But thanks."

Damn. Dom almost took Vinny up on her offer to help just so he could get her alone and peel that shirt off. Yeah, he liked Vinny.

But he hated this house.

Piewicket agreed. She only stayed in the house because Dom begged her to help with the spellwork. Otherwise, the cat preferred the verdant, hilly landscape outside.

Your focus is fractured.

Dom turned and saw Piewicket sitting just at the top

of the stairs he was climbing. For a cat, she was punctual.

"Is that your only insight?" he asked.

No. There is evil here, inside the bones of this house.

"What kind of evil?"

The cat lashed her tail once or twice. *I don't know.*

Cats hated to admit when they didn't know something.

As I said before. A malevolence…strong, yet hidden. Concealed.

"A ghost without a ghost story to go with it."

Possible.

"My other option is to think that the client, who paid a lot of money to get me here, is lying."

Humans lie as much as they breathe.

"Some more than others."

Piewicket yawned as the conversation shifted to the failings of humans, which was too broad a topic to keep her interest.

When we're done, I am going to hunt. I smell rabbits here. Rabbits are exceedingly stupid and fat. Piewicket licked her chops in anticipation.

"This shouldn't take long," he promised.

He looked around the room, an unfinished attic he'd noticed on his first exploration of the house. Judging from the size, the attic only covered one wing. There were probably other attics. This one was sufficient, though. It was almost empty, which was good, since he was going to cover the floor in symbols.

Using a piece of chalk, he drew a circle. Piewicket helped by walking it first. All he did was follow the path of her paws. He didn't know why she was good at circles—it was only one of many, many things that made Piewicket different from other cats. He long ago learned not to ask.

When the circle was marked out, he moved around it on his hands and knees, drawing symbols of protection and warding. Some of the symbols were ancient, but many spellcasters developed highly personalized versions of a circle of protection. His Uncle Patrick included both a Christian cross and an image from Space Invaders, because that worked for him. Magic was as much an art as a science. Dom liked it that way, perhaps because he'd always felt a more primal connection to magic, something that wasn't easily quantified.

Dom put eight candles around the circle, at the four cardinal points, and then the points halfway between each of them. Again, that was his preference. Others did it differently.

"I'm going to cast the spell now," he told the cat.

You hardly need me to do something so simple.

"But I like having you around."

Piewicket pretended not to be flattered. She remained outside the circle while Dom sat in the center of it.

Dom took a breath, calming himself, opening his senses to the otherworlds. He muttered a phrase in Latin, a basic spell intended to show the lines of energy running from the real world to the otherworlds. The circumference of the circle burned briefly, in a sputtering, dim green light.

He then cast the protection spell. It was one he'd cast so many times before that he no longer even thought about it on a fully conscious level. He held the image of the house in his mind, and more importantly, the people within it. He pictured Jonas, then Emma, then Vinny.

Vivid, Pie commented, as the image of Vin practically glowed in his mind.

Unfortunately, the spell prevented him from speaking

any stray words out loud. Dom settled for sticking his tongue out at the cat, and then proceeded with the spell.

He called up a ward for the house and its inhabitants, asking for aid from spirits of each element, as well as a personal request for Santa Muerte. Not an obvious choice on the surface, but to Dom, it felt basically like asking for help from his parents. While they'd been with him, they'd always helped.

He completed the spell and felt the power circle around him. Then it settled into the accustomed pattern. Good.

Dom stood up and stepped carefully over the chalked symbols to get out of the circle.

Piewicket meowed to signal that someone was coming. Dom looked toward the door. "Come on in."

It was Emma who appeared. She looked around the attic, at the candles and the chalk circle. Her expression swung between interest and skepticism.

"Don't worry. Nothing's permanent," Dom assured her. "And I won't set the place on fire."

"Is it magic?"

"Yes," he said simply.

"What's it for?"

"Protection."

"For you?" she asked.

He shook his head. "For everyone in the house."

"Hmmm." She shifted her attention from the surroundings to him. "You busy?"

"Nothing I can't stop doing. Something up?"

She glanced around as if to check that they were alone. Then she squared her shoulders. "I want to know what's up between you and Vinny."

"Why?" He'd expected her to confront him about the

job. A lot of people thought he was a con artist.

Emma stepped up to him. "Look, I'm not being nosy. Okay, I am being nosy, but because I love her, you know?"

"I don't really have an answer for you," he said.

"But there's something going on."

"Is that a problem?" Damn, Jonas had grilled him about Vinny the first day, and now Emma was too, though in a different way. Why was everyone so concerned about her? She was tough as nails. Even when she met a vampire, she snapped back to her normal self within a few minutes. "Vinny can make her own decisions."

"You didn't cast a spell on her, did you?"

Now he was angry. "What."

"The way she looks at you," Emma said. "I see her face, and it's different. Like she's… Let me put it this way. When she's had relationships, it was only after a multi-stage vetting process with background checks and interviews and probably some spiritual consultation with a Buddhist monk or something. She's careful. Presidential appointments move faster than Vinny. But she met you what, four *days* ago, and she's all twitterpated? No offense, but magic sounds like a pretty rational explanation to me."

"No offense?" he said. "Trust me, that's offensive."

"So you didn't magic her up?"

"No, because that's *wrong*. On so many levels I can't even get into it now. You don't cast at people without their knowledge. You just don't. Not if you've got a soul you want to keep."

"But it can be done?" Emma was staring at him intently.

"It can be done, yes," he said. "But it puts you down a

path that's hard to leave, even if you try to turn around later. And most people who do start down that path never try to leave it. I don't really want to discuss it. But believe me, I would never hurt Vinny. And messing with her mind through magic would hurt her."

Emma leaned back, drawing a long breath. "I'm sorry."

"Sure."

"I mean it. I can tell you're pissed. But I don't know you, and I do know Vinny. I don't want her to get hurt."

"Neither do I."

She tipped her head, considering. "Still doesn't explain how you got fast-tracked."

"I haven't been," he said. "You're reading too much into this. I just gave Vinny a ride."

"Yeah. And trounced a monster that was going for her. And slept with her every night since. She told me about the road trip."

"I didn't sleep with her."

Emma raised an eyebrow. "You slept *near* her, then."

"Not last night."

"You look a little sad about that," she said shrewdly.

He was a little sad about that. But he sure as hell didn't want to talk about it. "What do you want me to say?"

Emma's eyes narrowed. "I don't know. Maybe nothing. But Vinny's not as tough as she seems. If you hurt her at all, if you make her cry *once*, I will come after you."

He didn't say anything, but she caught his look. "Don't laugh, demon hunter. You might have magic or whatever. I have money. And lawyers. And I'm not afraid to use them."

"Vinny said you were her best friend. I can see why."

Emma suddenly smiled, all threat gone. "She is my bestie. We watch out for each other. Don't you forget it."

"Yes, ma'am." Only after he said that did Dom remember that he'd already made Vinny cry. Back at the motel room, when she almost left.

"Since you're here," Dom said quickly. "I have a few professional questions."

"Shoot."

"It's true that you and Jonas built this house?"

"Yup. About ten years ago, just in time for our wedding. We were married in the backyard."

"And since the house was built, there was no significant sad or painful event that you know about?"

Emma's face clouded briefly, but then she laughed as if there was nothing to bother her. "You mean a murder or a suicide? I'm sure Jonas told you already. Life in this house is pretty calm."

"He did tell me that, but…" Dom left the words hanging, inviting Emma to share more.

"Worst thing to happen was when—well, I'm not going to name names, but let's just say we had some very famous vomit in our pool after one party. That was years ago, though. I discourage that sort of party nowadays."

"You two don't always agree on those things, though. Right?"

"So now you're a marriage counselor?"

"Hell no. I'm just trying to figure out what's bothering my client. He's convinced there's something evil in the house, but there's no story behind his concern."

"Then maybe he's not telling you the whole story!" Emma burst out. Then she immediately backpedaled. "Sorry. I didn't mean that."

"Yes, you did," said Dom.

"I just meant…I don't know."

Dom could see her putting up a shield. He was a stranger and despite the already personal conversation, she wasn't going to confide in him any further. He didn't push the issue. Emma left quickly, obviously eager to not be around any longer.

Dom took a long breath. He was frustrated. Nothing in this house made sense. He wasn't being told everything. And it was hard to solve problems when people refused to tell him what the real problems were.

So he'd try it another way.

"I'm going to take a stroll," he told the cat.

It's dangerous, Pie responded. She knew he didn't mean an actual walk, but rather a journey into the otherworlds, so he could see this place from another angle.

"I've just cast the circle," he said, "It's strong right now, so if I keep my body inside, I should be fine."

He stepped back into the circle. This time Pie followed him.

"All right," he said. "Watch out in case I do something stupid."

That is my life's mission, the cat noted.

"Here goes."

Dom closed his eyes, preparing to open a pathway to the otherworlds. His grandmother had once explained the process—terrifyingly—as separating one's soul from one's body in order for the soul to travel where the body could not. The risk was getting lost, or being trapped while in the otherworlds. In that case, his body would basically remain comatose, a vegetable until it died. The risk was high enough that many capable people never even attempted it.

The Salem family always viewed danger a bit differently—each of the Salem brothers had to prove they could travel to the otherworlds before they were allowed to learn about "serious" magic. Lex described it as a bar mitzvah where one of your presents might be death.

But it did mean that Dom was now very comfortable doing this. He pictured the house again, keeping his breathing slow and even, just as in meditation. Idly, he wondered where Vinny was at that moment.

Not her, Piewicket told him. *The house. The land. Focus.*

"I'm trying."

Are you? All I see through your mind's eye is her.

"Sorry. She's…um…" As a rule, Dom did not get hung up on women. But Vin was different. "I don't know what's wrong with me."

Nothing. You're just human. Piewicket ran her head into his shin, an affectionate gesture. He picked her up and gave her a good minute of scratching behind her ears. Her purr rumbled to life. A second later, the little cat had insinuated herself into the crook of his shoulder and neck, purring contentedly.

"This isn't helping me find the ghost in the house," Dom pointed out.

Your mind is bent solely on her. Until you clear your head of this obsession, all other searching will be useless.

"I'm not obsessed with her. Just because I'm thinking about her…a lot…doesn't mean I'm obsessed. I mean, it's not my fault that we're in the same place and we keep running into each other."

Then whose fault is it?

"No one's. It's coincidence."

Pie's purr stopped short, just as a sick feeling hit Dom's gut, then his mind. Something, some supernasty thing, slid into his consciousness before Dom had time to put up any defenses.

A dizzying sense of vertigo gripped him. If he had been standing, he would have fallen down.

All around him he saw thin, glimmering threads criss-crossing each other, forming hatch marks and lines and random shapes. He could feel himself drawn into the maze of lines, aware that if he started falling, he'd never stop falling.

A sharp physical pain jolted his attention away from the hypnotic patterns. Pie's claws in his leg. She was helping him find himself.

He inhaled, trying to get control of his mind again.

The lines weren't entirely random, he realized. Some seemed to lead to...right here. The house. The house at the center of a web.

Because the lines were all part of a web. An image of Vinny surfaced again. Vinny in her dozens of necklaces, looking like the independent spirit she was.

Except she wasn't totally independent. She was being drawn along one of the lines to the center of the web. Because someone, something wanted to catch her.

Chapter 16

VINNY HAD RETREATED TO THE library to get her act together. She had to figure out how she was going to get through to Emma, and short of learning how to be a hacker to get Jonas's digital info, she didn't have any ideas.

She saw a bunch of old zines on a shelf and started paging through them. They all dated back to the years in New York City, when Vinny first got into the scene as a teenager, and met Jonas and later Emma. Even then, Emma was a writer, and she contributed to a lot of the magazines. She wrote accounts of shows, profiles of her friends' bands, and album reviews. The writing was raw, but Emma had a voice. Vinny could practically hear the younger Emma narrating the words as she read them. Vin smiled at all the photos, deliberately grainy to echo the look of original, photocopied zines. There was Jonas, in his pre-Mercury Thief days, just another kid with a microphone. Emma, during her brief stint as a very bad guitarist—she had been happy to move into freelance writing. She called it a grown-up move.

At the time, Vinny had been a little hurt by the comment. After all, she was still playing, and would play in one band or another for the next decade. But now, Vin wondered if Emma hadn't been referring to Jonas. There was no reason to think he'd make it big. He wasn't more talented or more hardworking than anyone else in the scene. But then he left his old band, started Mercury Thief, and overnight, he'd made it.

Leafing through a later, glossier magazine, Vinny stopped at a page with a photo of her and Jonas at a piano, a photo she didn't remember seeing before. The caption read: *Jonas Belling shows a fan how to play.*

"You fucking kidding me?" Vinny hissed. She was no fangirl, and she was approximately a thousand times better than Jonas when it came to playing piano. She checked the date on the magazine. Yep, Mercury Thief had just released their first album, to wild, voracious approval.

Just my luck, she thought. All those years of practice. All the times she had to turn down the chance of friendship or a fun time so she could perform or prepare a new piece. And it turned into *Jonas Belling shows a fan how to play.*

Vinny frowned when she caught a flicker of something out of the corner of her eye. It was like someone was sneaking up behind her, but when she turned, no one was there.

"Turning paranoid," she muttered. Too much hanging around Dom and thinking about the supernatural.

Then she heard something, this time in the hallway. Intent on catching whatever it was, she moved stealthily to the doorway. The sound kept coming closer—she imagined the footsteps of some spectral form, and then had flashbacks to Scooby Doo.

Focus.

Vin held her breath as the…whatever it was…approached and paused at the door. As a dark shape passed through the doorway, she lunged forward and grabbed for it.

"What the hell?" A startled Dom shook her off him.

"Oh, shit. Sorry. I thought you were somebody else."

He looked at her quizzically. "Yeah? Who?"

"I don't know," she admitted. "Look. Never mind. And next time, maybe say you're here."

"I didn't mean to sneak up on you."

"You didn't. I heard you. Obviously."

"Do you have a second to take away from your busy pouncing schedule?" Dom asked.

"Sure. What's up? You look like you saw a ghost." She realized what she said and added, "Did you?"

"Not exactly. I think I ran into one, though. If it's the one that's been worrying Jonas, he's right to be worried."

"So I take it it's not a friendly ghost."

Dom shook his head. Vinny did not like the way he was acting. Even when he fought the vampire, he hadn't seemed so off his game.

"Are you okay?" she asked in concern.

"Fine. Physically. Vin, can you tell me more about the nightmares that made you want to reunite with Emma?"

"Other than that they scared the crap out of me? I don't know. It was more the feeling than the specific images."

"The specific image being a spider and a web of crisscrossing lines, and below the web was a lot of nothing. A pit," he said.

Vinny frowned. "Hold on a minute. How do you know about a pit? I didn't say that to you. Why are you asking me this?"

"Because I don't think those nightmares originated in your mind. Something sent them for you to notice."

"Something got in my head?" she hissed.

"More or less. You were…"

"Manipulated," she spat, already getting angry.

"Influenced, yes."

"By a *ghost*?"

"There's a long history of ghosts doing exactly that, either through direct possession of a living person, or other means. This would be the second category."

"How do I stop it?"

"You don't. I do," Dom said quickly. "I will figure out what this thing is and how to get rid of it. That's literally my job."

Vinny knew he meant it to reassure her, but all she could think of was how helpless that statement made her sound. She was just meant to stand around and let a ghost take her over until Dom saved the day? "I'm not going to just wait for you to do your ghostbusting."

"If you want to help out, you can talk to Emma."

"About what?"

"Her marriage."

"Do all your clients know that you'll go poking around their private lives when they hire you?"

"Every job is different. Usually it's not this tricky to find out what the hell I'm supposed to be doing here. Emma definitely wasn't telling me everything when I asked about painful events in this house. She'll talk to you, though."

"And I'm just supposed to spill her secrets to you afterward?"

"If they seem like a reason for a house to be haunted, yes. I mean, you do want to help out, right?"

"Sure. Emma's my friend. But why are *you* helping out?"

"I'm being paid to," Dom said.

"Always with the money," she sniffed.

"Money's useful."

"I don't have a lot of use for it."

"You didn't stop me from using money on your behalf," he noted. "You seemed really okay with it, after a little light protesting."

Vinny about lost her mind when she heard that. "Don't you *ever* tell me how I feel about money."

He grabbed her by the wrists and pinned her against the wall to stop her from sliding away. "Did I hit a nerve, gorgeous?"

"Stop acting like a caveman and let me go," she hissed. "Or I'll hit a fucking nerve you won't forget."

Having Dom so close to her was throwing Vinny's emotions all out of whack. She was furious at him, but the last time he had her pinned against the wall, it had been in that motel room, and she remembered every second of that encounter. And she hadn't been angry then. She'd been turned on and practically feral, the way she'd been pawing at him.

Now he was just as close, just as aggressive. But it didn't feel the same. It felt wrong. Vinny took a deep breath and glowered at him. "You think this is going to make me all melty for you?"

"You've got to be kidding," said Dom, not looking the slightest bit interested in sexytimes. "I'm *working*. I didn't chase you here. You're the one who pounced on me."

He let her go and stalked back to the door. He muttered, "Let me know when you're normal again and we can talk. Meantime, how about you stay out of my way?"

Vinny glared at him. "Happy to. I'll stay so out of your way you won't see me again."

"Talk to Emma," he reminded her.

"Fuck you." Vinny should have had a better comeback, for a lot of reasons, but the rage running through her took all her words away.

She was not going to chat with Emma about some stupid ghost. She was going to do what she'd set out to do: find out just how badly Jonas had been behaving, so that Emma didn't have to be stuck in a shitty relationship ever again.

Feeling thoroughly out of sorts, and angry at men in particular, Vinny decided it was time to play detective.

Since rifling through the physical papers in Jonas's messy office offered no leads, she moved on. She wanted his phone. The trick, of course, would be how to get it. People liked their phones, and tended to notice when they vanished. Vinny would have to be sneaky.

She found Jonas in the studio, fiddling around on the production end, testing out different versions of tracks together.

His phone sat on the table off to the side.

She smiled as she came in, positioning herself near the phone. "How's it going?"

"Hmm. Pretty good," Jonas said in a distracted tone. This part of the process always absorbed his attention, and honestly, was probably his greatest strength. "There's some ambient noise mucking up the bass. Got to get that gone."

"Is that a notification?" she asked, pointing to the phone.

Jonas woke the phone up with his pass code, squinted

at the screen and said, "Nothing important." He put the phone back down. "I think I know how to fix this track."

"Ok, I'll let you work. See you later."

"Cool, cool." He barely glanced away from the monitor. So he didn't notice when she palmed his phone, touching the screen so it wouldn't go to sleep.

Tucking herself in the bathroom on the upper floor and locking the door, she started to go through his info.

Emails first. There were *hundreds*—Jonas wasn't an Inbox Zero guy. She scrolled through a bunch of them, pausing whenever she saw a woman's name. Lots of business related stuff. Marketing. Sales. PR. Nothing incriminating, and not worth plowing through when she had no clues to help her out.

She scrolled through his contacts. There were definitely a lot of women's names in there, and some of them looked a bit sketchy. Who was *Tansy—LA, Shaker Bar*? She could picture a cute cocktail server who just *loved* Mercury Thief, and she could easily imagine a flirty conversation turning into a hookup. But with only a number, she had no proof. It was just as likely that Jonas put Tansy's contact info into his phone with a promise to send her some autographed swag. He was a celebrity, after all.

Vinny went to photos next, and here there were plenty of images that would raise eyebrows. Jonas had tons of selfies with absolutely random hot women, and lots of pictures of just a woman, with no hint as to where it was or why Jonas had it. Some were risqué, others were straight up pornographic, like the one where a brunette dressed in a thong and nothing else perched on a hotel bed in a pose that made Vinny's back hurt just looking at it. The photo would have a different effect on most male viewers. But again, she couldn't prove anything with it.

The chick could have sent it to Jonas, and he just didn't delete it. Vinny had gotten really inappropriate things sent to her while she was in bands, and she never got even a little famous.

Emma would laugh it off. Jonas would have a story. Nothing would happen.

She sighed, wondering what to do.

A calendar notification popped up: *V Day*, it said, with her birthday marked. The calendar showed a big red dot on the day. Vinny smiled, and then felt sort of bad for snooping. Jonas was troubled, but he had a good side. Was she just making a mess with her quest to get Emma divorce dirt? Maybe what she should be doing was getting them both to talk to each other and work things out.

Not that she'd ever been good at that sort of thing.

Her mood soured as she remembered all the times she'd utterly failed to get both halves of a couple to talk to each other like adults, most memorably her parents. She was an idiot for thinking this would be different. Then she remembered Dom's suggestion that she'd been manipulated into coming here. That something snuck inside her head and played with her brain. She shivered, feeling violated just imagining the possibility.

Emma's voice echoed up the stairwell and through the door. "Where did you see it last?"

"I had it like an hour ago!" Jonas yelled back, fainter.

"I'll call your phone," Emma said. Vinny didn't have to see her to know she was rolling her eyes.

Vinny dashed down the hall and opened the door to the ridiculously huge master bedroom. She dropped his phone onto a plush sheepskin rug by his bed. Maybe he'd forget that he had it in the studio earlier. Anyway, plausible deniability meant she had to get out of the room before anyone saw her.

She almost made it.

Vinny left the door partially closed and was about to walk off innocently, just as Jonas's phone went off. His ringtone was the chorus of Mercury Thief's first hit.

Then she saw Piewicket staring at her from down the hall. The cat looked like she knew exactly what Vinny was up to.

"It's for a righteous cause," Vinny pleaded. "Don't give me away."

Pie didn't move.

"I'll get you some fish. Fish for silence. Deal?"

She mewed once and sashayed off, which Vinny took as a yes. She followed the cat and was out of the way before anyone knew she was there.

But just when she felt safe again, she saw another flicker in the corner of her eye. She turned her head, but saw nothing out of place. Yet she was positive something was there, watching her.

Chapter 17

AFTER THAT EXCHANGE WITH VINNY, Dom had a crappy rest of the day. He opted out of any socialization. He liked Emma well enough, but Jonas was an ego-trip pretending to be human, and Vinny glared at him every time she saw him.

So he stayed out of range. He called up his youngest brother Lex with a brief report.

"Ghosts have a pattern," Lex said when he heard what Dom gleaned so far. "At least, every account I've seen says that. You need a lookup on aberrant ghosts?"

"See what you can find," Dom said. "It's definitely not a typical haunting. Maybe check on any supernatural events or beings that have psychic pull, or the ability to draw people in."

"Hmm. There was a case in the 50s where a ghost exerted such a strong psychic force that it pulled people into an otherworld it created, like a pocket-sized recreation of its memory. Could be something along those lines. The house could actually have nothing to do with it."

"Maybe it's the land," Dom guessed. "See if there's something about that area that shows up in the records."

"Already did that," Lex said, sounding a little offended. "As soon as we said yes to the job. There's no history of paranormal events for that location. Not to say there's no potential for it. But that part of the world just doesn't have a long written history. It was barely settled outside the city, and there's no suggestion of any Native American accounts mentioning something—not that the records are that great when it comes to tribal histories. But that's what happens when you manifest destiny all the locals to the point of extinction."

"It's almost like the government didn't care about them," Dom agreed. "See if you find anything useful at all. I'll keep digging."

"Good luck," Lex told him. "Oh, did you get paid in cash?"

"Yeah, why?"

"Deposit it soon, okay? The water heater broke."

Dom swore. That house was going to drive him mad. The sooner he finished this job, the sooner he could take another one.

"I can install a new one," Lex was saying, "but I need to pay for it."

"Do it," Dom told him. "I'll get you the money. God willing, I'll be home soon anyway."

Lex said goodbye, and Dom mostly brooded until he got too sleepy to brood properly. He wished Piewicket would show up, but she was nowhere to be found, and she certainly didn't respond to his mental call. Cats, in general, didn't come when they were called, so that wasn't totally surprising. Just sort of sad.

The next morning, he awoke when Pie jumped on his

chest, her eyes gleaming.

I am hungry.

He yawned. "I'll feed you in a bit."

A paw swatted at his ear.

"All right, all right." Dom removed her and swung out of bed. "It's not like you're starving."

Pie let out the softest, most piteous meow, and looked up at him with big eyes.

"Whatever, drama queen. Where were you last night?" Dom asked as he grabbed his clothes.

I slept with her, the cat replied.

Cats rarely bothered with proper names. Dom knew Piewicket meant Vinny, and he got unreasonably jealous. "I thought you were a Salem family pet."

Pet?

"You know what I mean."

She was plagued by nightmares till I calmed them.

Dom felt worse than before, remembering how ripped up Vinny had been when she told him about the nightmare that spurred her whole journey. "Nightmares of what? Not the same one she talked about?"

The cat flicked her tail in the feline equivalent of a shrug. *I can't see into her mind. But she was restless.*

"You don't usually go out of your way for strangers."

She is not a stranger. And I prefer a companion who doesn't toss and turn. It disturbs my own sleep.

"God forbid," Dom muttered. "Are you helping here, or not? This whole situation is messed up. I don't know what I'm dealing with. If there's a ghost, it's a very coy one."

Agreed. I've seen no ghosts, though there are strands of power wrapped all around this place.

"We've got to get someone to talk. I feel like everyone's lying. Not Vinny," he amended. She was pissed at him, but she never lied.

He followed Pie down to the kitchen, where he served her some canned tuna on a plate. She was devouring it when Emma walked in. Car keys dangled from her right hand.

"Heading out?" he asked.

"Yeah, got some errands. You need more holy water or candles?" she quipped.

"Cheese and crackers," he said, before he knew he would say it.

"Ha, you have been hanging around Vin." Emma smiled. "I always laughed so hard when she said that, back when we first met. She's so punk rock, and then she's got this hokey little phrase."

"She said she picked it up in Catholic school."

Emma snorted. "It wasn't school that kept her saying that. You can blame Sister Stellamaris, her first piano teacher. Vinny did everything that lady said. It's funny. I can't remember anything Vin's own mom told her, but I know all the sayings her piano teacher taught her. Cheese and crackers...Vinny just says it to make her happy."

Piewicket turned and mewed. Dom said, "Pie would love some more tuna."

Emma smiled at the cat, her mood shifting to pure happiness. "For you, sweetie, anything."

Pie walked over to Emma's feet, purring. Emma bent down to pet her, but she looked up at Dom.

"How the ghost hunting going?"

"Slowly."

"That typical?"

"There is no such thing as typical in my line of work."

"That makes sense. Need anything besides tuna?"

He said, "Can I ask you a question about Vinny?'

"What?" Emma eyed him warily.

"What's her deal with money?"

Emma's face cleared. Whatever she thought he was going to ask, it wasn't that. "It goes back to when she was a kid. You should hear it from her, though."

"I don't think she wants to talk to me."

"Really? What happened?"

"We got into a bit of a fight."

"A fight? Vinny's super chill, though."

"Not yesterday."

"Well, try to talk to her." Emma gave Piewicket a few scratches behind the ears, then reluctantly stood up. "If you think it's worth it. Which I think you do."

He did think it was worth it. Dom knew that in a few days he'd leave and never see her again, but he wished that when he left, she would no longer be mad at him.

He tried to work that morning. But no matter how hard he tried to concentrate on figuring out exactly what the hell was haunting Jonas and Emma's house, he kept coming back to Vinny. She was like a magnet. All Dom wanted was to find her, get close, and learn every little thing about her. Not to mention finishing what they'd started that early morning before they got here. Every time he closed his eyes, he could see Vin standing there, topless, with just those necklaces. He couldn't wait to get the rest of her clothes off and see what she looked like then.

Too bad he'd already messed things up between them with his weird behavior before. Dom hardly ever touched a woman he wasn't actually dating, and he'd never touched any person with violence unless it was out of pure self defense. His dad had made that lesson clear from the very beginning, when Dom's biggest problem was learning how to share toys with other kids. So what the hell made him grab Vinny like that?

He had to talk to her.

He found her by following the sound of a piano. She was playing on a big black grand at the end of a longish, narrow room that looked like it rarely ever had any people in it. Dom had an aunt who kept her living room perfect and closed up for all but the most special occasions. This room had just the same vibe. Beautiful and off limits.

And of course Vinny was right there in the middle of it.

She noticed when he passed through the doorway, and lifted her hands from the keys.

"Don't stop just because you have an audience," he said hurriedly. "Aren't you used to that?"

"I stop when I feel like it," she said. "How long were you there?"

"Not that long." He walked over to the piano. "You said you played guitar."

"Not many punk rock pianists," she said. "Hard to pack a baby grand in a van."

"That makes sense. You can play more. Just ignore me. You sounded good."

"Oh, a compliment. Does that mean you're done embracing your inner troglodyte?"

"I'm sorry about before," he said. "I never should have grabbed you like that."

"No kidding." Vinny didn't look at him.

"Will you forgive me?"

At last, she looked up. "Seriously?"

"If you can. I actually don't know what got into me."

Vinny paused. "Could it be related to the house haunting?"

"You mean I'm stressed out? Stress is no excuse for hurting someone."

"You didn't hurt me. But I meant what if there's something…making us not normal?"

"Do you feel not normal?" he asked intently.

"I feel…not centered. Not since I got here, pretty much."

Dom sat on the bench next to her. "Tell me more."

"I can't really describe it. Things are just off. Jonas and Emma are totally on edge. With each other, with this haunting thing. With you, for sure."

"I'm used to that. People don't usually like having a demon hunter in their house."

"But Jonas hired you, so he must want help. And you're helping."

"Doesn't matter," Dom said. "It's still awkward."

"Well, it's not just that," Vinny said. "I'm on edge too. Even without nightmares, I didn't sleep great the past couple of nights."

"Even with Pie in your bed last night?"

"How do you know about that?"

"She told me."

Vinny shook her head. "We're going to have to clarify what you mean by that someday."

"Why wait for someday? The short version is that my cat talks to me. Telepathically."

She looked at him with narrowed eyes. "You can talk to cats with your mind?"

"It's more that Pie chooses to speak to me with her mind. Because I'm a Salem and she's a Salem family cat. The Salems have always had a few cats around. It's a tradition." He never told people about this, but it felt important to tell Vin.

"How long of a tradition?" she asked.

"Generations. Many of them."

"I bet you have a few ancestors who got burned at the stake," Vinny said.

"That's a whole other story," Dom told her. "Let's get back to your feelings. How have you felt in the house, besides on edge?"

"I don't know," Vinny said, with a roll of her shoulder. "A little…creeped out."

Dom reached for her hand. "I'm a professional demon hunter with a telepathic cat. I'm not going to laugh at you if you say something a bit unusual."

"Remember when I said I felt watched that first night? It's happened more," she admitted.

"All the time? In certain places?"

"When I'm alone. When it's quiet. I'm not a look over the shoulder kind of girl, but…I've been looking over my shoulder a lot lately."

"That's not surprising. You learned some dark stuff about the world. But there's something here. You're *not* paranoid."

"I feel paranoid. And out of control. I got so angry at you, even before you…got physical."

"I am sorry about that," he said again.

Vinny nodded. "I know. And I have to admit I provoked you."

"What set you off?" he asked. "Lots of people have strong feelings about money, and not always rational. But you obviously have some…issues with who pays for what."

"Yeah."

Dom inched closer. "Tell me."

"Will it help you unhaunt the house?" She looked skeptical.

"Maybe it'll help unhaunt you," he said. "Figuratively."

"That's not in your job description," she said. "And I'm not your client."

"I'm doing it on spec."

Vinny laughed a little. Then she said, "Okay. But stop me when you get bored."

"I'm listening."

"I grew up rich," she said. "Doesn't look like it, but it's true. And I mean *rich* rich. I went to boarding schools. Ski trips to Switzerland, Christmas in Paris, that kind of thing. My parents know people. They're all chummy with European royalty, and Chinese nouveau riche, and oil magnates. My best friend growing up had a bodyguard— all the time. Even posted outside the bedroom door during sleepovers. I didn't have a normal childhood."

"Okay."

"And not to sound like poor little rich girl, but I was miserable. I didn't know it when I was little, but eventually I could see it. Our family life was hell. Huge fights and lots of icy silences and passive aggressive bullshit. Not that I had terms for that back then. My parents got a divorce when I was eight. On cold nights, law firms still tell stories about the case to their junior partners. It was *nasty*. Armies of lawyers. They fought over every house, every piece of art, every bank account."

"And you."

"Yeah. But I was at the bottom of the list," she added bitterly.

"I'm sure that's not true."

Vinny shook her head. "I'm not exaggerating. I was

just a piece of property. They fought over me because they each wanted to own me. It wasn't because they loved me."

"Vin…"

"I was a musical prodigy," she said. She ran her hand along the keyboard and a rippling arpeggio of notes filled the air. "Piano. I got a lot of attention. Lot of special treatment. Classes from the best in the world, with fees that would make you rage. There was talk of me maybe being the next big name in classical piano. If I panned out, of course. Lots of child prodigies can't hack it or deal with the pressure. They just fade away. But both my parents felt like I was a worthy investment risk. And they each wanted to be *the* parent of the prodigy, the one who nurtured me into greatness. They each tried to convince me to choose them. That was what I had to look forward to when they shared custody. And because they were who they were, they did their convincing with gifts. Trips and horses and shiny things and everything they thought a girl wanted."

"What did you want?"

"I wanted my parents not to fight. I wanted two happy parents in the same house. But that was the one thing I'd never get." Vin splayed her left hand wide and hit a few heavy bass chords. Dom recognized the first notes of the song cartoons always used to signal doom.

"Beethoven's Fifth," Vinny supplied helpfully. "Anyway, when I got older—when I was a teen in those fancy prep schools—I saw guys doing the same shit my parents did before. Take me out to dinner, and they get some action. Buy me some present…action. Exclusive dating? Might as well come with a contract saying blowjobs on demand. It was just the market to them, just the way things were. They believed anything or anyone could be bought. I wanted to burn it all to the ground."

"You sound like an anarchist." And those guys all sounded like assholes.

"Close," she said. "One day, when I was at school in New York, fifteen years old, I met some kids in the subway, busking in the tunnels to make enough money to buy something to drink. Punk rockers, hardcore kids. Didn't have a dime, but they were sure they could change the world. I loved the music, I loved every word they said. I ran away from home to be with them. I cut and dyed my hair. I used a different name. I destroyed my ID and my credit cards so no one would track me down. My dad eventually hired a P.I., and it took him two years to find me." Vinny grinned, pleased at the hassle she must have caused.

"So when I covered your meals and the motel room, you thought I was trying to buy you?" Dom asked.

She shook her head. She looked so unhappy. "I don't know. No, not really. It was just circumstances. And you did way more for me than you ever had to, and you were nice about everything. But when you mentioned that I let you pay for me, I just…freaked out. Sorry."

"It's okay. My reaction wasn't great either. Truce?"

"Truce."

"So we're clear on this, you know I don't expect anything from you, Vin. Want, yes. Expect, no."

"Yeah, I know."

"Good." He smiled. "Because I don't want to have to tell you *no charge* every time I get you some coffee. Or pull out a calculator whenever I get close to you."

"Hey, what makes you think I want you close to me?" Vinny asked, her sarcasm not quite up to its usual level.

"If you didn't," Dom asked, "why are you trying to shred my only clean t-shirt?"

Vinny looked down to where she was gripping the shirt in both hands, as if he'd otherwise slip away. "Oh, right."

"I don't mind," Dom said. Then he kissed her.

Chapter 18

GUESS SHE HADN'T LEARNED HER lesson about steering clear of this guy. Vinny leaned in and did everything she could to make that kiss count.

She let go of his shirt and slipped her hands underneath it, feeling how warm his skin was. Dom groaned a little at her touch, then doubled down on the kiss. Damn, he was good with his tongue.

Vinny caught her breath and leaned back, hitting a few keys as she did. Dom used the space to slide one hand under her shirt and up along her back, feeling for a bra that wasn't there.

"Didn't wear one today," she muttered.

"Mmm. No complaints here." Dom took his hand back, and gathered up her chains to make the necklaces hang down her back. "You and your damned jewelry," he said.

Then he lifted her shirt up. The cool air would have perked up her nipples if they hadn't been perked up already. Dom ran his palm lightly over her left breast. "This do anything for you?"

She wriggled, feeling heat between her legs. "You know it does."

Dom pulled her close again, his mouth on hers. Vinny rocked against him, her body waking up with every little touch of his hands and his mouth.

Judging by the bulge in his jeans, he was enjoying this too. "So much for staying out of your way," he said.

She remembered telling him that. She'd been so sure that her thing for him was just a momentary madness. That now that she was here, she'd be able to get back to her own life and forget about him.

Yeah, right.

"Let me get my shirt all the way off," she said. "Or get yours all the way off. Come on, Dom."

He shook his head. "Not here."

"Why not?" God, she wanted to see all of him. "Just so I can see all your tattoos again."

"All? Then you'll need to get me naked."

"Really?" That was a very interesting bit of info.

"Yeah. But trust me, Vin. When we get all our clothes off, we are going to fuck, and talented as I'm sure you are at piano, I do not want to fuck you on one. I prefer a bed. And a whole night to spend in it."

Vinny rolled her eyes. "Traditionalist."

"Traditions get to be traditions for a reason."

He kissed her again, slowly this time. Then he murmured, "You know what. I could forget about tradition. You tell me, Vin."

Go for it. The words were on the tip of her tongue, a command for herself as much as him.

Then something caught in her peripheral vision. At first she thought it was a shadow, or something dark. But when she turned her head and looked harder, she saw what must have distracted her. A little blinking red light.

"Cheese and crackers," she muttered.

Dom paused. "What is it?"

"Um, don't freak out. I think there's a security camera. I can see the recording light."

"Are *you* freaking out?" he asked quietly.

"Little bit, yeah." She hated getting her picture taken, and she hated cameras in general, even when she was wearing all her clothes.

He went still for a long moment, then sighed and pulled her shirt back down. Vin saw the frustration on his face, and she completely understood.

"Sorry," she whispered.

"Not your fault." Dom glanced around, his gaze locking onto the red light. "Your friends are serious about security, huh?"

"I guess. Side effect of having money. You worry people will steal it."

He looked back at her, his hands resting on her hips. His touch was grounding now, not tantalizing. "Maybe the cameras are why you've been feeling watched."

"Maybe. Anyway, they sure work to kill the mood." She wriggled off him and stood up. "I gotta get out of here for a bit. I'm going to take a walk." Anything to work off the sexual frustration she was feeling.

"Mind if I tag along?"

Vinny nodded, glad he asked.

The moment they got outside, Vinny felt better. Well, on one level. She was still feeling worked up after a couple of minutes alone with Dom. Maybe she should be grateful for the stupid security camera. It stopped her from making what was probably a terrible decision. Getting attached to Dom would be pointless, and if she slept with him, she'd get attached. Vinny knew herself well enough to know that. Relationships always turned sour. They were best avoided completely.

Meanwhile, Dom was looking around, taking in the scene. It was an amazing scene. Emma had selected the property very carefully, and she chose it because the view was gorgeous from every direction.

Especially gorgeous in Dom's direction.

Stop that, Vinny told herself. God, she was turning into an idiot.

Dom said, "Hard to believe a place this pretty can have such bad energy. But then, looks aren't everything."

"You sense energy? Like auras?"

"I'm not great at auras. I know some people who are astonishing. It's not mind-reading, but it's the next best thing. A little scary, really." Dom looked around. "I just recognize the more basic levels of energy, especially any-thing that leads from this world into the otherworlds, or a place of power, or some spot that has some unusual con-centration of energy—like a grave, or a doorway."

"That sounds pretty astonishing to me," Vinny said.

"It's just practice." Dom sounded a little embarrassed, and Vinny got the impression he was playing it down a bit. He clearly had gifts. It couldn't be just practice. Then he said, "It's a mental technique, really. We use it to see what's happening around us more clearly. It's like being able to see several layers of reality at once. It tends to blur out what doesn't matter, and make what does matter stand out more."

Vinny asked, "Are you special? Is it like a superpower that only you have?"

"No. Anyone can if they know how. It just takes train-ing."

"Then train me."

"Training takes a little longer than that. Months. Years."

"Come on, Dom. Something. I want to help."

He thought about it. "You can't walk into the other-worlds, but there's something else you could try that might help. This is a bit easier to do if you can be surrounded by nature, so we may as well do it here."

"Do what?"

"Do you meditate?"

"Never got the hang of it. Are we meditating?"

"Not exactly. We call it centering. It's a really useful trick when things are getting complicated and overwhelming in a supernatural way. Centering helps a person kind of pull themselves back into one place, shake off psychic angst."

"I'm all for that."

He stopped when they were out of sight of the house and among a stand of pine trees. "Here's a good spot. Sit down. Close your eyes. Take a few deep breaths."

She did all that, then waited for his next instructions.

He sat near her, saying, "Keep your eyes closed. Try to empty yourself out of your surface thoughts. Oh, crap. I forgot that it helps to have a focus when you're just learning this."

"A focus?"

"Like a totem. Something to ground you."

She looked down at her necklaces, then selected one, an enameled oval of a female saint. "How about Cecilia here?"

"Patron saint of music. Perfect," Dom said happily. "So close your eyes, hold onto St. Cecilia, and take a few deep breaths. Keep calm, and try to let go of all the stuff that's been happening."

"That sounds impossible."

"That's the hard part," Dom agreed. "But try your best. Now, you're going to open your eyes in a second, but here's the key. Don't use your regular eyes. Use your firefly eyes."

Vinny opened what she assumed were her regular eyes. "You said what?"

Dom looked a bit shy as he repeated, "Your firefly eyes."

"What the hell are you talking about?"

"Have you ever watched for fireflies at night, when you were a kid?"

Vinny nodded slowly. Dom's questions were bringing up long-forgotten memories of childhood evenings when she waited for fireflies to come out, anticipating the magic of that brief time just after sunset. A time when no matter what else was happening with her life, no matter how her parents fought, Vinny could see a little glimmer of magic in the world.

"Do you remember *how* you looked for them?" he went on.

And then she remembered the trick of seeing fireflies. You couldn't search for a particular lightning bug, or try to find their dark bodies against the shadows. You had to unfocus a bit, wait for the next moment, and not look for anything. Then you'd see hundreds of fireflies, blinking madly in the night.

"I got it," she said.

"Okay. Start with that sort of seeing. Close your actual eyes, open your firefly eyes, and go from there. Don't try to see anything in particular. Just concentrate on your own breathing, and your own sense of self."

She took a few deep breaths on Dom's recommendation, and closed her eyes again.

At first, it was just…her sitting there with closed eyes. Vinny hoped for some magical revelation. But evidently, magic didn't work like that. It was just this dull place of black and white. And more black and white. And more.

She realized she was standing up, looking at her feet. She stood on a path of black and white stripes. Wide white stripe, a slightly shorter black stripe. Then white, then black.

A piano keyboard. Well, that just figured. Centering brought her directly to music. She used to live and breathe piano, and her subconscious must still have it locked in. It was like she was still twelve years old.

She took a step, and another, walking the striped path into a landscape that otherwise looked just like the real world she'd left. Pine trees everywhere, and thick mists hanging in the highest branches, the suggestion of mountains beyond. Somewhere, she heard a faint roaring sound…a river.

It was all quite pretty and peaceful. Vinny resolved to give meditation a try, if it was like this.

Looking around, she became conscious of thin, shimmering threads in the air, almost like spidersilk or those long threads some little green caterpillars used to sail through summer. But when she reached out, her hand passed right through them. They weren't tangible. They weren't anything she could grab. But her skin tingled with a sort of vibration when it made contact with each thread. Like a harp string vibrating under her fingers.

Emma.

Vinny touched the last thread again, curious as to how it seemed to want to draw her toward her friend. Then she noticed how this particular thread actually emanated from her own self. *This thread connects me to Emma,* she thought. It was thin, but strong and tight, and it glimmered brightly, as if the sun shone on it, despite all the mist around.

Vin saw another thread, thinner and wispier. *Jonas.*

Then another, one that led back where she'd walked from. *Dom.* Vinny was a little alarmed at how tough the thread looked. For something that only existed a few days, it seemed awfully...real. She passed her hand through it, and her whole body resonated with the hum of energy it sent through her, leaving a warm glow she would have called golden if she were a more poetic person.

Firefly eyes, she told herself, willing herself to lose focus on the thread leading to Dom. A moment later, she realized the misty air was concealing hundreds of thin, silvery threads running out from her to...everywhere. Vinny had always thought that connections mattered. But this was the first time she'd actually *seen* it. No wonder she always felt so weird about relationships everyone else seemed to charge into without thinking.

She paused on the path, and heard an odd sound behind her, as if something had been matching her pace, and got caught out when she stopped.

She turned, looking around. The mists that seemed charmingly mysterious before now seemed menacing, hiding something within.

Vinny was not going to call out *hello* like a horror movie victim, but she kept turning in a circle, hoping to catch whatever was out there. She no longer felt centered, if she ever had been.

She couldn't see anything, but the sense of being

watched made her shoulders bunch up. She told herself to calm down, to stop freaking out.

Then she felt it. A hot breath on the back of her neck.

She jumped, turning a full 180, ready to punch whatever it was in the face.

Nothing there. But she heard an odd hissing noise, like a far away, staticky radio.

It was still just Vinny, standing alone in the mist. She noticed, though, that in her hand was a knife, one that looked a lot like Dom's knife. She took a breath. She could do some damage with that.

The second she started to feel better, the hot breath returned, joined by a lick of a tongue across her neck.

Delicious.

Vinny screamed.

Arms wrapped around her from behind. Vinny strained hard, trying to free herself.

"It's me," Dom said, still holding her tight as he shifted around to face her. "You're okay. Vin, what *happened*?"

She felt like she had a fever, and her heart raced as if she'd run a mile. "What the hell was that?"

"I don't know, Vin. Centering is supposed to be peaceful."

"Well, it wasn't," she snapped. "There's nothing peaceful about being stalked in some creepy shadow world. There was something…behind my eyes. Like it was hiding inside my brain."

He frowned. "Shadow world?"

"It looked like here, but black and white, like a keyboard, on the ground."

"Shit."

"What?"

Dom was staring at her like she'd grown an extra head. "I think…Jesus." He pulled out his phone. "I gotta ask Lex about this."

"About what?"

"I think you walked into the otherworlds."

What was an otherworld? Vinny asked, "Is that bad?"

"Not inherently," he said as he texted a message to his brother. "But it is dangerous, and it's not easy to do."

"So probably that's not what happened," she said quickly.

He still looked concerned, and Vinny could tell she wouldn't be getting out this easily. He said, "Tell me how it felt. Or smelled. Anything that comes to mind."

Vinny squeezed her eyes shut, trying to put words to what just happened to her. Dom's arms still circled her.

"It was fine in the beginning. I was just noticing all the threads."

"Threads?" he echoed. "You've mentioned something like that before."

"Yeah, but this time, I could really *see* the threads. You know, all the threads that go from person to person. I saw the ones to Emma and Jonas…and you. And a hundred others."

She noticed a tiny shift in Dom's eyes. He was surprised.

"You don't know about the threads?" she asked nervously.

"I do know about them," he replied, his words slow. "But most people don't see them, even in the otherworlds."

"Oh, I've always known about them. Since I was like eleven or twelve. I tried to explain it to my therapist once. She convinced me I was being too literal about how my parents were each tugging at me. My dad would pull his thread, then my mom would pull hers, and I always felt it, even when they were talking with each other and I wasn't supposed to know." Vin paused. "I think I would have felt better if I'd known those threads were really there."

"They were," Dom said. "It was unusual that you saw them, but they're real." He leaned in a little, then said in a low voice, "Now you have to tell me about the other thing you saw."

Her shoulders tightened up instantly.

"It's okay, Vin," he said quietly. "Just talking about it can't summon it back."

She swallowed hard before bile could rise in her throat. "What if it never left?" she asked. "What if it's still here?" She was shaking, her muscles reacting to the anxiety she felt.

"It's not here," Dom said, his voice steady. He released her. "It's not in the real world, at least. It's in the otherworlds. I promise. It might still feel close but it's not here. Tell me whatever you remember, Vin. That will help me fight it the next time it shows up."

The idea of a next time made her woozy. "No."

"Yes, Vin. Start with something simple. Was there a smell at all?"

She took a few breaths, remembering. "Um, yes. Sort of…hot. But not fire. Like hot asphalt? Hot, but…dark. Tar. It was tar."

"Good. Keep going. Did you hear anything?"

Vinny shuddered. "Oh, yes." She didn't have to try to remember that. "There was this growling sound. Like an animal." A big, scary animal. "A slobbery growl. I thought it was about to eat me. Do demons eat people?"

"Some do. Did you hear words? Did it speak to you?"

Vinny frowned. "Maybe? There was something I heard that I almost understood. Or like when someone is talking on the other side of a wall and you know it's words but you can't make them out. Or maybe it wasn't talking to me. I'm sorry. None of this is useful."

"Let me decide that," Dom said. "I thought centering would be good for you, and it never occurred to me that you might be able to see an otherworld. Sorry. That had to scare you."

Vinny bowed her head. "Scared doesn't begin…that was terrifying. It was nice at first, and then it wasn't. It was like a trap. I don't like your stupid otherworlds."

"Most people don't," he said, turning his head. "Oh, hey. Look who's here."

Vinny looked over to see Piewicket approaching. Dom stepped away to give her space. Vinny picked the cat up and held her, craving the normalcy and warmth of a little cuddly being. Pie tolerated it for a minute, then wiggled.

Vin put her back down. Pie meowed, then looked at Dom.

"Yeah, I was teaching her how to center, and by accident, she sort of walked into an otherworld." He paused, evidently listening to something Piewicket was telling him. "Not sure," Dom said after a minute. "Vinny didn't really get a visual sense. More the usual creeping dread sort of thing."

"Not creeping," Vin corrected, ignoring the fact that Dom was having a conversation with a cat. "There was nothing creeping about it. It wasn't there, and then it was. It was a rushing dread. A pile-on of dread."

"Okay." Dom squeezed her shoulder, then looked toward Pie again.

The cat's tail lashed once.

"Pie, she doesn't know how to describe a demon. She's got no training." Dom sounded angry. Then his expression changed. "Oh."

"What?" Vinny asked anxiously.

Dom shook his head. "This is bad. When I got here, everyone said it had to be a ghost. But this proves we're dealing with a demon."

Chapter 19

PIEWICKET HISSED AT THAT. THE cat looked directly at Vinny, then back to Dom, who was still trying to fit everything together in his mind. Vinny accidentally strolled right into an otherworld. And that meant a doorway, which meant a demon.

He said, "Pie thinks you would be safer if you leave. I think she's right."

"Leave?" Vinny gasped. "When you guys are all still here? When *Emma* is here? I'm not running away like a wuss. And besides," she added, "if there's something scary around, doesn't it make sense to stick close to an actual demon hunter in case things get bad?"

Dom frowned. "Or you could be out of actual danger by leaving. You can take Emma with you, if you want. You can go to Seattle for a few days. Why don't we see if Emma will do that?"

God, how had he missed it? This house wasn't haunted by a ghost. After Vinny's brief glimpse into the otherworlds, it was now clear that whatever was causing trouble had to be a different—and more powerful—type of supernasty.

To find it and identify it, Dom had to shift strategy.

Now that he knew about the security cameras, Dom had an idea. He thought he might be able to view some footage to find out if they showed any evidence of a supernasty hanging out in the house.

He said, "I gotta go take care of something. Will you be okay on your own?"

She looked surprised, but said, "Yeah, of course."

After getting her to promise she'd find him if something else bad happened, Dom left her on the terrace where they'd eaten dinner the first night.

He went in search of Jonas, and found him pacing in a circle in a small room on the first floor, which appeared to be an office. Jonas was on his phone, yapping to someone on the other end, exchanging clipped phrases and looking annoyed.

When he saw Dom in the doorway, he said, "Call you back," and quickly turned off the phone.

"Sorry to interrupt," Dom began.

"Just yelling at lawyers. Some of these assholes forget they're working for me."

Dom didn't try to hide his reaction.

Jonas huffed out a breath. "You can say it. You think I haven't heard it all before? You think I'm shallow. Some bonehead who got lucky and doesn't deserve what he got." He sounded both defensive and proud.

Yup, Dom thought. *Basically.*

"Well, I worked. We all worked. Yes, I got a break. But I made sacrifices too."

"What kind of sacrifices?"

"Life sacrifices. Shitty living, weeks on tour, long days, lots of owing favors and reminding people who owed me favors. This is a tough business." Jonas let out a breath. "Maybe not as tough as ghosthunting, but don't judge me."

"I didn't come here to judge you. I came to tell you something."

Got news?" Jonas asked hopefully.

"Yes and no. I figured something out, but it's not the end of the problem."

"Go on."

"So," Dom said. "What would you say if I told you that the house isn't haunted by a ghost?"

"Um…you're saying you can't find anything?" Jonas looked crestfallen.

"No. I'm saying that instead of a ghost, you've got a demon. Or something like it."

Jonas expression shifted to alarm.

"Any chance you know something about that?" Dom pressed.

"What would I know about a demon?" Jonas asked. He wouldn't meet Dom's eyes.

"Some demons are good at looking like normal people—for a while anyway. Do you remember any interaction with a stranger that was a bit…odd? Or someone who came to the house that you don't remember seeing leave the house? Does anyone besides you and Emma have access to the property?"

"No," Jonas said. "At least, no one can get in without us knowing about it."

"And the doors to the house are alarmed, I assume."

"Absolutely. Doors, windows, everything. Not to mention the cameras. I'd know if someone snuck in."

Dom frowned. So much for that avenue. "I want to look at your security feed."

"The cameras? Why? Demons don't sit around getting filmed, do they?"

"Not exactly, but there's a chance that the cameras will show something useful. I might be able to pin the disturbance down to a specific room or object. That will help a lot. Where's the control panel for the security cameras?"

"Uh…not here."

Lying. Dom wasn't psychic, and he didn't need to be to know that the guy was lying.

"Where?" he asked, to play along.

"Security firm," Jonas said. "Everything just goes to them."

Which didn't jibe at all with Jonas's comment that he knew if anyone had come onto the property.

"So there's no place in the house with all that info?" Dom asked, very deliberately.

"No. Sorry."

"Worth a shot." Dom left the office and immediately sent out a mental call to Piewicket.

Shortly after, the cat appeared, a dead mouse in her mouth. She dropped the mouse at his feet.

"Hey, thanks." Dom nudged the little brown mouse with his foot. "You going to eat that?"

Naturally. What did you want?

"The owner of this place denies there's a way to watch the security camera feeds in the house. I think he's lying. I did my best to put the idea in his head, and I think he'll go to the place soon. Tonight or tomorrow." It was basic psychology. People trying to hide things had a tendency to go directly to them, even when common sense suggested it was a stupid thing to do.

And you want me to stalk him, so he can lead me to

his den.

"Yes. Except the den is filled with information, not snacks for you. Sorry."

You will reward me later?

"All the cuddles you want," he promised. "Or fish."

Both.

"Deal. Please go hunt him, okay?"

Piewicket ate the mouse first. Cats had priorities.

While waiting for Pie to return with news, Dom decided to be conspicuous about not following Jonas around. Instead, he helped Emma and Vinny move a few pieces of art Emma had purchased but hadn't yet unpacked. Dom hadn't realized that all the stuff hanging on the walls was actual art—as in, original works worth thousands of dollars each. And Emma was the person who selected it all, according to Vinny. "She's got a good eye for this kind of thing," she concluded.

"And Vin would know," Emma chimed in.

Vinny's expression darkened momentarily, and Dom figured it had something to do with her upper-crust childhood. But he didn't want to push for more details. He was just happy that Vinny seemed recovered after her accidental stroll into the otherworlds.

Jonas didn't show his face more than a couple times. When he skipped dinner, saying he had work to do, Emma rolled her eyes. "Musicians!"

That evening, Dom made a call to his brother. Lex sounded sleepy, and Dom remembered it was later there.

"What's up?" Lex asked. "How's the ghostbusting?"

"Well, I'm pretty sure it's a demon, not a ghost," Dom explained. "So that changes things."

"Whoa." Lex suddenly sounded much more awake. "How do you know?"

Dom told about Vinny's encounter in the otherworlds, and Lex predictably interjected, "Wait, this person just strolled into the otherworlds, no problem? No practice?"

"She says no, and I believe her. So it must be the environment itself that caused it—it basically invited her right in."

"That's not good," Lex muttered. Dom guessed he was scribbling down notes in his ever-present notebook. "I'll do a lookup on demons that can open paths to their worlds. You know this means it's a pretty nasty supernasty, right?"

"I figured," Dom said dryly. "There's something else."

"Lord, what?"

"Vin—the person who walked into the otherworld—she described seeing energy lines while she was in there. And she said that she's seen those lines before. Or sensed them. She's done it most of her life. She described them as threads, but the way she talks about them going between people, how some are light and some are heavy..." Dom trailed off, sure that Lex already knew what he was thinking.

"She can sense ley lines and ties, just naturally?" Lex asked excitedly. "I remember how tough those were to see, even when I knew where to look. That's so cool!"

"It is *not* cool when one of those lines might lead a demon straight to her," Dom said, thinking Lex wasn't seeing the main point here. He remembered the first full day he'd been here, when the supernasty had snuck up on him in the attic and sent him into that vision of falling through twisting lines, and his sense that some of the lines led to the house. "We've been approaching this problem as a haunting focusing on the location, because that's what the client said it was. But *I* think that whatever it is

—demon, probably—it wants a person. Not a place."

"I get it," Lex said. "Now that you're sure it's a demon, we'll figure out what's what. Keep an eye on her, and I'll let you know as soon as we find something. Lily can help, so it'll go fast. Meantime, can Pie seal up that door to the otherworld?"

"I'll ask. She's already doing some spying for me, though."

"Keep us updated. I'm going to make some coffee." Lex hung up. Dom knew his little brother would be up all night. Though easy-going by nature, he was tenacious when he was given a problem to solve.

* * * *

Piewicket was not to be found the whole night. Dom had no idea if she slept at all, or where she was. But in the morning, she leapt up onto his bed.

Cuddles?

He reached out to pet her. "Find anything out?"

Late at night, when all were sleeping, he went to a room in the level below ground, at the very end of the passage. He spent a few hours there, staring at pictures of the house and those in it. He did not see me.

"Well done."

Salmon is an acceptable reward.

"We're in the right area of the country for that. Let me see what I can do."

Dom almost fell asleep again—a purring cat on your chest tended to do that—but the sounds of an argument downstairs got him moving.

When he got downstairs, he overheard Emma saying, "Why is my lawyer calling me with papers to sign?" She was glaring at Jonas. "We agreed on the payment structures for the royalties from those songs. What's changed?"

Jonas shook his head in exaggerated annoyance. "God, you'll get a higher percentage after this. What's your problem?"

"My problem is that you're not telling me why."

"Don't worry about it! Jesus." Jonas looked to Vinny, who stood close to Emma. "Vin, explain to my wife that more money is better than less money."

"It isn't always," Vinny responded evenly. The day before, Dom would have missed the heavier meaning her words. Now that he'd heard a little bit about her past, her attitude made much more sense.

At that, Jonas just turned on his heel and left the room, unwilling to face two women who didn't agree with him.

"Um, is there coffee?" Dom asked. Whatever was going on, it had nothing to do with his job.

"You bet," Emma said. "Full pot in the kitchen. Help yourself."

Dom caught Vinny's eyes and smiled. She grinned back, but stayed with Emma, who'd gone back to frowning at the paperwork in her hands.

Dom drank two cups of coffee. Then he went in search of wherever the security camera feed ended up.

He found it in a closet-sized room in the basement, not far down the hall from the now-deserted recording studio. Dom wondered briefly where Jonas was and if he'd come back down to work on his song, but pushed the worry aside. After all, Jonas did hire him to fix his problem. And that meant looking at some video.

Even though demons and other paranormal forces tended to muck up any attempts to record them, sometimes those same acts could be useful indications of their presence, if you knew what to look for. Dom could check for odd blips, static, errors with the time stamps—all hints of demons' innate ability to thwart modern technology.

Unlike the rest of the house, this room was painted utilitarian grey and had no windows. It was all business. He sat down at the computer, ready to work. He wasn't a hacker by any means, but when his client didn't want to be forthcoming, Dom had to get creative.

The screen prompted him to enter a password. He hit enter, hoping that Jonas bypassed that little bit of security.

Nope. The prompt appeared again.

"Okay. What's your password, egomaniac?"

What did Vinny say the name of Jonas's band was? Oh, yeah. Dom typed *Mercury* in the field. Accepted.

"In one," Dom muttered. Of course the band that made Jonas rich would be his password.

The files were ordered by date, so Dom started looking at the most recent files.

"Music room: V." Did the V stand for Vinny? He clicked. A video feed from the day before popped up, showing the exact time he and Vinny had been making out. The camera had been in a perfect position to capture Vinny during the encounter. Yeesh. If she hadn't noticed the recording light, that video could have gotten NSFW very fast.

Which brought up the question of why it was recording at all. Motion sensors might automatically cause it to record. Or, someone chose to hit record, which was a lot creepier.

He saw a folder marked "Blue Room." The bedroom Vinny had been given was called the blue room. He clicked and saw a number of files, all within the last two days. Clicking one at random, he watched as a video started playing. It showed Vinny's room, and there was Vinny entering the frame, evidently walking in from the bathroom, because she was wrapped only in a towel.

Well, that was not cool.

He remembered how insistent Jonas had been that Vinny get the blue room. Apparently, that was so Jonas could get video of her. Vinny would go through the roof if she ever found that out.

Dom closed the file before the video hit the point when the towel came off. He clicked on the next one. Vinny sleeping on the bed. She didn't wear much, though the bed sheets hid most of her body. She tossed and turned a lot, Dom saw as he hit the 8x button to speed it up. Why the hell did Jonas need footage of Vinny sleeping? Aside from being really stalkerish, it also seemed pointless. The next file was just single images. Still Vinny sleeping, but these were pulled from the video feed at a point where the bed sheet had come down to expose her breasts.

So Jonas looked through the whole feed to grab images of Vinny to jerk off to.

Angry, Dom deleted the images before realizing that they might actually be helpful if he needed to convince Vin that her supposed friend had a serious boundary problem.

There were more videos. He didn't want to, but he quickly scanned the rest, just to make sure there wasn't something horrible on any of them.

They were mostly boring. Aside from invading Vinny's privacy, the videos were nothing to get worked up about. Nothing showed anything she had to be ashamed of. A few were crappier than the others, blurry and grainy for a few minutes, but still viewable.

Dom got to the end, and wrestled with whether to

delete them now, or wait. He didn't like the idea of the files existing. But what if he needed them to show Vinny later?

"Damn." He had to keep them there for a little while.

He scanned the rest of the folders. Nothing spying on Emma. Nothing spying on Jonas. Nothing on Dom either, though he did see that his guest room had a camera in it. He noted the image and guessed where the camera must be installed, in a high corner of the room. He'd block the lens the first chance he got.

Curious, he switched over to the live feed, which skipped to a new camera view every thirty seconds. There were a ton of cameras set up throughout the house and grounds, especially at the doorways and the entrances to the property. Jonas was paranoid as well as pervy.

The video jumped and went staticky for a second, then settled.

"Jesus Christ." Dom sat up. He'd been so angry about the videos of Vinny that he forgot he was looking for footage like this. Footage with flaws.

There was a supernatural presence in the house. Right now.

Noting the room that the footage showed—the piano room, in fact—Dom jumped out of the chair and ran up to the first floor.

The piano room was empty when he got there, but he was alert, and the whiff of tar and brimstone was real.

This house wasn't being haunted by a ghost. It was inhabited by a demon. Somehow, it had found a way through the otherworld to this house. Vinny hadn't just got unlucky in her first foray with opening her eyes to the otherworlds. That thing was close in the otherworld because it was here in the real world too, or at least very,

very close. The borders between the worlds could be as thin as a soap bubble sometimes.

And soap bubbles broke easily.

He took a few breaths. Knowing it was a demon changed his whole approach. First, he had to get Vinny and Emma out of the way. Jonas too. The house was too dangerous for regular people to be hanging around.

Plus there was that whole spying thing. Extra motivation to get Vinny out of here.

Chapter 20

Jonas was out of his mind.

Vinny watched her friend, who was slouched across the long leather sofa in the great room. His expensive clothes were rumpled and streaked with…something, and his head fell back onto the back of the sofa, his mouth open as he stared at the ceiling.

"Jonas. Jonas Belling!" Getting no response, Vinny leaned forward and grabbed his shoulder. He moaned and slid to the right.

"It won't do anything," Emma said, standing at Vinny's side. "He's completely gone right now."

"What's he on?"

"Hell if I know. He picks up these whack designer drugs when he goes to LA, and then waits till he's home with me to try them out!" Emma's voice rose to a wail by the end, her fists clenched as she considered her husband.

"Safety first, I guess," Vinny muttered.

"It's not funny!"

"I'm not laughing." Vinny reached for Emma's arm. She'd been so fixated on finding evidence of Jonas's philandering, she'd overlooked a much easier route to Emma's independence. All Emma had to do was to use the drug angle. She'd get a quick, easy divorce in no time.

"How long will this go on?" she asked, pointing to Jonas.

"I don't know. Hours, probably. He does this when he's on edge. He says he needs to relax."

Vinny squinted at Jonas. He didn't look relaxed. He looked nearly braindead. Was the paranormal activity getting to him that badly? She tried to ask him, but he only blinked when she spoke. His hand waved languidly, the moment looking like it was happening underwater.

Dom strode in, banking when he saw Jonas on the couch. "What's wrong with him?"

"Nothing. He's high."

"On *what*?" From Dom's reaction, he wasn't used to seeing people in Jonas's state, a fact that comforted Vinny a tiny bit—for all of Dom's strange experiences, he did not know everything.

"Does it matter?" she asked. "He's out. You could light a firecracker in his face and he'd barely blink."

"That's…convenient," said Dom, now frowning at Jonas.

"Convenient for who?" Emma asked.

"Um. Never mind." Dom faced the two women. "I wanted to find you. You should leave," Dom said. "We talked about it yesterday, but I mean it this time."

"Why?" Vinny asked.

"This house is less safe than I thought. You and Emma should both leave for a while."

"Why not Jonas?"

Dom's gaze slid to the bombed-out Jonas for a moment, assessing the other man. Whatever Dom was thinking of, it made him huff out an annoyed breath. "He's not the target."

"The target of what?"

Dom shook his head. "Can we talk about it later? If you girls can just go—"

"We're girls now?" Vinny asked. "What, are we too weak to hear what you think is going on?"

Emma pressed her hands to her temples, her eyes shut. "Oh, God."

Vinny turned to her. "What?"

"Migraine coming on. Ugh, this one's gonna be bad." Emma opened her eyes to glare at Jonas. "Like I don't have enough on my brain already, with his behavior, and now an actual headache."

"You should lie down," Vinny said, concerned. Emma had struggled off and on with migraines her whole life, and Vinny knew how debilitating they could get. No wonder she was getting one now, considering the stress and bad feeling building up in the house.

"No, you should both leave the house," Dom said, more urgently.

"If Emma gets in a car while she's got a migraine, she'll be ten times worse. Nothing can be so bad we need to leave before you tell us what's wrong."

Dom grimaced. "I don't want to get into it."

"Well, I do. You say what's happened, or you shut up." Vinny put an arm around Emma's shoulders, intending to walk her to the bedroom.

Emma didn't budge. "No, I want to hear this. What did you find out?"

Dom looked very uncomfortable. "The details can wait."

"Why?" Vinny noticed how he kept looking over to

the barely-conscious Jonas. "Does it have to do with Jonas?"

"Um. Sort of. Yes."

"So tell us," Emma insisted.

"I'd prefer to do that when he's…"

"Not high? Me too," Emma snapped. "But guess what. He is, because he doesn't give a damn about anyone but himself!" She clutched at her head again, moaning. "Christ. Fuck this. I'm going to my room. Vin, please get an answer from this fucking con man."

"Count on it," Vinny told her.

Emma stumbled off through the far door. When she was gone, Vinny turned to face Dom, who seemed unmoved by the con man remark.

"Well? What's the big secret?" she asked, curious. "What's so dangerous that we have to run away?"

"I found some compelling evidence that there is something from the otherworlds in this house. Now, at this moment. Can't you get Emma in a car and out of here?"

Vinny shook her head. "No way. Not when she's already suffering. And I don't get it. Why is this dangerous for us, but not Jonas?"

"That's a different thing."

"How?" Vinny's patience, which had been low ever since she got here, evaporated.

Dom said. "Please. I need you to trust me."

"I want to trust you," she said, "but you've got to do something besides say *trust me*. You have to show me something."

"I can't. It's not a visible thing."

"Then how do you know it is a thing?"

He said, "It's the absence of a thing—blips on the video footage."

"What video footage?"

"Shit." He looked away, and she knew he said something he hadn't meant to. "There's some footage from the security cameras."

"Really? Where?"

"In a room. It's not important."

"Sure it is." The news that the security cameras actually had footage to be viewed could be helpful for Vinny's personal quest to get dirt on Jonas. "Show me."

Clearly unhappy about it, Dom lead her downstairs to a small room at the end of the hall. It was windowless and filled with electronics. Some were related to the recording studio, but some were obviously connected to running the house. And a utilitarian desktop monitor showed images that had to be from the security cameras.

Vinny sat down in the chair before Dom could, and began to scan through the apps and files listed.

It didn't take long for her to see what she was never meant to see. She guessed something bad was here. She read it in Dom's too-stiff posture, his repeated, restrained movements toward the computer. But he didn't say anything, so it was still confusing to open a file and see a picture of herself.

She blinked in noncomprehension at first. The grainy, green-tinged image didn't help. But then she saw it. Saw her. Lying on the bed she slept in last night. Naked, except for the sheet. Because why would she cover herself when no one could see her?

Except someone could see her. There had been a camera. In her room. *Her* room.

She felt sick to her stomach. Vinny had never felt so betrayed since she was a child, and this time, it came with a rush of fury because the assault on her had a sexual edge. It didn't matter that her body hadn't been touched. The video proved that something had been taken from her, without her knowledge and definitely without her permission.

"You weren't going to tell me about this." Her voice came out surprisingly calm. Vinny knew it wouldn't stay that way.

He didn't look at her. "I thought it should wait."

"Wait for what? This is my life. It's me in that clip. Pictures of *my* body. Is this some guy code thing? Not rat each other out when you catch each other being pervy?"

"No." Dom's eyes flashed once, and she knew she'd made him angry. Too bad.

"Then why didn't you want to tell me?" she pressed.

"I knew you'd get mad, like you are right now."

"Damn right I'm mad! Forget not telling me, why didn't you delete it?"

"If I deleted it, how could I prove it happened?"

"You weren't going to tell me it happened!" Her throat tightened up, and her eyes went hot, sure signs she was about to lose her temper. Why, why, why had she trusted Dom? She'd been so good for so long, keeping herself out of emotional bullshit. Then one guy came along and acted like slightly less of a dick than most guys, and she was willing to fold, just because he was hot. Stupid.

Well, he'd win one thing. Vinny was leaving this house. Right now.

"I'm out of here." She turned on her heel and stalked out of the grey room, slamming the door shut with Dom still inside.

As Vinny pounded up the stairs, taking them two at a time, she struggled not to cry. She swallowed compulsively, her throat dry from yelling.

"Getting out," she muttered. "Not staying here one more minute."

She reached the front door and stopped short. What was she doing? She couldn't just run out. Her wallet and her backpack and her everything were all upstairs in her room. She had to get them.

She moved to the staircase, going up at a slower pace than before. Was she nuts? Maybe. Then she remembered the grainy shot of her own body, lying there helpless on the bed. Nope. She couldn't stay in a house where that happened.

Entering her bedroom, Vinny instinctively sought out the place where the camera had to be. She saw a little gleam from the lens and smiled, flipping her middle finger to the camera. "Save the shot of this moment, asshat," she said, though she knew there was no sound.

She started to pull her things together, stuffing them into her ratty backpack. She took a break only to grab some water from the bathroom. Man, anger made her parched.

Once all her clothes were packed, Vin took another drink of water. Why did her throat feel so tight and itchy all of a sudden? And it wasn't just her throat, it was the skin of her neck too.

She yanked at her necklaces. She'd worn them for years with no problem and yet now they were causing some reaction. That was just her luck. She pulled off a few of the longest ones, thinking that maybe the base metals in the chains finally triggered an allergy.

It didn't help. She pulled off a few more, and then a few more. She picked up her backpack, but doubled over, coughing. The discomfort only worsened, and she started to get scared.

One by one, each necklace came off, until only the gold one was left. The irritation didn't stop, though. She fumbled with the clasp of the gold necklace, but her fingers wouldn't work. It felt like it was coated in oil, and she couldn't get a grip on it. In a fit of anger, she curled her hand around the chain and yanked hard, determined to snap the thing off.

Nothing.

She yanked again, harder.

The chain actually seemed to grow tighter. Vinny took a breath, but barely got any air. Was this what drowning felt like? The room started spinning.

She blinked several times. Was she on the floor?

"He—help," she said. Or tried to say. Even she could barely hear the word.

Dom. Pie. Emma. Anyone. Help.

No help.

"That's what you get when you do it all yourself, morsel."

Did she just hear something hiss?

Vinny opened her eyes wider, but couldn't see anything else in the room, and certainly not something that would have spoken those words.

She pulled at the chain again, wincing at the effort it took to do so. The idea of getting up from the floor seemed like so much work.

She closed her eyes for a second, and when she opened them again, the light had changed. The clock on the bedside table indicated an hour went by. An *hour*. And she was still on the floor. Vinny tried to get up, and failed.

She couldn't move, but then something made a sound. A…skittering.

Nothing good ever skittered.

What's wrong with me? she thought, on the edge of panic. She could barely breathe, and she felt too warm, even hot.

She heard the skittering again, and no matter how much she blinked, everything went slowly black.

Did I get in an accident? she wondered. *Am I in a coma?* She tried to speak, but heard nothing. The panic edged closer. What if she was paralyzed, she thought suddenly. Was that why she couldn't move?

Just then, she did hear something. A voice, familiar but not one she quite understood. She strained to hear what it said, but was distracted by a flicker. *My sight's coming back*, she thought. Good.

Or not so good. Vinny saw something moving toward her. A dark, low something, sprawling on the ground, its limbs long and twisted.

Recognition nudged her. This was the same shadowy something she'd sensed when she'd accidentally walked into what Dom called the otherworlds. The thing that sent her running in a panic.

It was back. Closer. The pungent smells of burning tar and smoke fumes surrounded her.

Then it tipped a head up to her, and she saw its face for the first time.

Huge teeth gleamed at her from a mouth too wide to be real. Like a lizard, but way too big. A nightmare.

That's it. I'm dreaming, she told herself frantically. This is a nightmare and I'll wake up and it will all be over soon.

"Hello, morsel," the lizard mouth said. Huge, yellow-red bloodshot eyes filled her vision. "You're not asleep."

Vinny tried to scream one last time, but not a sound came out.

Chapter 21

After Vinny stormed out, Dom just sat there for a few minutes, unsure of what to do. He messed up. Was there a right way to tell someone they were being stalked? Maybe not. But there was a wrong way, because that's the way he just did it. Sure, he was just the messenger. But with a message like that, it didn't really matter that he wasn't actually responsible for the videos. Just letting Vinny know they existed was enough to spark her fury.

Dom fiddled at the keyboard for a little bit, then abruptly leaned forward. He deleted all the files from the time Vinny arrived here. Jonas would have to get his kicks some other way. Maybe once he finished whatever trip he was on, Vinny could yell at him properly and Dom could stop feeling like an asshole for just knowing about the videos.

He should look for more of the discrepancies in the live feed so he could track…whatever was in the house. But he was too disgusted with the whole surveillance system just then, so he turned the computer off and got the hell out of the grey room.

Heading directly outside, Dom took several deep

breaths as he looked at the perfectly still water of the pool. Lord, that house had some *bad* energy, and it had built up fast over the past day or so. Part of the problem was the sheer strength of personality among everyone inside. Jonas was a drug-addled, fame-addicted celebrity. Emma was boiling over with thwarted ambition, obviously unhappy with her life path but unsure how to change it without breaking everything she knew. And then there was Vinny, whose personality might as well have gravitational pull.

He should go see how she was doing.

Then he remembered her *I'm out of here*. Did she mean that literally? He'd told her to leave the house, but he didn't want her to rush off while she was furious.

Dom headed back inside. The house was eerily silent. No sound from the living room, where Jonas had been last. No hint of Emma. And nothing from upstairs. Maybe Vinny had just left the house without another word. She was definitely capable of a solid Irish goodbye.

Wait. There was something. A scratching.

He climbed the stairs and turned toward Vinny's room.

Pie was in front of it, stretched to her full length, clawing uselessly at the door.

Open it! the cat demanded.

"Vin? It's Dom. Can I come in?" Dom tried the handle. It was locked. "Vin, I'm serious. We need to talk. Open up."

The sullen silence continued, though he heard something thump, like Vinny dropped—or threw—something. She was in there.

Fed up, Dom threw his shoulder into the door. It wasn't very tough, and he barreled inside, anticipating more resistance.

"Vinny, we have to talk—"

He stopped in shock. Vinny lay on the floor by the far wall. Her body was twisted as if she'd been writhing in pain.

Silver threads lay all around her, and it took him a second to understand that they were all her many silver necklaces, the ones she wore like an elegant Mr. T. She'd ripped them off as if she were desperate to get rid of them. Only one necklace remained, a thin gold chain with a little gold pendant. Dom didn't remember seeing it before.

Kneeling beside Vinny, Dom tilted her face to his. Her eyes were wide with fear, and her breath was choked. Her throat worked as if she was trying to speak, but nothing came out. Vinny's fingers twitched.

"I'm here, Vin," he said, trying to reassure her as he checked her over. The gold necklace was tight around her neck, rubbing the skin red, even cutting trails into her flesh. He could barely work a few fingers between the metal and her skin. He tried to snap the chain without hurting Vinny, but it held fast.

He stared at the pendant, an unfamiliar symbol of a circle overlaid by a triangle. Though he didn't recognize it, he recognized the dread rolling over him. Nothing he tried could remove it. Even cutting at it with his silver knife—which normally sliced through bones like butter—did nothing to the seemingly delicate gold chain.

This was *bad* magic. How had this happened without him knowing about it?

"Vin, I'll get this thing off you, but I need to be outside to do it. Can you walk?" He grabbed her hand, but she only gave a tiny shake of her head, that one movement costing her serious energy.

She was in a state. Not paralyzed, not catatonic. But

definitely cursed and unable to help herself at all.

Piewicket was still in full-on attack mode. Take her and go. Find running water to work your spell. I will remain here and guard against whatever may come.

"Okay, Vin. Good thing you're skinny," he said. He picked her up in a move that landed her body over his shoulder. The classic get your buddy out of the war zone carry, not the cradling the damsel in distress carry. He couldn't care less if it was unromantic. Vinny would run out of breath soon.

He got to the giant garage and started to head for his bike. Then he glanced at the red Porsche. The keys were handy, on a hook on the wall. He didn't think twice. Putting Vinny on the passenger seat, he drove away from the mansion, the gates opening just in time for him to get through.

Dom pushed the car as much as he dared. The twisting roads forced him to drive way slower than he wanted, not to mention he couldn't risk getting pulled over. Piewicket had said to find running water. He had to find it within the next few minutes. Out of the way of people, and with enough natural energy to work a fast spell.

The car zipped across the bridge they'd taken to get there. A river ran furiously in a gorge far below.

"Running water," Dom muttered. "Perfect."

He nearly missed the dirt turn off just past the bridge. The tires squealed as he turned onto it, and then went quiet when they left the pavement and hit the dirt. He followed the path, turning two hairpins to get to the bottom of the river gorge.

He looked over. Vinny had stopped breathing.

His own breath caught, and he almost swerved off the road. Instead, Dom hit the brakes and slammed the car into park.

Her eyelids only fluttered up briefly when he shook her. She was losing the battle she was fighting against the spell. That gold necklace was the magical equivalent of snake venom, and he needed an antidote, fast.

Running water was the best antidote he had right now. He hauled Vin out of the car, carrying her to the river. At the water's edge, he paused, then walked into the freezing, fast-flowing water.

With every step, the water rose around him, till he was waist deep and ten feet from the shore. Despite being summer, the water was icy. No sane person would walk in here fully clothed. No wonder they were the only people around. Which was good, since he was about to cast a spell.

"Listen, Vin, I'm going to almost put you under the water. I'll watch you, okay?"

No response, not even a flicker in the eyes.

Dom had to risk it. He slipped one arm around her shoulders to support her as best he could. Her head rolled back a bit.

God damn, this water was cold. Pure freaking snowmelt from the Cascades or wherever. Dom had to work fast, or the cure would kill Vinny.

With the other hand, he got his knife out. Muttering well-known words, he touched the tip of the blade to the pendant, channeling all the energy he could summon down to the point of contact. The metal of the pedant should shatter.

But it didn't. Dom recited the words again, a little louder. This spell was so familiar he could work it in his sleep.

The pendant remained whole, though Vinny's skin

began to turn pink, either from the rush of magical energy, or from the intense cold of the water.

Dom flipped the knife away, afraid that another attempt would harm Vinny's flesh. But though her chest was turning pink, her lips looked blueish.

"Vinny, *breathe!*" he yelled, hoping his voice got through to her unconscious mind.

He had to get the necklace off her, but he couldn't destroy the object. It was too powerful, even against this glacial river full of its own power.

Wait. He didn't need to break the curse itself. He only needed to separate it from Vinny.

He pulled out his silver knife again, this time laying the edge of the blade against the chain, working it between the metal and her skin. There was no established spell for this process. He had to wing it. He had to trust whatever words and actions came to him in the moment. That was his one true skill, the innate connection to the magic that was always flowing though the world.

"Lavinia Rose Wellington Wake belongs to me," he said, in English, not sure what words he would say until a moment before he spoke each one. "*I* claim her. Take your curse elsewhere. I release her with silver and water and—" he broke off.

Just say it, wuss. This is life or death.

He took a breath. "I release her with silver and water and love." Three of the most potent forces in magic.

He drew the knife blade against the chain. Aided by the rushing water, the silver was stronger, and two links of the chain snapped. The tip of the blade caught a bit of skin at Vinny's neck, and blood beaded up before the river took it away.

Dom grabbed the necklace just as the current seized it.

He stuffed it in his shirt pocket.

Then Vinny gasped, her whole body convulsing with the removal of the cursed item. "Dom!" she screamed hoarsely.

"I got you," he said, pulling her body tight against him.

"So cold," she gasped.

"I know. We're getting out." He carried her to the bank, the water keeping her buoyant. When the water went down to his waist, he tipped her to her feet. "You can walk, Vin. It's okay."

She put her feet down with a splash. "So cold," she muttered again.

"Keep walking. Get out of the river," he said. "We're done. It's over. You can come out. You're soaked and you're going to get sick if you don't get dry."

Vinny just stared at him, her eyes gigantic. "I couldn't talk, Dom. It was like I was screaming and nothing came out…"

He grabbed her by the hand and pulled her toward him, walking them both out of the river.

"It's okay now. It's over." The effort of the spell had him a little shaky too, but he was much better off than Vin.

She was shivering from the cold and the shock. He needed to get her dry. No help from the sun—it was already close to setting, and the river gorge was completely in shadow. He opened the trunk of the car. By pure dead luck, there was a bag full of beach gear, plus a blanket. He grabbed everything and rushed back to her.

"Vin, you have to help me out here. If you stay in those clothes, you'll never warm up."

"What about you? You're all wet too."

"Yeah, but I wasn't also choking to death. You first."

She yanked at the hem of her shirt, trying to pull it over her head, but the sopping wet fabric just clung to her body.

Dom peeled it off. "Put your arms up," he said. He got the shirt off and pulled the blanket around her shoulders. "Good girl. Halfway there."

"You've…been…waiting for this," Vinny got out between her chattering teeth. He saw that she was trying to smile.

He grinned back to show her things were all right. "You got me. I was just waiting for you to get cursed so I could get your pants off."

"Your lucky…day," she said, her teeth still chattering. Then she worked at her belt and unzipped her jeans. The tight jeans were even more molded to her skin than the shirt, and they weren't coming off easily.

"Okay, babe. Lie down. I know you've been hoping I'd say that."

Vinny laughed, or tried to. Dom pulled the blanket off her shoulders to put it on the ground, then Vinny lay down. He knelt in front of her, peeling the jeans off inch by inch, so finally Vinny was only wearing her bra and panties. Both were wet, but she was better off than before. He folded the top of the blanket over her. "Dry off. Then you'll warm up."

"Help me," she said.

"Help you get dry?"

"Warm me up." Vinny reached for him. "Please."

He took off his jacket and stretched out beside her, and before he could say a word, Vinny rolled the blanket and herself on top of him. She bent down to kiss him. "Warm me up," she said, her voice rough. She was pulling at his shirt, getting it over his head in no time.

"Vin, this isn't the best—" he began, then had to stop because Vin was kissing him, biting him, pawing at him. And holy hell, did he like it. Maybe it was the best.

"No one's here," she said in a hiss. "We're alone." She reached down for his belt.

Dom had a sudden and very bad thought. He rolled so Vinny was on her back again, and pinned her arms with his hands. "Don't take this the wrong way, Vin, but are you damn sure you're feeling like yourself?"

Vinny didn't struggle, or get angry. She looked at him with very shy eyes. "I'm me, Dom. Lavinia Rose Wellington Wake. And I'm not always very good at going after what I want, but I really want you. Please don't turn me down. Not now."

He kissed her, and felt her whole body relax and then tense again as he deepened the kiss. He took a breath, then said, "You got me, Vin."

Chapter 22

VINNY SIGHED WHEN SHE SENSED him give in. At last.

She knew something unreal had just happened, and she couldn't face it at the moment. What she could face was her need to be as close as possible to the one person who stuck by her while whatever weirdness took over. The one person she wanted to be with.

He started running his hands all up and down her body. She was still cold from the river, and that felt amazingly good. She said so.

"Good," Dom muttered. "If we're going to get all naked, I need to know you're not going to die of hypothermia."

She laughed, the sound coming out husky from the ache still lingering in her throat. "You're so sexy when you talk first aid." She slid her hands down his chest, all the way to his waist. "Can I take your jeans off *now*?" she asked. "I'm not possessed, just really into you."

He was too intent on warming her up to laugh. "You do whatever you want, Vin. Whatever makes you happy."

"Actually, can you do it?" she asked. "Turns out my fingers are numb. The river was freaking cold."

He got his jeans off without getting out from under the blanket, then covered her with his body. She felt how hard he was already. But he reached to take one hand, kissing her cold fingers, then sucking one at time.

"You're warming me right up," Vinny whispered.

"Tell me how to get you from warm to hot."

"You know already," she said. "Each time we started something, the way you handled me, I was dying for you…until you walked away."

"I'll make it up to you," he said. Then he lowered his head to kiss her chest, and her breasts. He sucked both nipples through the thin fabric of the bra until Vinny was moaning. "Keep going," she urged. "Touch me."

He slid one hand down, under her panties. Vinny stretched her whole body against his. "Yes. Keep going. Please."

He slipped one finger inside her. She was wet, instantly and insanely wet. Then she had a bad thought.

"Oh, no," she moaned. "I don't have any protection with me."

"You can reach my jacket," he said, not moving. "Inside pocket has a condom."

"Mother of Christ, thank you."

"Is that really the best person to direct thanks to?" he asked, choking back a laugh.

"Now is not the time to talk about it." Vinny worked to get the condom out of the jacket. The task was made more difficult because Dom didn't stop touching her, and she was crazy with desire. At last she had the condom packet in her hand.

"Let me put it on you," she said.

"Whatever you say."

She was still shaky, not from cold anymore, but from excitement. She reached down, and wrapped one hand around him.

Dom closed his eyes. "That's good."

"You're so hard," she said, stroking him. "I could get you off this way, if you want."

"Next time, Vin," he said, opening his eyes again. "Unless you're having second thoughts?"

She shook her head. "No way. You?"

"I want you so bad, Vin, you have no idea."

"Then let's get this party started." At the moment, she had zero interest in foreplay. She ripped the packet open and got the condom out. She rolled it on, making it a game, playing with him the whole time. She could tell he liked it by the way he teased her back, slipping another finger into her body and making her squirm.

Then he moved back a bit, pulling his hand away from her, sliding her panties down her legs till they were gone gone gone. She got her bra off just as fast.

He was obviously stoked at her enthusiasm, settling his body between her legs the second she lay back down.

She put her hands on his shoulders, smiling up at him, loving how his hair hung down nearly to his eyes. "What's keeping you?"

"So," he said cautiously, "I just had an idea. And you can say no, because this is a thing that definitely won't work unless you want it to."

"Go ahead. I've heard plenty of kink. You won't surprise me."

"I want to cast a spell."

Vinny bit her lip. "Forget what I said about not surprising me. You're serious? What is it? A sex spell?"

He looked very serious. "Sort of. A protection spell. Sex is powerful, and it creates some pretty amazing energy."

"I'm listening." Hell yes, she was listening.

"I can cast a spell to harness some of the energy to help protect you from, well, let's just say evil. Which you probably could use, considering what just happened to you."

"A sexy protection spell," she said, to make sure she was getting it right.

"Yeah. Essentially. It's just words. And I'll trace some symbols on you—not visible ones. But mostly sex…and it'll work best if you, um, enjoy it, so there's that."

"Well, when you put it that way, how could I say no?"

"You can always say no," said Dom. "Magic isn't for everyone, and you did just get free of a pretty nasty spell. Maybe you don't want more magic in your life."

"But you really want to protect me?" she asked, touched more than she dared to think about.

Dom nodded. "Any way you'll let me."

"Then I want you to do it," she said decisively. "Cast your spell."

He kissed her. "You don't have to do anything special. Just relax."

"Wait. Will it hurt?"

"Absolutely not," he said with a smile. "Just the opposite."

Dom kissed her again, murmured something in what sounded like Latin and then her name, then drew on her skin with his finger, just over her heart. Then he repeated the kiss and the words, drawing on her forehead. He did it again, drawing on her belly, and then her back. His expression was calm, and a little distant, and intriguing as hell. She'd been wrong about skipping the foreplay. Vinny wanted him so much it almost made her faint.

Finally, Dom whispered something else, said her full name again, then kissed her on the mouth. Vinny opened her mouth and let him in, wondering what spells tasted like.

He tasted good.

"Here's the tricky part," Dom said then.

"What is?"

"I need to fuck you so you come, and it'll help if you love every second of it. So tell me what you need, Vin, because I want to make you delirious with joy and completely exhausted from feeling good. Whatever you want, just say it and I'll make it happen."

That was a turn on. "Why not start with, um, well, I like to be bitten, actually. Not too hard."

"Guess that vamp would have had a good time with you," Dom muttered.

"Don't be snarky," Vin breathed. "Just be sweet."

He bit her shoulder gently, and pleasure washed through her.

"Just like that," she moaned.

So Dom nibbled his way across her skin, every limb, and special attention to her neck. Vinny begged him to keep going even when she came, hard, when his teeth grazed on one nipple. "Oh. Wow." She couldn't remember ever being so wired.

Then Vin gasped as he slid into her. She hadn't done this in a while, and she'd almost forgotten how incredibly good it felt to be with a guy she liked, and maybe more than just liked. She contracted around him. "Mmmm," she said. "I love this."

"You feel good," he said in a low voice. "Really

good."

Dom went slow, and he plainly enjoyed feeling her outside and in. Vin let him play with her, loving the feeling of him. She reached up, running her fingers through his hair.

His eyes were locked on hers. God, he was intense. Shyness spread through her and she glanced away.

"No," he said. "Look at me."

He said that to her before. "Why's that your thing?" she asked.

"Because it makes it better. And I like your eyes."

"Really?" For some reason, him telling her he liked her eyes melted her almost as much as the sex.

"Yeah. Really." Then he worked a hand between their bodies to cup her breast. "You like this?" he asked.

"Yes," Vinny said, arching her back as she pressed closer to him. "Love it."

"Tell me another thing you like," he said. "Please."

"I like to be on top," she said. "I'll be good," she added. "I'll go slow."

He rolled so she was on top. Vinny straddled him and sat up slowly, surveying the man under her, liking every inch. "That's nice."

Dom watched her, because of course he did. "Do what you want," he said.

Vinny bent down, kissing the tattoos on his chest, then running her hands over his skin, following the dips and ridges of his muscles.

"You look good," she said, still feeling shy, despite everything.

He didn't say anything, but put his hands on her hips, and pushed her down a bit.

Vinny gasped, feeling how hard he still was.

"Can I get you off again?" he asked quietly. "Tell me how."

She took one of his hands and guided it right between her legs. "Touch me."

He took his spell casting seriously, Vinny thought as she felt him touch her and thrust in her. The pressure built fast, and she wanted desperately to come again, and come big. She put her hands on her breasts. "Can I do this?" she asked.

"Hell, yes," he said, his own breathing hard.

She teased her nipples as Dom found the rhythm she needed, and Vin collapsed with another orgasm, letting her upper body lay on Dom. His arms went around her, and held her tighter against him.

"I want you to come," she murmured.

"Don't worry about me," he promised her. "This is good."

"But I want you to come," she repeated. "I mean that *I'll* feel good when you come. I need to make you happy, too. I need it."

"You're making me happy, Vin," he said. "Being this close to you feels so good. I..." he hesitated. "I don't want this to be the only time."

She lifted her head to look at him. "You mean that?"

He said, "I don't want to talk about this now, but just know...yeah." He took an unsteady breath. "Now let's get back to you. What can I do to make you feel good?"

"You can fuck me till you come."

"I said don't worry about..."

"You want to know what, Dom? It's my birthday tomorrow. And for my present from you, I want you to hurry up and use me. Understand?"

"It's your birthday?"

"True story. Fuck me."

In a second, Vinny was on her back again. "Wrap your legs around me," he ordered.

As she'd asked, he put aside the slow approach, and fucked her, hard and fast. Vinny moaned each time he thrust.

"That's it," she begged. "Don't stop."

His breath was ragged, so was hers. Vinny felt the second when he stiffened and came, holding her tight. She wrapped her arms around his shoulders, keeping him next to her. She whispered encouragement, ridiculous compliments that were absolutely true, and secrets she never thought she'd say out loud. He bit her neck, then licked her fevered skin, and Vinny closed her eyes as she felt a final, unexpected aftershock roll over her.

She relaxed against Dom, telling him she was done for real. He pulled out, and did whatever he did with the condom. She was not paying attention at all. Seconds later he was on his back with her in his arms, half slung across him.

He said something, and it took her a second to realize it was also Latin, and he wasn't speaking to her. She didn't know whether the spell did anything, but she had no complaints. She was gloriously warm, and delightfully tired, and pretty pleased with the world in general and Dom in particular.

Vin kissed him softly. "If that's magic, I like it."

"It's one kind of magic," he said. "Thanks for letting me multitask there."

"So does the mystical protection kick right in? Or is there a delay?"

"I don't know. This is the first time I've ever done it."

"Oh?" she asked archly.

"I mean that particular actual spell, I mean, like, for real, in um, the field, as they say." He sounded so flustered that Vinny couldn't stop from laughing out loud. Flustered Dom was adorable.

"The other part I have done a few times before," he added.

She didn't need to be told *that*. He definitely knew how to show a girl a good time.

"Did you like the non-magic part?" she asked shyly. "The ordinary sex part?"

"You have a weird definition of ordinary," he said.

"And you don't want this to be the only time."

He turned his head away. "I don't mean to rope you into anything."

"Rope me?"

"Figuratively speaking," he said hastily. "I'm actually not that kinky. Sorry."

"I'm not sorry."

"I just meant I know you weren't planning on me. Or this."

"Dom. I wouldn't have asked for this if I hadn't already…um. God, this is embarrassing."

"What is?"

She squeezed her eyes shut. "I really like you. And I don't just like a guy. Certainly not after a few days. But you're different, and oh, God, I like you, and I don't know what to do about it."

He held her close. "Vin, you don't have to have all the answers. We'll work it out."

"We will?"

"Yes. *We.*"

Vin drew her hand across his chest. Saying she liked him out loud took more guts than asking him for sex.

What the hell was up with that? But she was glad she said it, and she trusted him when he said they'd work it out.

Silver and water and love.

Vinny blinked, wondering why those words came into her head. *Silver and water and love.* The phrase warmed her, though she didn't know why.

He tilted his head up, examining her neck. The skin felt raw where the necklace had cut into her.

"Does it hurt?" he asked, worried. "Honestly, that mark might not fade." He kissed the spot as if that might help heal it. It felt good, whether it healed her or not.

"It's fine," said Vinny. "I'd rather deal with the scar than whatever the hell was after me."

Dom shifted, pushing off his post-sex lethargy. "Tell me what happened. Was it like before? And I mean details. What you saw, what you felt. Everything."

She recounted the ordeal, from the first flickers of darkness to the mood swings she felt, to the sudden paralysis and the nightmarish monster she saw when she was lost in unconsciousness.

"I don't know if I'm describing it right," she said nervously. Just thinking about the thing's eyes and mouth made her start shaking again.

Dom held her close until she stopped shivering. Vinny's mind was still reeling, feeling both the remembered fear and the lingering warmth of the sex and possibly the spell.

After a moment, Dom moved again, fishing the gold necklace out of his discarded shirt. "I had to cut this off you in the river. Which brings up the next question. How long have you had that necklace? I never noticed it before. It only started acting up after you got into the house, right?"

"Um," she said. "I just got the necklace from Jonas. The night we got here."

Dom went still. "He gave it to you."

"Yes. As a birthday present. I didn't know…"

"Of course you didn't know it was cursed, Vin. It's not your fault." He was very alert now, and angry. "He gave it to you for a reason. And not a nice one. I have to find out what it means."

"Wait, wait, wait." Vinny took a breath. "It has to be a mistake. He wouldn't have tried to hurt me."

"Oh, really?"

"Yes. You don't know him. I do. Listen, we go back years and years. Jonas is not perfect—he's not anywhere close. He's done some fucked up shit with the cameras, and I'm going to do something about that. Trust me. But there's *no* way he'd knowingly pass out cursed jewelry."

He took a breath. "Maybe."

"Definitely," she said, hoping she sounded convincing. "He cares about me, Dom. Maybe in a messed up way, but he likes me, right? You said yourself he was all salty to you when you met. That was because, whatever else he's into, he doesn't want me to get hurt."

"If that's true, we still need to know how he got the necklace. Where it came from, how long he's had it, if there was a reason he gave it to you in particular."

"No problem. I'll talk to him."

"Don't be alone with him when you chat."

"You're paranoid. He's not after me."

He put both hands on her head, making her look at him. "Vin, you nearly *died*. I almost didn't get that thing off you in time. There's no paranoia at work here. That was real."

"But so was your spell, yeah? I'm safe."

He shook his head, and let her go. "You're safer than you were. But I don't know how nasty this could get. You need to be careful, Vin. Please."

His concern was so raw that she knew he was being honest. "I'll be careful. But we're not interrogating Jonas. I'll talk to him, one on one."

"I want to be close by."

"You will be. I'll put you on white knight alert."

"Count on it." He kissed her, his mouth hot on hers. "Now, as much as I want to get you a thousand miles away from here, we need to go back. There are way too many questions, and I *am* being paid to find the answers."

They got dressed and walked to the car in the now violet twilight of the ravine. She slapped a mosquito away just before she opened the car door. "Some protection spell," she told him. "I almost got my blood sucked just now."

"The spell repels evil," he said with a grin. "You want to repel insects, buy some bug spray."

"Smart ass," she muttered.

As she got in the passenger seat, she realized something. Dom and she had just had some mind-blowing, magical sex, and here she was joking with him like they were pals for years. She could practically feel the thread between them, the invisible bond that was going to hurt hard when it was inevitably broken.

Chapter 23

BEFORE DOM STARTED THE CAR, he remembered something and pulled out his phone. "Just a sec. I need to get a hold of someone."

He called Lily, then waited for her to answer. While doing that he stared at the thin red wound on Vinny's neck where the necklace chain had tightened so much it cut her flesh. Dom was going to make someone pay for that.

"Hi!" Lily's voice chirped.

"Lily! Hey, I need—"

"You've reached my voicemail because I'm doing something more important. Leave a message and I might call you back."

He grimaced, waiting for the beep. Then he said, "It's Dom. *Please* pick up. Pick up no matter what. I need a lookup and I need it fast. Anyway, call me."

"Who's Lily?" Vinny asked curiously.

"She's a witch. And a friend. She lived close by us growing up, and her family has a link to..."

"Magic. You can say it."

"Basically, yes. Lily studied magic and the supernatural and all the occult stuff alongside us. She's like our little sister. She's almost Lex's age. Lex is my youngest brother," he added. He was rambling a bit, mostly out of nervous energy. The full realization of everything that happened was hitting him, finally. Including the realization that he'd been subconsciously denying the web of connections around the house and the job and him and Vinny. "Lily will help. She's crazy smart and is great at research."

"Is she great at returning phone calls?"

Just then, his phone buzzed. Lily. "Hey, you busy? I need a thing."

"Hello to you too." Lily's voice crackled a bit.

"Sorry," said Dom. "I'm in the middle of something. I'll be polite when it's done."

Her tone turned professional. "What's up?"

"I need a lookup on a symbol."

"What is it? Wait, back up. Is it on something?"

"It's the pendant of a necklace. Looks old."

"Material?"

"Gold. Both the pendant and the chain."

"How'd you find it?"

He glanced at Vinny. "Had to cut if off the person wearing it. It was killing her."

"I was going to ask about the vibe next," Lily said. "But now I'm just going to guess evil."

"Very evil. Feels like ice. Hasn't warmed up and I've been holding it for a bit."

"Well, stop holding it," Lily snapped. "Get it into a binding pouch pronto." Lily was several years younger than Dom, but that never stopped the witch from giving orders.

"Don't worry, I got one with my gear."

"Ok. Describe the symbol."

Dom tilted the pendent in his palm. "A circle, intersected down the middle by an upside down isosceles triangle. Narrow, like an arrow point. And there's a line overlaying the triangle's top side. The length of the line just extends past the circle's width. There are jagged edges at each end of the line. Does that make sense?"

"I think so," Lily said. "I'm drawing it out in parts."

"I could send a picture."

"No! We don't know what effect ascribing the symbol to any medium could have. Digital counts!"

"Got it. Can you look it up?" he asked.

"How fast do you need it?"

Dom needed it now. He said, "Sooner is better than later."

"I'll do what I can," she promised. "Give me a few hours, and I should have a little information for you."

"You're the best, Lily."

"I try." She ended the call.

Vinny looked at him with interest. "You said research. Do you have a Hogwarts sort of place? Or a secret government agency? You can tell me."

He shook his head. "It's not that organized. There are other folks who fight evil, and hunt demons. The world's a big place. But it's not a global conspiracy. I mean, maybe somewhere, some secret society has an underground compound or a mansion where they do secret anti-demon stuff, but if they do, they've never invited a Salem to join. My family just kind of has always done this. So what we know, we know because it's been passed down over time."

"Too bad. A secret underground compound sounds cool."

"Sounds expensive," he said.

"You do worry about money, don't you?"

"Somebody has to," Dom said. "I'm the oldest, so it's my responsibility. I've always handled the finances, even before I was legal age—our grandparents were great, but not great with money. And it's sort of hard to hold down a nine-to-five job when demons are involved."

"I bet they like midnight," Vinny said.

"They do."

She absently brushed at the reddened skin of her neck, and Dom pulled her hand away. "Don't. We should get that cleaned and disinfected. Spells are one thing, but Neosporin has its place."

She smiled, squeezing his hand. "Then we should get back."

Dom looked over at her. "Your birthday is tomorrow."

"Yeah. Why?"

"Dates like that tend to be significant. And Jonas was pretty insistent about the end of the week being the deadline. And that's where we are now."

She frowned. "But I didn't summon a demon, so why would it care about my birthday? Can't it just be a coincidence?"

No. On some level, Dom knew this was coming. He'd ignored the signs, largely because acknowledging them meant admitting that Vin was at the center of them, and he didn't want Vin at the center of anything dangerous. But all he said was, "When the occult is involved, coincidence usually isn't."

Vinny looked thoughtful, staring out at the intensely green landscape surrounding them.

Dom started the car and drove back to the house, obeying the speed limit this time.

The Porsche Dom stole had a button to open the security gate at the house. He stopped at the gate and was about to push the button when Vinny, who'd been silent the whole way back, said, "Wait."

"What is it?"

"I just remembered something." She looked over at him, her eyes big and troubled. "When Jonas gave me the necklace, he said Emma was the one who found it."

"Do you believe him?"

"I don't know. I didn't even think about it at the time, but that's maybe important."

"Yes." It meant that either Jonas lied about it, or Emma was much more involved in this situation than she seemed, or worse, that both of them were in it together. Dom wished he knew their personalities better. He didn't think Vinny could see things clearly where her friends were concerned. It was natural for her to think the best of her friends, despite evidence of their worst impulses. "I think we both need to be careful about mentioning anything related to the necklace or the demon you saw."

"Okay." Vinny's tone was meek, like a little girl's. Dom could guess why—it sucked to think someone you trusted was actually not on your side. He remembered exactly how he felt when Rachel revealed her true nature, and he'd had practically his whole family to back him up in the aftermath. Vinny had almost no one. Except him.

It was nighttime when they pulled up to the garage. The house had lights on, but they were all automated, so it didn't mean anyone was awake or around.

Just as he got out of the car, Dom saw the familiar shape of Piewicket approaching.

"Pie," he said. "Come here."

The cat slinked over, curious.

Dom dangled the necklace in front of her, the pendant tumbling down the chain.

Piewicket hissed and leapt backward, her tail puffing out.

"That's exactly what I thought," Dom said, tucking the necklace back in its pouch. "What happened while we were gone?"

The humans here did nothing. They slept off their respective ailments, though the evil in this place is getting stronger by the hour.

"Did you see anything?"

The cat flexed her claws in and out. Not seen. But smelled, yes. Sensed, yes. Something is pushing into this place from the otherworlds, and it will break through soon.

"Tomorrow," Dom said, in a tone low enough that Vinny couldn't hear.

Very likely. The cat looked at him. You should rest. If it is tomorrow, you need to be ready for it.

"What's going on?" Vinny asked.

"You're heading up to your room," he told her. "Pie will go with you."

"Because I need a bodyguard?"

"Because Pie likes you."

"What about you?"

"I want to renew the wards I cast, just in case. I'll check in before I go to bed."

Vin nodded, relief on her face.

Dom left her to go up to the attic where he first cast the circle of protection. The physical markings looked undisturbed. He lit the candles and quickly went through the spell to strengthen the ward he put up before.

This time, though, he knew what he was dealing with,

so he added a few lines to his recitation, ones specific to demons. Then he recited the names of everyone in the house, including himself this time. Pie was always telling him he forgot that part when he cast protection spells.

After he was done, he extinguished the candles and returned to the second floor.

He knocked on the door of Vinny's room. "Hey. Can I come in?"

"Yup," she called. "But you'll have to get past Pie to get to me."

Dom came in, noticed Piewicket in a corner, and then saw Vin had been busy. She'd dragged the dresser over to the corner of the room where the camera was embedded high up on the wall. The spot where the camera used to be was now a largish hole in the drywall. Shards of either plastic or glass were scattered on the carpet.

He sized up the height of the hole. "Do you have a crowbar around that I didn't notice?"

Her lips curved into a smile. "Hey, you got skills. I got skills. The point is that I solved a problem." Vin's smile faded then. "A problem that never should have existed in the first place. I'm sorry I got angry at you when it should have been Jonas's ass I kicked."

"You can do that tomorrow," he said.

"Unless a demon comes to kick his ass first. You really think he…how do you put it…consorted with the powers of darkness?"

Dom nodded. "Someone consorted with something dark. You did say that it might have been Emma who was the source of the necklace."

"But it was Jonas who…" She glared at the shattered camera.

"The two things don't have to go together," Dom said

cautiously. "Jonas is guilty of creepy ass voyeurism, but it *could* be Emma who made a deal with a demon."

"Emma is my friend," Vin said, her arms tight around her body, as if she was warding off cold.

"I've seen friends and families sell each other out," said Dom. "Jonas has a thing for you…obviously. What if Emma wanted to remove competition?"

She shook her head once, saying decisively, "There is no competition. I do not want to be with Jonas in that way, and I would never, ever cross Emma like that. I've been trying to get some concrete evidence on his cheating—because I *know* he's cheated—to convince Emma that she doesn't have to stay with him."

"You're advocating for a divorce?" Dom asked, at last seeing all the parts according to Vinny's point of view.

"I'm advocating for the truth," Vinny said. "Emma can do what she wants with it…unless she hired a demon to kill me, in which case I'm going to have to take back her half of the best friends charm." She put a hand to her chest, then blinked as she remembered she still wasn't wearing her necklaces. "Oh, well. I have one."

Dom held out a hand. "That reminds me. Did you clean that cut?"

"Not yet." Vinny walked to the bathroom and started running water.

He followed her, and she threw a quizzical glance at him in the mirror. "I'm perfectly capable of doing it myself."

Standing behind her, he put his hands on her hips, just at the hem of her shirt. He watched her face in the mirror. "Let me."

Vin's breathing changed, and that was enough answer for Dom. He pulled the shirt up and over her head, revealing the lace bra. Keeping his gaze locked on hers, he un-hooked the bra. She let the straps slip down and then tossed it away.

Dom liked everything he saw in the mirror. Vinny leaned back against him, and he liked that even more.

The water from the tap was steaming now. He reached for a washcloth, soaking it. "Tilt your head up," he said.

Vinny complied, and he used his last bit of composure to clean the long cut in her neck. It wasn't too bad, but the sight of the darkened, dried blood put him in mind of Rachel, wounded in the neck by a monster and then turned into one. He inhaled, suddenly feeling a sense of vertigo.

He felt Vin's hands slide down his body to rest on his thighs. "You okay?" she asked.

In the mirror, he caught a glimpse of her concerned gaze. He exhaled. "Yeah. You'll be fine. This cut isn't too deep."

"You sure, doc? You could kiss it to make it better."

He kissed her neck, just outside the cut. She sighed, and all thoughts of the past evaporated. He watched Vinny in the mirror as he ran his hands over her half-naked body. He played with her breasts, teasing her until she molded herself against him, her ass brushing him in just the right way.

God, he wanted her. "Bed. Now."

Catching her satisfied smile in the mirror, Dom suddenly had a bad thought. "Fuck."

"Yeah, I figured," Vinny replied, laughing.

"No. I mean, fuck as in I just remembered I only had the one condom." Watching Vinny's face fall would have been gratifying if he wasn't so worked up right now. "I don't suppose you have one."

She shook her head. "Sorry. You can't just cast a spell that…you know…."

Now there was a terrible idea. "Nope. Magic is about intention. And if the only thing I can think about is how much I want to bone you, then any spell I cast is going to…um…intensify that."

One eyebrow rose up. "Interesting."

"Please forget I said anything."

"What's it worth to you?" she teased.

He didn't tease back. He was too invested in the idea of getting to spend a night with her, in a bed, together. "Vin, I need you."

Her eyes closed. "Say that again, because I really like hearing it."

"I need you," he repeated. "In a bed. Right now."

"Um, one thing. Where's your cat?"

"She's a very considerate roommate. She won't get in the way."

"And the whole lack of protection thing?"

"I know what's off limits," he promised.

Then she smiled, very slowly. "We'll just have to be inventive about how we get each other off."

She proved to be plenty inventive, and very, very dedicated to exploring basically every way other than penetration to have a good time. Dom thought the sex by the river had been amazing, and it was, but this was a whole other experience. Vin told him exactly what she wanted, whether it was his hands or his tongue. That wasn't something he was used to. He loved it. He loved hearing her reactions, and seeing every move she made.

Making her come could be his new hobby. She looked so great afterward, relaxed and breathing heavy, and sweaty in a way that made her skin extra fun to touch.

"Oh, my God," she sighed. "You gotta lay down."

"I'm not tired," he told her, even as he moved to stretch out beside her.

She pushed him onto his back. "Good. Neither am I."

When she put her mouth on him, he damn near went crazy. He would not last long at all.

But Vin decided to take her time, and he realized he didn't know anything, and he should just let her do whatever she wanted. She was the hottest thing to ever happen to him, and he didn't even know a tongue could do what hers was doing to him right now.

"Vin," he moaned at last, just before he lost it. He came. Hard. He thought his heart might have stopped for a second.

Then Vinny was sliding up to lie next to him, a sweet smile on her face. "Hey. Like that?"

"Holy Christ."

"Is that really the best person to address right now?" she asked.

Dom reached out and pulled her over to him. "No teasing. You just broke my brain."

"So that's a yes you liked it?" She paused. "You don't mind I didn't swallow. I never got into that."

"Hey, I'm just happy to be here." Here was the only place he wanted to be, as long as here meant with Vinny.

He turned his head to take in the sight of her, running a few fingers over her body, enjoying the way she shivered in reaction. She looked so beautiful, and even a little vulnerable.

"What is it?" she asked.

"I was thinking about how different you look without all your necklaces."

"Which look is better?"

"The necklaces are definitely a signature." He paused, then said, "You look good no matter what."

"So I could skip the necklaces for a while?"

Something in her voice made him pull her closer, wrapping her in a hug.

"Why did you do that?"

"You looked like you needed it," he said easily.

Dom let her go after a moment, and Vinny laughed softly. "You sure you're not a mind reader?"

"Very sure. But that wasn't a hard call. Just because the one necklace was cursed doesn't mean you have to give them all up."

"I know it's irrational," Vinny said. "But all of today has been way past the edge of the rationality scale."

"You can wear your necklaces, and you'll be fine," he said. "In fact, you should definitely wear the ones with the cross and the little bottle of salt."

"Are they special?"

"Short version? Yes. Where'd you get them?"

"One of my first piano teachers was a nun, actually. Sister Stellamaris. She gave me the cross when I completed my lessons from her and moved on to my next instructor. Said she asked the holy family to watch over me."

"It holds a blessing in it," Dom told her. "It's really possible that if you weren't wearing it up to the end, you would have been hurt a lot worse. What about the salt charm?"

"Um." Vinny's forehead wrinkled. "That I got in Vienna. I was twelve. I was wandering around this crazy flea market one night..."

"What, alone?"

Her voice turned icy. "Yeah. Alone."

She started to pull away and he tightened his grip,

saying, "Nope. Not till you finish the story."

"Fuck you."

"Give me a few minutes. Until then, tell me what happened."

Vinny huffed, but said, "All right. I was in Vienna for a competition. Piano. Big international competition, one that actually matters in terms of proving that you're the real deal or not."

"At age twelve?" he asked incredulously.

"There were several age levels," she explained. "If you place, you get scholarships and offers to exclusive schools or programs and stuff like that. It matters. It was one of the times I was with my father, because it was a summer competition, and he had custody when I wasn't in school."

"What happened?"

"Well, my dad was telling everyone that I was the best, and no one had heard Debussy like I played Debussy, and I'd blow the competition away…yadda yadda yadda."

She took a breath, and Dom felt the pain in it. She went on, "I played. I played it perfectly, and better than I thought I could. Out of forty competitors, I took second place."

"That's amazing."

Another breath, one that suggested what was to come was not amazing. "I was on stage to get my trophy, and they invited my family up to get pictures. Which meant my dad. But he didn't come up. Because he wasn't in the theater. He wasn't in the building. He wasn't even on the campus where the competition was. Turns out he was at the airport, flying back to New York. He'd scheduled a bunch of interviews with some TV people and magazines, but when I didn't take *first* place, he just left. He didn't want to deal with a second place girl."

"He left his twelve year old daughter alone in a foreign city?"

She sounded resigned. "Yup. No one knew exactly what happened at the time, of course. It was a while ago, I was a kid without a phone, and everything was pretty chaotic. But the upshot was that I walked off the stage into the loving arms of no one, and then just kept walking. Walking around Vienna, with no real idea of what to do or even where I was."

Vinny took a breath, gathering herself for the next part. Dom was careful not to interrupt. She went on, "I ended up at this…place. An old train station, maybe, with stalls and stalls of vendors selling everything. Lace and incense and weird animals and soap and jewelry. And it was night, but it was jam packed. I ran into this woman. She just looked at me, really the only person to look at me. She gestured for me to come over and I did. I asked her directions to the hotel I was staying at. She didn't speak English, but her daughter did. And I told them the whole story, and I was crying and they probably thought I went completely bonkers. But at the end, the daughter said she'd take me to a taxi and tell him where to go. Then the older lady gave me the salt charm necklace. I gave her the trophy to pay for it. It was this big gaudy crystal thing, and she just took it like that was totally normal. The daughter said her mom was a good witch and the charm would protect me from evil spirits.

"And then I got in the cab and got back to the hotel," Vinny wound up with a sigh. "Found out that my dad left me behind. Called my mom international long distance. She was so happy, because she could bring Dad's neglect up in the next hearing. I flew home the next day. First class, of course. And somewhere in Vienna right now, there's probably an old lady with a trophy that says Lavinia Wake is second place."

"Holy shit." Dom wasn't good with words just then. He wanted to find Vin's father and stare him down, or possibly just punch him.

"Downer story," she said apologetically. "Sorry to kill the mood."

He shifted to draw her closer. "I asked."

"You did. Serves you right." Vinny yawned, and then tucked her head so it rested on his chest. One hand curled around his other shoulder. "Dom?"

"Yeah?"

She didn't say anything for a moment, and when he moved his head to look at her, she was asleep. He kissed her once and then stared at the smashed remains of the camera in the wall. He didn't sleep for a long, long while.

Chapter 24

It was Vinny's birthday, and waking up next to a hot guy was a fantastic present she didn't know she needed. She looked over at the still sleeping Dom, and smiled because looking at him first thing just felt so right.

Then the second guessing hit her. Was she literally the most gullible person ever? The day before, she'd basically broken every rule about relationships she had, twice, just so she could get it on with a guy she didn't know nearly as well as she should. And yes, it was level-up sex. But did she really think she was somehow magically protected because he said so? Or was that just some ridiculous role-play shit she bought into because she was overly emotional and horny and Dom was convenient? And then what explained the second act, other than the fact that the first act was just so good?

But she *saw* the demon, she reminded herself. The necklace physically contracted and tried to choke her to death. No matter how weird Dom's tales of magic and monsters still seemed, that stuff happened. The vampire attack before happened. She wasn't hallucinating it.

She told herself to stop looking for the cloud in every silver lining. Maybe some good things could occur in her life. Reaching out, she traced the outlines of the tattoo on Dom's arm, then moved to run her fingers lightly down his back. He made an *mmm*ing sound, but didn't open his eyes.

The sound echoed by the foot of the bed, and Vinny saw Piewicket curled up there, her eyes on Vin.

"Hey, cat," Vinny said quietly. Before she could do anything else, another wave of sleepiness came over her. She inched closer to Dom and closed her eyes.

The next time she woke up, the light was brighter. Dom was awake, propped up against the headboard, and peering at the screen in his hand. His other hand was entwined with hers, and when Vinny realized that, she sort of went mushy.

"Hey," she whispered.

Dom glanced over, his frown transforming into a smile just for her. "Hey."

She sat up, disentangling her hand so she could drag her fingers through her hair, which was probably a horrendous mess. "What are you up to?" she asked, nodding to the screen.

His frown returned. "We found some stuff out. None of it's good."

"Tell me."

"Well, Lily found the true name of the demon associated with the symbol. Which is very good news, because I'll need that if I want to get anything done against it."

"What's the name?"

He showed her the screen. "Read it. Not out loud."

She looked at an incomprehensible string of letters. "I couldn't pronounce that if I tried."

"Yeah, demons' names are hard to pronounce on purpose. Cuts down on the accidental summonings."

"What's the bad news?"

He exhaled. "The necklace is a problem. As far as we can tell from previous reports like this, the necklace is basically Cinderella's shoe. You put it on and the magic will find you anywhere. Doesn't matter where you are or what you're doing."

"Ugh. This is the worst version of Cinderella ever. If it's what you say it is, then why did it start choking me before the stroke of midnight tonight?"

"Not sure. I think maybe part of you knew, subconsciously, that the necklace was dangerous. Your body was reacting to it, trying to tell you to get it off. But it's magic, so when you actually tried to remove it, it tightened up like a noose so you couldn't get it off without some countervailing power."

"Which you cast."

"With the help of the river, yes. For future reference, binding magic and running water do *not* get along."

Silver and water and love. The words echoed in Vinny's head. But Dom was still explaining things, so she put it away and listened.

"The bad part is that even though I got the necklace off you physically, I think you might still be connected to the curse within it. It all depends on the details of the original deal. But because it's your birthday, I'm pretty sure you were mentioned in the deal. It also explains why I was having so much trouble finding the source of the evil in the house when we first got here. When I reached out to search, I kept getting images of you. I couldn't get you out of my mind. But now I know it's partly because you were already wearing the necklace."

"So your seeing me was like a false positive?"

"Or noise hiding the signal. Now that the necklace isn't being worn, I can sense everything a lot more clearly. Including the fact that the curse inside it is still active."

A wash of cold edged up her spine. "What does all this mean? For me personally?"

He put the phone aside, and pulled her over to him. "It means I'm not going to let anything bad happen to you. So all day long, even if it seems like I'm not too concerned, everything I do will be necessary to break this curse. I need you to trust me on that."

Vin really wanted to trust him. "I—"

Without warning, the bedroom door swung open. "Vin, you better be here—"

Emma stopped short when she saw Dom and Vin together, naked except for the sheets. Her eyes wide, she mumbled, "Um. Okay. I guess…you're here. We can talk later. When you get, um, dressed."

"Down in a second!" Vinny called, but Emma had already skedaddled, the door pulled tight behind her.

Vinny bit her lip. "Welp. Cat's out of that bag, I guess."

"Was it supposed to stay secret?" Dom asked, sounding a little offended.

"Of course not," Vin said. "We're grownups, right? Besides, after what you just said, Emma knowing we spent the night together is literally the least of my worries."

Vinny scooted out of bed and got dressed fast. What Dom said hit her all at once. By the end of the day, she could quite possibly be a demon snack. And yeah, he said he'd try to stop it, but Dom was just a guy. And the demon was a demon.

And this morning her best friend was going to tease the hell out of her for hooking up with a random monster hunter.

It was going to be a weird day.

Downstairs, Emma was evidently over her surprise, and was now grinning like she won a bet. She had three mugs of coffee already poured. "So," she said, on seeing Vinny and Dom enter the kitchen together.

Vinny sat at a tall stool and reached for a mug. "So."

Emma's grin widened. "Have a good night?"

I will not blush. I will not blush. I will not blush. Vin took a sip of scalding coffee so she wouldn't have to answer immediately.

"She did," Dom said, casually reaching for his mug. "So did I."

Blushing. "Yup," Vin managed to say.

Emma actually giggled. "Awesome!" she squeaked out.

"So you busted into my room why?" Vinny asked.

The grin slid off Emma's face. "Are you kidding me? What happened yesterday? The migraine nearly killed me, and then I woke up in the afternoon and you were gone, and a car was gone and I nearly called the cops."

"We, uh, had to borrow the car for an errand," said Vinny. "Sorry."

"I was worried! Jonas has been recovering from his damn stupidity, so he's useless. I didn't know what happened."

"Sorry, Emma. Really. It was unplanned."

"You okay? What's wrong with your neck?" Emma asked, squinting.

Vinny raised her hand to cover the scratch. "Um, nothing. Do you have a scarf or something?"

"Sure, but it won't match your style. Speaking of, where'd the necklaces go?"

Dom's foot nudged Vinny's, a warning to watch her mouth. As if she needed the warning. "They're safe. I'll put them on again after breakfast."

Emma drained her coffee. "Guess what."

"What?"

"Side effect of Jonas's boneheaded move yesterday." Emma smiled. "We had a really good talk this morning. The first good talk in a year, honestly. He woke up, his head clear, and he told me he was so sorry for all the crap he put me through these past months. He's tossing the stash he's got in the house, and he's going to get help for his addiction. He says he's committed to starting a new life. And I didn't even say anything! He came out with it. I'm so relieved."

"That's great," Vin said. Emma's eyes were full of hope, and Vinny knew she'd lost her chance to tell her that it was highly likely her husband made a deal with a demon and nearly killed Vinny with a necklace.

"Oh, and in case you forgot, it's your birthday! I got a birthday cake all ready. So let's have a little party tonight."

"Sure."

Emma beamed and then said she had to take care of a few things.

After she left the kitchen, Vinny shot a look at Dom. "Ixnay on the urse-kay, mmkkay?"

"At least till after the cake," Dom agreed cautiously.

Fortified with coffee, Vinny went back upstairs, Dom at her heels.

"It's not Emma," she told him as she put her necklaces back on. "She's got nothing to do with it."

"She noticed the necklace was gone."

"No, she noticed *all* my necklaces were gone. She didn't ask about the gold one, and she didn't look weirded out. So she's innocent."

"Maybe," Dom said. "Listen. Try to keep a low profile today. I have to scope out my wards, and check in just in case Lily or Lex dig up more info. If *any*thing happens, tell me instantly. Text. Scream. Whatever. I'll join you as fast as I can. And Pie will be around."

She nodded.

The day was actually pretty quiet, considering. But Vinny was also conscious of a feeling building up in the air, the sort of atmospheric shift before an electrical storm. It made it hard to concentrate.

In the early afternoon, Jonas found her on the patio. "Vin," he said. "I have to apologize."

Was he confessing to giving her a cursed gift? "For what?"

"For yesterday. For more than that, but yesterday especially. I'm so sorry you saw me like that. Strung out. I never meant for that to happen. And definitely not for you to see it."

"Oh. It's okay." She was nonplussed. She'd never seen an apologetic Jonas.

"It's not okay, but I'm going to try to be better. Emma deserves it. I fucked up, but I can't let a bad choice define my life."

"I hope you turn things around," she said.

"I will. Anyway, I just wanted to let you know I'm sorry."

How was she supposed to ask about a curse now? How awkward.

"No worries," she managed. Then, because the seriousness was killing her, she added, "Don't think you get to have a bigger slice of cake tonight."

He held up his hands. "Wouldn't dream of it."

Time came for dinner. Emma went all out, and every dish she put out was one of Vinny's favorites.

It should have been fun. It was almost fun. Emma and Jonas held hands, and they looked happy. Dom was outwardly funny, but Vinny could tell he was anxious.

"Sorry I didn't make your deadline," he told Jonas suddenly, before dessert.

The mood shifted, as Dom brought up the one thing they'd all been avoiding talking about.

Jonas jumped a bit in his seat. "Oh. Right. Well. You tried. There was never a guarantee it would work. Some ghosts are tricky."

"Demon," Dom corrected.

"What?"

"I told you it wasn't a ghost. It's a demon."

"That sounds less good," Emma said.

"It is less good," Dom told her honestly. "But I'm going to try one last thing tonight. It might work, it might not."

"What are you doing?" Vinny asked.

"A different spell. I have to use the attic. And it'll take me a few hours."

Jonas said, "Wow. Sounds serious."

"Yeah." The way Dom looked at him almost made Vinny wince, because it was blindingly obvious to her that Dom wanted to throttle Jonas. But Jonas seemed unaware.

"I hope it works," he said.

"Me too." Vinny said. He hadn't told her a thing about this new spell, but she knew he'd been talking with his family all day about what to do. Maybe they'd found something.

"Okay," Emma said, too brightly. "I'm getting the cake."

She brought out a tall, white frosted angel food cake, with burning candles in a circle around the top. Vinny smiled at her friend, grateful that at least this one relationship seemed to hold tight despite everything.

They sang the song, and then Emma said, "Make a wish!"

Vinny didn't know what to wish for. Should she wish to break the curse? For Jonas to go to hell? For Emma to get happily divorced? For world peace? For a fresh box of condoms?

I wish for life to be better tomorrow.

The wish formed in her mind, and she blew out the candles. They sparkled briefly before going out, leaving long trails of thin, twisting blue smoke.

The cake was delicious, but Vinny kept thinking of Dom alone in an attic, with a demon on the loose.

When everyone got up from the table, she took Dom by the arm, whispering, "You didn't do anything to the cake, did you?"

"What do you mean?"

"Those candles acted funny."

"Maybe Emma bought trick candles."

"Emma *hates* trick candles. You cast a spell on them, didn't you."

"I don't know what you're talking about." Dom looked way too innocent.

"Whatever." She looked him over carefully. "Are you going to be okay? With whatever you're doing in the attic?"

"Don't worry about me. But do me a favor. Don't go upstairs. Hang out on the main floor for a while."

"Why?"

"Trust me."

She nodded. She'd trust him. "Good luck."

He smiled at her, then left.

Vin helped Emma clear the dishes. In the kitchen, she noticed how tired Emma looked. "You okay?"

"I'm just really wiped out all of a sudden," Emma said. "Am I the worst friend if I turn in super early on your birthday?"

"Of course not. It was a perfect birthday dinner."

"I didn't even get you a present," Emma said. "How could I forget that?"

"You know I'm not a material girl." Vinny gave her a hug. "Get some rest. We'll party tomorrow."

"Cool."

Emma went to her bedroom, leaving Vinny alone in the great room, except for Piewicket, who commandeered a couch to herself. Vinny sat on another couch, staring out the window at the sunset.

"Not exactly a night at the club."

She turned to see Jonas standing there, skinny and stylish and hair perfectly done. He looked like the celebrity Jonas Belling.

"It's fine," she assured him. He didn't want to go out to the clubs in the city, did he? Why was he so slicked up?

Jonas said something, but it was weird and garbled and Vinny didn't catch it.

"What did you say?"

"Nothing." Jonas smiled as he sat down on the couch. "You hearing things, honey?"

"Must be. I swore you said something."

"Well, I'll say something now. Happy birthday, babe."

"Thanks." What was with all the *honey* and *babe* stuff? Vinny hated that kind of talk.

He moved a little closer to her. "I'm really glad you came out to visit."

"Well. I guess I felt compelled."

Jonas slung an arm on the back of the couch, but then moved it to her shoulders, his fingers threading the chains of her necklaces. "What'd you wish for?"

"I can't tell you that. First rule of birthday wish club."

He laughed, then leaned over and kissed her.

"What the hell?" She pulled away, angry. She hadn't planned on confronting him about the camera until tomorrow, but maybe it couldn't wait.

"Come on, Vin. Loosen up."

"How loose do you think I'll get?"

He tried to kiss her again, as if that were normal. Vinny edged off the couch and stood up. She glanced over to where Piewicket had been. The cat was gone. Oh, great.

"You're all uptight. What's wrong with you?" he asked, standing up too. Standing way too close to her.

"Wrong with me? You're the one acting all horny with your wife sleeping a few rooms over."

"I'm just being honest. You're hot, babe."

"Are you high again? Seriously. Are you on something?"

"I want to be on you."

Gross. Vinny pushed him away, hard. "What. The. Fuck."

Jonas lost his balance and was now on his ass in the middle of the room. He glared at Vinny as he climbed to his feet. "I take it back," he said. "You're not hot. You're a fucking ice queen. It's like you got a wall around you."

All at once, she got it. She did have a wall around her —the one Dom so very lovingly put up to protect her. And it was working.

"You're trying to use magic," she accused him. "To get me in bed. That's low."

"What the hell are you talking about? You're crazy."

In any other context, it would sound crazy. But Vinny was utterly certain of what was happening now. "Don't lie to me. You're using some kind of magic. What's the matter, out of roofies?"

"You're insane, Vin."

"That's what guys say when they want women to shut up. I'm perfectly sane. And pissed. I'm going to wake up Emma. It's time she gets the full story on you."

"No!" Jonas grabbed her by the arm, twisting it painfully in his attempt to keep her from leaving. "You can't tell her. I'll lose everything."

Vinny pulled her arm free. "Too late."

Jonas grabbed at her again, this time wrapping his hand around the chains of her necklaces. "Where is it? Where's the one I gave you?"

"I got rid of it," Vinny said.

"Got rid of it? You can't! It's impossible."

"So you did know it was cursed."

He stopped moving, just for a second. "I don't know what you're talking about."

"Yes you do." Dom came into the room, holding the gold necklace up. "And it's time you stop lying about it."

Chapter 25

VINNY HAD NEVER BEEN SO happy to see two guys about to argue.

Jonas turned on Dom. "You said you were going to be in the attic all night."

"I told people what they needed to hear." Dom walked toward Jonas, who shrank away as soon as Dom held the necklace out toward him

"Get that thing away from me!" He glared at Dom. "I *paid* you to fix my problem!"

"You lied to me," said Dom. "Made the job pretty hard."

"Fuck you."

"No thanks. But if you really want, you can try your secret code word."

Behind Jonas, Vinny watched him with narrowed eyes. She remembered the garbled sound he'd made. "I knew there was something weird about what he said."

"Yeah. I guessed as much," said Dom. "It's a pretty typical piece of the deal when someone bargains with a demon out of lust." He looked back to Jonas. "Was that the only sin? Lust?"

Jonas shook his head, not meeting Dom's gaze.

"It can't be just lust." That comment came from Emma. She'd been woken, somehow, and now rejoined them all. "It was money too. And fame."

Piewicket padded into the room, silently taking it all in.

"Jonas was never that talented," Vinny noted, slowly putting it together. "But all of a sudden, he had an agent, and an album deal, and distribution, and tours."

"Not everyone is as lucky as you, Vin!" Jonas snapped.

Vinny felt like he'd hit her. "Lucky? I wasn't lucky. I worked my *ass* off. I practiced every damn day just to keep up. That's your problem, Jonas. You never wanted to put the time in. You just wanted to magically be rich and famous."

"What happened?" Dom asked. "How'd you run into the demon?"

Jonas looked around at the three people surrounding him, cutting off every point of escape. He looked up at the clock on the wall. "It's too late."

"It's not," Dom said sharply. "But you have to tell the truth. What happened?"

"There was a party," Jonas said, his voice barely loud enough to hear. "A birthday party. In the Bronx."

"Malika's party?" Vinny gasped out. "That was years ago."

"Thirteen years ago." Jonas looked lost. "She threw that party for you, Vin. And I went because I wanted to see you so bad."

"You were already dating Emma by then."

"Off and on," he said, defensively. "But it was you, Vin. It was always you."

Emma's mouth just hung open, and Vinny felt sick to her stomach.

"What happened at the party?" Dom asked quickly.

"I couldn't get close to Vin. So I just drank. Dropped some acid. And I saw this chick looking at me. She said there was a way to get everything I wanted. But I had to make a deal."

"She was the demon," Dom guessed. "Demons often take on human appearance to get close to victims. She offered you a bargain. What was the deal you made?"

Jonas grimaced, but didn't say anything.

Vinny glared at him. Time was draining away, and Jonas was just now having his come-to-Jesus moment? Jesus. "Jonas! Spit it out!"

"I got thirteen years till she came back for the payment," Jonas said, dully. "Thirteen years. Over a decade. I thought it would be plenty of time to figure a way out."

"You called the Salems two fucking weeks ago!" Emma yelled.

"I was scared!" Jonas yelled back.

Dom stepped in front of Jonas, blocking his view of his furious wife. "Jonas, look at me. What was the deal? I need details."

"It was simple," Jonas said. "She said three sins could be satisfied. Greed, envy, and lust. One sin, I'd get 39 years. Two sins, 26. Or all three, for 13 years. I wanted it all. So I took the bargain. Money, fame, sex. All I could handle, and then at the end, I had to offer up the one thing I desired most. Whatever I put the necklace on. If I chose nothing, it'd be my soul. I didn't ever even feel my soul, so I said yes. I figured it was like getting something for nothing."

Vinny laughed, nearly hysterical. "Something for

nothing? From a demon? Have you never seen a movie?"

"For all I knew it was a bad trip!" he insisted. "What did I have to lose?"

Dom snapped his fingers to return Jonas's focus to him. "Keep going. Say what happened next."

"What happened is that I got everything. I got famous. I got rich. I married Emma, who's smart and gorgeous. And Vinny just drifted away. Not famous. Not rich. Playing at being a punk."

"Playing?" Vinny hissed.

"I wanted to show her what she missed," Jonas said. His words came fast now, after years of keeping silent. "I wanted to show her what I'd accomplished."

"You mean what your demon accomplished," Vinny said.

Jonas rambled on, unhearing. "But when she got here, I could tell nothing had changed. She was too fucking proud to admit that I was good enough for her. She still looks like she's real people, but she's a spoiled princess and she'll always think she's better than everyone else."

Vin realized tears were streaming down her face, and she wanted nothing more than to feed Jonas's soul right over to the demon.

Emma rushed over to wrap her arms around Vin. "Don't listen to him," she whispered. "None of that is true."

"Stop that!" Jonas yelled. "Fucking stop that, both of you! It's driving me nuts!"

Dom looked disgusted. "They're not doing that to turn you on, idiot."

Jonas stared at Vinny and Emma, as if he couldn't look away. "I said fuck it! I gave her the necklace. I wasn't going to, but then I thought why should I give my soul up for Vinny? She's so high above everyone, on her own plane. Who would miss her?"

Vinny buried her face in Emma's shoulder, as if that could keep her from hearing Jonas say things like that about her.

"Even if you gave her the necklace, it doesn't mean anything," Emma said triumphantly. "She's not your obsession. That's *bullshit*."

Jonas glared at Emma. "Shut up. You don't want to win this contest, Emma."

"That's not what I mean! This demon's supposed to get the thing you want? That's the deal? Years of fame and fortune and fucking random chicks in exchange for the one thing you desire most?"

"It was a good deal," Jonas hissed. "Look what it got you!"

"Vinny's not the thing you desire most," Emma said, her voice hot. "Neither am I. I know you, Jonas. The only thing you really love is yourself, your own image. You'd fuck a mirror if you could. After ten years of marriage, believe me, I'd know."

"It doesn't matter!" Jonas bellowed desperately, trying to drown out Emma's words. "It's too late anyway."

"No, it's not." Dom said. He grabbed Jonas's shoulders to get his attention again. "It's not midnight yet. It's not too late if you let me work."

"You're still going to help?" Jonas asked incredulously. His breathing was shallow, uneven. His eyes were unfocused.

"That's what you hired me for."

Jonas began to smile, the smile of a gambler who just got the card he needed.

Then the house began to shake. Piewicket yowled a

warning.

"Oh, my God, what's happening?" Emma shouted, far too close to Vinny's ear.

The electric lights flickered off, leaving only the candles Emma had lit around the first floor to make the birthday dinner festive. Now, the sparse, guttering flames just looked weak.

The acrid stench of tar and brimstone began to the fill the room.

Dom said, "Your business partner is here."

Vinny smelled the smoke filling the air and wanted to run away. But her feet were nailed to the floor. She remembered the smell from her dream, and the surprise walk into the otherworlds.

Before she could do anything, the smoke began to take shape.

The same long, twisted limbs and body. Like a lizard built wrong. Then eyes, huge bloodshot eyes, peering through the smoke. And that smile full of teeth.

She was going to throw up. Vinny swallowed. She did not want birthday cake vomit to be her last taste of food on earth.

"You made a bargain with *that*?" Emma shrieked, terrified.

Jonas was white-faced. "It didn't look like that before."

"Why are you here?" Dom asked, his voice remarkably calm.

The demon turned fire-bright eyes to each of them. "Why does a lion find a lamb? I'm hungry. So many kinds of hungry, and this little world offers such delights. The air is sweet, and the sins are sweeter. All these tiny, delectable souls with such tiny desires. Ah, I want to eat them all!"

Then it sighted Jonas. "There he is! This mortal, Jonas August Belling, made a bargain with me. I granted him fame and material wealth, so that others envied him, and so he could indulge in avarice by spending profligately on whimsical, useless things. And then the lust...I gave him means to seduce whoever he desired, a spell to speak that rendered the listener open to seduction. It was a gift he used again and again and again."

"Ew," Vinny muttered.

Unfortunately, that comment got the thing's attention.

"Ah, the one to whom he gave my symbol. A pretty thing indeed, with a prettier soul." The demon reached out toward Vinny, a glow suffusing its clawed hand. "He wants you most, so it's you I take."

Vinny couldn't even scream. She had her crappy little knife out, but the demon only laughed, the sound filled with flames. "Come, my child."

"No," she hissed.

"Ah. You wear charms against evil. How quaint." A huge claw sliced at her neck. The necklaces, including the cross and the bottle of salt, fell to the floor.

Vinny fought back a sob. She could barely breathe against the stench, and she wanted nothing more than to crawl into the smallest hole next to the smallest mouse and hide forever.

"Come. There's no stopping it, sweet dear. You're a pawn, a payment. Most deaths are pointless. At least you'll see the glory of my hell before you die."

No. She wasn't sure if she said it or thought it or screamed it.

The thing swiped again. Vinny's stupid, cheap knife clattered against a wall somewhere. She shrank back farther, trying to be a mouse, a flea, anything small enough to ignore. Why did she have to be a thing to be taken? Why didn't she have a say? Why was nothing fair?

Hot breath rushed over her face. She squeezed her eyes shut, terrified of seeing this nightmare one more time. *What do I have to do to keep living?*

The demon reached, and paused just before grabbing her wrist. "What is this?" it asked, puzzled.

She opened her eyes a slit. The demon made another grab, but its claws seemed unable to actually take hold of Vinny. "What surrounds you?"

"Cheese and crackers," she whispered, a wild laugh starting to well up inside her. "That spell totally worked."

"You're *protected*?" The demon winced, then whirled around. Vinny gasped in relief, no longer in its crosshairs.

It found Jonas, and stooped low. "What is this game? You seek to play with *me*? Putting a lock on my prize?"

Jonas said in a panic, "I don't know anything about a lock. I'm sorry!"

"Sorry, mortal? Sorry?"

Dom stepped forward. He looked totally unintimidated, despite the fact that the demon was twice as tall as him, and oh, yeah, a *demon*. He said, "The protection spell is mine."

Chapter 26

DOM FACED THE DEMON HE knew was Azthaanethmaoul, and took a breath, trying to not inhale too much of the nasty brimstone stench. "I cast the spell on her."

The demon turned its full attention to him, which was never a place he wanted a demon's attention to be. It hissed, "Who are you? Some dabbling mage?"

"I'm Dominic Salem."

"That name means nothing to me." The demon sneered at him.

He slowly, deliberately recited the names of a few other demons. "Heochxiomon. Zaeasbathcaiphon. Zaphelal, Erosorsacer."

The creature in front of him considered the names. Then it said dismissively, "Those ones are all destroyed."

"I know. My brothers and I killed them all."

The demon paused, reassessing Dom. "Or you are lying."

Dom shrugged. "Whatever. I don't care if you believe me."

"Just as well, since you'll be too dead to care about

anything in a moment. And then your little spell on her will die too."

It lunged toward Dom, but then stopped, pushed back by some invisible force. "What now?" it roared.

"Oh, you missed it, with all the smoke and confusion and threatening mortals' souls. But that cat just ran around you in a circle—she's great at circles. And I fired up a ward, because I'm great at wards. So now you're stuck inside."

"You can't cast without a ritual!"

"Just did." Dom kept his voice as steady as he could, partly to piss off the demon, and partly because he'd freak out if his concentration slipped even a little. And that would shatter the ward.

"I don't believe you!" the demon screeched.

Piewicket hissed and spat at the demon. You will remain confined within this circle. I have eaten fiercer creatures than you before my morning nap, and I will eat you if you pass the border.

The demon snorted fire, but didn't try to cross the line Piewicket had created. Still, it laughed. "You may confine me for a few moments. But no more than that. You're still a mortal, Dominic Salem." It intoned the syllables of his name precisely, lovingly, hoping to use his name against him if it could. "Such power in a mortal, though. Fascinating. What is your full name?"

"You're kidding, right?"

The demon hissed out a laugh. "Power doesn't equal wisdom. I have tricked greater mages than you into giving me every...last...bite...of their souls." It made a gross, smacking sound. "Let me eat a soul. Choose one you like the least, put the necklace on them and send them to me. Then I'll go."

"No." Dom resisted, because the offer *was* tempting. Jonas would be so easy to give over.

"You want more?" the demon asked. "Then say it. Say your desire. More power? I can offer you a deeper look into the well of magic. You'll gain knowledge others would weep over."

"No." He didn't need power. Power couldn't give back what he lost.

"Oh…" The demon's voice changed. It became gentle. "What you've lost. What your family lost. Do you want to see them again? Speak to them, the ones who gave you life and then gave their lives to keep all of you safe? My symbol back, and a promise to give me your soul when it's all used up and old…"

"No!" Dom burst out. Hate filled him like a flash flood. How dare this thing look into his memories, his mind. He should just give Jonas to it. That's what the asshole deserved.

Keep silence! Offer nothing! Piewicket's voice echoed through his mind. *It's scared.*

"Of what?" he breathed.

Something you have.

Dom wasn't that powerful. What did he have that could scare a demon? He held his knife in his right hand. It was more magical than most knives, but nothing against a millennia-old creature of flame and smoke. He had a cat, also more magical than most. He had…the necklace.

Now he knew what he had to do. He had to break the necklace. The necklace served as the representation of the contract in the real world. In one way, it *was* the contract. But Dom had to be sure the contract was severed before he could try to destroy both the physical object and the magic within it.

"I'm going to pull the contract from this symbol," he said.

The demon's eyes flared. "You may try, you stupid mortal. But such a ritual would take you weeks. Months! Gather your ingredients and map your sky. I'll have a soul by midnight."

"Or I'll just break it." Dom raised his knife, preparing to bring the blade down onto the symbol. Now that he had the demon's true name, he could mangle this thing like tinfoil.

"NO!!" the demon shrieked, the sound echoing in many worlds. "You cannot! Please, I beg you, stop!"

He stopped, and smiled.

"You can't make more symbols," Dom said, enlightened. "Something went wrong, sometime, a long time ago, and now you're bound by the ones you still have. You need each one back, whole and unharmed, or you lose the chance to get another soul from it. It's why you're so hungry. You have to wait for your meals, and you don't have as many coming as you used to."

"I'll tear your soul from your veins," it hissed. "You're nothing! A speck. I hold multitudes! My domain is vast, with oceans of black flame."

"Empty oceans." Dom held the necklace tight in his fist. "You want this back to get more? You agree to my offer."

The demon's head ducked low, a bull waiting to charge. "An offer?"

It thinks it can outwit you, Piewicket warned. Be simple.

"Here's the deal." Dom thought a minute, his eyes flicking toward Piewicket, getting her read. "If you release Jonas August Belling from his contract, and forgo all claim to the humans and cats in this house, I'll toss the necklace back to you, and without offering further harm or bargains, you will leave the real world for your own place in the otherworlds."

"Surely I can bring something to this offer," the demon countered slyly.

"Shut up," Dom warned. "There's one bargain on the table. Mine. Listen. You can say yes or say no. Or I'll use your true name to destroy your necklace, and you'll get one measly, shitty soul for it, and lose all hope of more."

The demon hissed. "Not that, I pray you."

"Then what's your answer to my offer?"

"You could get so much more. No negotiating? No haggling? No sweeteners?"

"Try no fucking patience." Dom twirled the knife.

The demon hemmed and hawed, but couldn't find a way to wiggle past the very basic parameters of Dom's offer. Every time it tried to speak, Dom just ran the tip of the blade across the metal of the symbol.

"Very well!" it screamed, minutes to midnight. "I accept your offer."

"Then pronounce the contract with Jonas August Belling null and void. Say it!"

The demon ground out the statement.

"Pronounce all people and cats and living creatures in this house safe. Pronounce that you will leave the moment this necklace crosses the border of the circle."

The demon did so, ending with "So I say it. Done and done! Now uphold your side, Dominic Salem."

Dom bunched the necklace in his hand, then threw it in an easy arc toward the demon, who outstretched massive, reptilian hands to receive it.

But just when the necklace glittered in the fey light of

the circle's edge, a swift shadow flew past, capturing the necklace, eclipsing the shine in a dark shape.

And then Piewicket landed lightly, on four paws, the necklace secure in her jaws.

Mine.

Dom probably could have reminded the demon that cats can cross borders. But then, the demon should already know that. It was an old timer, after all.

The demon started to shriek at an unbelievable, unholy volume. Vinny and Emma both clapped their hands over their ears in a vain attempt to block out the sound.

"Lies! Cheating! Abomination and trickery!" the demon wailed.

"No," Dom said firmly. "I held up my end of the bargain. I tossed the necklace across the border. The cat was not a party to the contract, and you have no grievance."

"I want it, I want it! Give it! Pretty kitty, please bring me my toy."

Pie's ears were flattened, and she bit down on the charm. The snapping sound was absurdly loud.

The demon wailed again. "I will destroy you!"

"Nope." Dom held the knife out, blade down. "You have to leave now. Rules are rules." He shifted his tone to the more formal language of the banishment spell. In Latin, he said, "I abjure thee. Go."

The demon hissed and flailed. Plumes of black smoke gushed forth.

"Azthaanethmaoul." Dom spoke the demon's true name, carefully, clearly, then stooped down, plunging the tip of the blade into the floor. "Be gone."

There was a flash, and the smoke in the room *ungushed*, falling back into the circle, into a pinpoint. The demon vanished from the same rift it entered, and the last thing it left was a scream on the air.

"What the fuck just happened?" Jonas yelled, panicked.

"Show's over," said Dom.

"What?" Emma said, taking her hands off her ears.

"The contract is severed. The charm held it, and we've destroyed it. And then, since the demon had no claims on anyone's soul, I sent it back to hell. It's all good."

Or maybe it wasn't.

Piewicket mewed, and dashed over to Vinny, who was huddled on the floor in a tight ball, not responding to anything.

Chapter 27

VINNY MOANED IN PAIN, HER body overwhelmed by the deep, soul-scorching reality of what just happened. A tiny lick on her cheek made her jerk sideways. Then she realized it was just Pie. The cat looked at her with what Vinny could swear was concern.

Then Dom was there, pulling her up, holding her tight. "You okay?" he asked. "What's wrong?"

"There was a demon that tried to eat my soul," she mumbled. "Don't know if you caught that."

"Yeah. It's gone now."

"Thanks." *Thanks* was so inadequate a word. Vinny wrapped her arms around him to let him know how she felt. "I'm so glad you're here," she whispered.

Then a sob broke through her thoughts. Vinny looked over to find Emma standing over Jonas, who was literally on his knees. The sob came from him.

"Don't, babe," he was saying. "I'm so sorry about everything, but it's over now. We can move on."

"You can move on," she said. "You can move on tonight, out of *my* house."

"Your house?"

"Yeah. I'm keeping the house. And half of everything. That's what my divorce lawyer will send over to your lawyer. If you fight it, I will spill so much shit to the public, you won't get a gig for an infomercial."

"Emma, please. Give me another chance."

"You've had a whole marriage worth of chances. Pack a bag. Pick a car. Movers can take care of the rest."

Vinny saw resolve in Emma's eyes, something she hadn't seen in a long while. Jonas must have seen it too, because he got up off the floor without trying to convince her again.

But then he looked over to her.

"Vin…"

She turned away from Jonas, toward Dom, who didn't say a word. He just held her, and that was all Vin wanted.

What seemed like mere moments later, Jonas drove off. He had a bag full of clothes, and his soul. But he'd lost everything else. Emma locked the gate behind him, and then changed the code. "That's good for tonight," she murmured.

She turned to Dom, who still had an arm around Vinny. "Did you trick a demon? Was that a thing that happened?"

He said, "The offer was real. I did everything I said I would. I just left out the part where Piewicket has her own agenda. And besides, I couldn't just give that necklace back knowing more souls would get taken with it. That would make me a pretty bad demon hunter."

Emma nodded slowly. "I guess you're the real deal. What's the etiquette on tipping?"

"Pro."

She smiled. "Can I take care of it tomorrow? I'm about to collapse."

"I'll tuck you in," Vinny said suddenly. She could see the loneliness in her friend right then.

Emma looked like she might burst into tears. "That'd be great."

Vinny took care of Emma, then returned to the great room, which was a hot mess. Dom was attempting to clean up, but it was beyond one tired human.

"How are you?" he asked.

Vinny rubbed at her ears, trying to knock out the ringing. "Say what you will about club sound systems," she muttered. "That demon screeching just made my tinnitus ten times worse than touring ever did."

"How's Emma?"

"Emma's out of it. She took something to help her sleep, and I put her to bed and stayed until she drifted off. She can't deal with anything more now."

"It's really late," he said. "You should get some sleep too."

"Tuck me in."

He walked her upstairs. Vinny stripped off her clothes without even thinking about it, then slipped under the covers. Dom pulled the blanket up to her chin.

"Dom," she said, catching his hand before he could step away, "Stay."

"You're perfectly safe now."

"It's not about safe. Please. Just sleeping. Just to not be alone…after that."

He hit the lights, and a second later slid into bed beside her. Vinny curled up on him the second he lay down. "Can I ask you something?"

"You just did."

"Smart ass," she said. "I'm serious."

"What do you want to know?"

"Tonight, when all that happened. When that *thing* showed up. Were you scared?"

"Yes," he said simply.

"You didn't act scared."

"Well, I was. It's always smart to be scared around the supernatural. The universe is way bigger and meaner than most people dream of."

"I was terrified," she confessed. He tightened his arms around her, and Vinny sighed with contentment.

"Terror is a rational response," he said then.

"Dom, I don't want to be terrified if it happens again."

"How many friends of yours made a deal with a demon?"

"I mean running into *any* of your supernasties. I want to be prepared."

"It's not that simple. But it's also not that likely. Most people live their whole lives without ever having an encounter."

"Yeah, well I seem to be an outlier."

"Maybe just because you're around me."

"Or maybe the only reason I got more than one encounter to my name is because you were there to save my butt," Vinny said.

"You have a butt worth saving."

She smiled in the darkness. "You think?"

"Pretty sure."

She thought about what happened, then said, "If Piewicket eats demons for breakfast, then why didn't she just eat this one? Wouldn't that have solved everything?"

"No. First, the demon's death wouldn't necessarily have saved Jonas's soul—we had to sever the contract to do that. And second, Pie says this type of demon tastes really bad."

"I can never tell if you're joking when it comes to Piewicket."

Dom laughed softly. "She's a cat, and therefore transcends human understanding."

Vin nestled closer to him, breathing in the smell of him—not exactly glamorous, just sweat, and smoke, and something else she could only label as Salem. She didn't want to let him go.

"Stay all night," she whispered.

"You didn't even have to ask."

She drifted to sleep while listening to him breathe. She'd never been so happy in her life.

* * * *

Despite the late night, despite his exhaustion, despite his fear that he'd lose Vin and her soul to some demon, Dom slept great. It was because he had Vinny right next to him. Naked, yes, which was nice. But more importantly, alive. That was what he liked best.

He drifted in and out of sleep until the morning sunlight got too bright to ignore. He picked up his phone and suppressed a snarl. Dom saw a string of texts from Mal, all basically saying *we need to talk*. He sighed. He really didn't want to know what happened, because chances were he'd have to leave this place fast. And that meant a very uncomfortable talk with Vinny.

She was asleep, though. If he kept it quiet, he could talk without waking her, and without leaving the bed.

He dialed Mal.

His brother picked up instantly. "Hey, where the hell have you been? I texted a million times. Are you done out there? How'd it go?"

"Fine. The client nearly died, though, so it might be hard to get referrals."

"What? What did you *do*?" Mal demanded.

So Dom explained everything that happened. Mostly. He scaled back all the events with Vinny.

Mal said, "Why aren't you on the road back already? What's the hold up?"

"Um. I thought I'd stay to help Vinny get things under control."

"Who's Vinny again? I thought the client's name was Jonas."

"It is. And I did get paid. So it's okay."

"So who's this Vinny dude?"

"Vinny's not a dude. She's a girl. Woman. Lady."

His brother pounced on that info. "Are you into her?"

Dom squeezed his eyes shut, as if that could shut out his brother's questions. "Yes," he ground out.

"Is she a vampire?"

"No."

"Holy shit. You got paid beaucoup bucks for a job that nearly killed our client, and you got tangled up with a chick named Vinny, which believe me we're going to talk about, and you're just hanging out there like you're on vacation. What the hell, bro? Explain."

If there was one thing Dom really didn't like talking to his brother about, it was anything to do with women. "You didn't call to give me dating advice. What's happening back home?"

That worked. Mal burst out, "Oh, man. That hellhole across the street—it's suddenly crawling with people. Workmen, county inspectors, utility workers. Whoever owns that place is no longer content to let it crumble away. It looks like a full restoration. From the outside anyway. Who knows what's going on below the house. Behemoth says he can feel the hellhole now. Something in the otherworlds is waking up, right underneath that house."

"Ok. I'll get on the road and come back as soon as I can. Do whatever you have to in the meantime."

He hung up and then saw Vinny watching him. She'd heard his side of the conversation, and she knew what was coming.

"Vinny," he said. "Listen, I need to get home."

"I was wondering when you'd say that."

He'd been dreading this moment. As long as neither of them said anything, he could pretend it didn't matter. But it did matter. They didn't live here, and their home bases were hundreds of miles apart.

"Can we talk?" he asked, feeling absurdly nervous.

"Hope so. We're adults, yeah?"

"I can play one pretty well," Dom said.

Vinny said, "Depending on what you want, it's either going to be a very short conversation, or it could go longer."

He took her hand in his, flipping her palm up. "I was not expecting you, Vin. Not picking you up on the road, not letting you know what I do, and definitely not getting into a relationship with you. But I'm not sorry I did any of those things."

"Good. Neither am I."

"So," he said, "this is where it gets awkward."

She said, very quickly, "I really like you. Let's get that out of the way."

"Okay."

"I need some time to think. About everything. But I really like you."

"It's mutual," he assured her. "You should take as much time as you need."

"I mean I'll need days. Maybe weeks. You'll be long gone before I know what the hell I want."

"But you're smart enough to use a phone, yeah?"

She laughed. "Yeah. We can talk later. Assuming you're not locked in battle with an undead wereferret or something."

"Unlikely."

"You said that like there was still a slight possibility. Wereferrets aren't real, right? I just made that up."

"I can research it. I promise that most nights, chances are way better that I'm doing research instead of kicking ass. Sorry."

"No, that's good to hear."

"Vin, I want you to be happy."

She waited, her eyes bright. "Was that the beginning of something?" she finally asked, when he didn't say more.

"That was it," Dom admitted. God, he was crap with words around her. "I want you to be happy. You have to decide what will make you happy. I've got a few opinions, but it's your choice."

"You've got a choice too, you know."

"I already made mine," he said.

"And?" she asked pointedly.

"Understand me here, Vin. You are amazing. In every way I can think of, you're amazing."

She frowned. "But?"

"I've got a steady job, a vocation, even if it's a strange one. I have a life and house and family around me. I'd say that I'd give all that up, but I'd be lying. I can't give all that up. It's part of who I am. So the person who has to decide what you want is you. I'm not pretending that's an easy decision. You value your independence more than anything else. And accepting me…for whatever…would mean accepting a lot more than just me. It's the job, the strange, the Salem clan—which is its own brand of strange. I'd never blame you for choosing another path."

"A path without you," she said. Her words sounded a little clipped, a little too precise.

"If that's what you want," he said, fumbling over the words. Those sounded like the right words, but he got the order wrong. Or something. If this were a spell, he'd be in trouble right about now.

Vinny looked him over, her expression cooling by the second. He'd stood under a solar eclipse. The air went cold all at once, the moment the sun went away. This was the same feeling, but worse. Because after the eclipse, the sun came back.

Vinny wasn't going to do that. She pulled away from him in her own mind. She was right next to him in the bed, but a million miles away. She was the aloof, untouchable woman he'd met the day he pulled to the side of the road to pick her up.

"At least you're honest," she said. "You never pretended this was anything besides…what it was."

"Vin." He didn't know what to say, and he knew it was already too late.

"I still like you," she said, without cruelty, even though it hurt to hear it. "But you're right. You have a path. You should follow it."

Chapter 28

DOM DROVE FOURTEEN HOURS THE first day, and another six the next. By the time he got home in the early afternoon, he could barely see straight and he still felt the road under him, the miles passing one by one.

When he pulled into the driveway of the Salem house, Lily was the first person to see him.

She'd been sitting on the porch, and now walked down to the crumbling concrete front path. "Wow. You look like hell," Lily said by way of greeting.

She did not look like hell. No matter what, Lily always looked neat as a pin, thanks to a super-strict upbringing by her Chinese-born parents. Long, perfectly straight hair the color of midnight—except for the purple-dyed ends—framed her face. Her brown eyes missed nothing, particularly not the way Piewicket bounded out of her confinement at the side pannier of the bike. The cat sashayed toward the house without a glance back at Dom.

"You made her mad." Lily bent down to pet Pie as she passed by.

"I've been making a bunch of people mad," Dom said after he got off the bike. He stretched, relieved to be done with the road trip. "You're staying here?"

"For a bit. I need to go back to the library again for the research I'm doing. This is as good a place as any to get some work done."

"You'll get mad at me too, before you leave."

Lily shook her head. "Whatever, Dom. You guys already had plenty of chances to offend me. I'm sticking around."

"Thanks." He meant it. Lily was good people. "Your research helped with getting rid of that demon. It helped a lot."

"Good, though I bet you being a badass spellcaster helped more. Why don't you come inside? It's your house, after all."

Dom followed her in, wishing the house felt more like home.

Seeing his youngest brother helped Dom feel a little better. Lex leaned through the doorway of the room they called the study—which was jam-packed with boxes of books and other materials they hadn't managed to unpack yet. "I heard you like a girl."

"Shut up."

"Is it true?" Lex looked sweet, but he was implacable when it came to getting info out of people.

"I'll tell you the story if you do a lookup for me."

"Eh." Lex paused, considering. "What's the lookup?"

"Wereferrets."

Lex shifted his gaze to Lily, who merely shrugged. "Got me," she said.

"You want a lookup," Lex said slowly, "on wereferrets. Were. Ferrets."

"Just find out if they're real or not. And if they can be turned undead."

Lex narrowed his eyes. "Is this a hazing?"

"Nope. It's a lookup."

"Things I do for a story," Lex muttered. "All right. Lily, are you in on this? I might need someone else around, if only to remind me that I'm doing a lookup on wereferrets."

"Sensible," Lily said, with a sharp nod. "I'm in."

Dom left them arguing about the best way to start a lookup on wereferrets. Once he reached his bed, he crashed, sleeping five hours on top of the covers, still fully clothed.

He woke up when a heavy weight landed on his back.

"Ugh," he grunted. "Get off me."

Dom managed to knock the massive black cat off him as he flipped over. He blinked, utterly disoriented. The light in the room was strange. "What time is it?"

Time to eat, Behemoth told him, his green eyes gleaming. *Past time, in fact. You are summoned.*

"All right, all right."

He changed his clothes and stumbled downstairs, where everyone else had already gathered for a late meal. He sat at the long table in the dining room, surveying the action in the kitchen. Mal yanked out a chair on the other side, sitting down.

"Watch the floor," Dom muttered. "You'll scratch it."

"Have you seen our floor?" Mal responded. "It's made of scratches."

Lex pulled the big ceramic crock out of the oven and put it on the table. Lily leaned over and removed the lid, releasing a cloud of fragrant, savory steam that smelled better than any magic ever could.

"Cheesy Beany!" she declared, with a hopeful look on her face.

Dom knew the two of them had chosen to make

Cheesy Beany specifically to cheer Dom up. It was *the* Salem family meal for all the brothers, something that their parents used to cook, and something all the boys clung to in that dark time afterward when they struggled to hold onto any sort of normalcy. Essentially it was a very bastardized, mashed up version of frijoles charros and masa harina cornbread. Over the years Cheesy Beany had never failed to make Dom feel better.

In addition to Cheesy Beany, there was rice, grilled corn on the cob, fresh pineapple, a green salad, rolls… basically enough to feed all of them twice with plenty of leftovers.

"Thank God. I'm starving," said Mal, who'd never skipped a meal in his life. He reached for a roll, only to have it slapped down by Lily.

"Grace first," she said. "Barbarian."

"Jeez," Mal muttered. "Whose turn is it?"

"Mine," said Lex, his hands already folded. "May this meal feed us and bless us, and give us the strength to fight evil and stand for those who cannot fight for themselves. Those we love who cannot be at this table in the flesh, may your spirits always be welcome. Amen."

"Amen," Dom echoed.

"Amen," said Mal. "Now eating."

They all dug in. Dom was hungrier than he thought, shoveling in nearly as much food as Mal. He'd only had coffee and eggs for breakfast.

He looked around the table, at his brothers, at Lily, who was family in every sense but blood, at the two cats who had been around his whole life. They were family too. Everyone was here, all safe, and well fed. And it was all happening here in their own home. It wasn't quite Dom's dream, but it was pretty close. So why didn't he feel happier?

Because Vinny was over a thousand miles away, and not getting any closer.

There were several minutes of near silence, punctuated only by someone asking for more of a certain food. Dom ate a lot of Cheesy Beany. The meal did help him feel marginally better. The combination of three different kinds of beans, baked with massively spiced tomatoes, mixed with a metric crap ton of cheese and topped with cornbread…unequivocally his favorite food.

Mal finally stopped stuffing his face. He leaned back in his chair. "So. Let's hear it. You like a girl. A real, live, corporeal girl. There's hope for you!"

"Please shut up."

"I mean, not a lot of hope," his brother went on. "After all, she's not here, is she? And you look like you lost a puppy. So what went wrong?"

"Nothing. She stayed to help her friend get her life back on track. It's called priorities, bro."

Mal's eyes widened. "Oh, shit. You really like her."

"Yes," Dom admitted. "And no, I don't know if I'll see her again."

"She's got your number, though, right? Don't just ride off into the sunset and forget that part. The giving of the number is pretty important."

"She's got my number. She's got my everything." He did ride off into the sunrise, though.

"Right, right, right. As the Salem who understands ladies, I am going to offer you some advice."

Lex and Lily both broke out laughing. Even Behemoth gave a suspiciously timed meow.

Mal glared at them all, then turned back to Dom. "The laid back approach is bullshit in this case. Don't wait for her to come around. She'll just come up with reasons why she shouldn't. Let her know you're thinking of her. Especially if there's shit going on in her life."

"That's actually not terrible advice, Mal," Lily said.

"Try not to sound so shocked," he retorted.

Dom just shook his head. "I don't want to get in the way."

"Believe me, she wants you to get in the way," Mal insisted, leaning over the table. "Or at least, she'll want a tiny bit of a distraction from the shitty part of cleaning up after Senor Demon Deal."

"All right. I'll think about it."

Lex scooped a bit of the Cheesy Beany into a small, blue-enameled bowl that had sat empty until then. He wordlessly handed it to Dom.

Dom took it and got up from the table, heading to the side hutch, where the brothers had set up a permanent ofrenda. The shelf was covered with pictures of relatives and friends who'd passed away, along with dozens of little statues and candleholders. Most looked like traditional Mexican crafts, but there were other things mixed in too —the tall porcelain Kwan Yin statue with the broken-off hand, a Venetian carnival mask of Death, and some unexpected elephant figurines painted black and white. A pot of marigolds bloomed profusely.

In the center of the shelf was a framed picture of his parents, dressed up for a Dia de los Muertos parade. His mom, beautiful as La Calavera Catrina, flowers in her hair and her face painted to resemble a colorful skull. His dad, dressed in a perfectly tailored Spanish-style suit in black and white, with a face also made up into a skull, though not with as much detail.

He put the bowl in front of the picture. He didn't remember when they started doing that. Probably only a few months after their parents died. But it was now an ingrained habit to not just light candles, but also to offer food when they had the chance.

"Miss you," he said quietly.

When he walked back to the table, Lily stood up. "Let's clear this table. Mal, you're on kitchen duty."

"Why me?"

"Because I'm not your maid," Lily said with a deceptively sweet smile. "Not to mention that Lex and I are doing some very important research."

While Mal bitched about being forced to do actual chores, Dom wandered over to the living room and stretched out on the long, low, spectacularly ugly plaid couch that had come with the house. It was incredibly comfortable, which was the only reason they hadn't burned it.

The meal threw him into a food coma, and he stared into space while listening to Mal knocking around in the kitchen. The candles burning on the ofrenda flickered. When he was little, he told himself a story that when the candles flickered, it meant his parents were nearby. It was nicer to believe than the more prosaic truth that they always lived in drafty places.

Dom directed his thoughts toward the ofrenda anyway, looking at the picture of his mom. He told her about Vinny, about how fucking scared he'd been when he thought the demon was about to take her soul. He didn't tell Vinny that. He didn't tell his brothers that. But he could tell his mom.

I can't watch someone else I love get taken, he thought. It almost killed me the first time. What if it happens again? He'd rather die.

You'd better live.

The words came to him so distinctly that he wondered if one of the cats was yelling at him. The candlelight grew brighter, obscuring his mother's picture.

Death comes to all. If you fail to live and fail to live with the one you love while you live, I will find you in the afterlife and beat you until you wished there was a death after death, and let me tell you, my Dominino, there's no Child Protective Services in the Realm of the Dead.

"Wake up." Lex nudged Dom's foot.

He blinked and shifted to a sitting position. What the hell did he just dream? "Sorry. Didn't realize I fell asleep." He saw Lex and Lily standing in front of him. Behind them, the candles at the ofrenda were burning like perfectly normal candles. He shook his head to clear it. "What's up?"

Lex announced, "There are no documented cases of wereferrets."

Dom waited. "That's all you got?"

"We can't prove a negative," Lily said. "Theoretically, there could be. Ferrets are mammals, so physiologically, it could work. But there are no documented cases. At all. And yeah, they could be turned undead, but they'd have to exist first."

"Thanks."

"That's it?" Lex looked annoyed. "We do a lookup on undead wereferrets and we get a *thanks*?"

"Vinny asked about them. She'll be relieved to know they're not a big deal."

"Vinny. The girl."

"Yeah."

"The one you said you'd tell us about in exchange for your stupid lookup. What you said at dinner is insufficient."

Dom got the message. He explained about meeting Vinny on the side of the road, taking her along for a few days, fending off the vampire that went for her, and then discovering they had the same destination.

"Fate reboot," Lex said thoughtfully.

"Fate's not a thing," Lily countered, her voice very firm. "*Pattern* reboot. The fabric of the universe reweaves itself in similar ways if possible. So Dom meets a woman he's interested in, like before, and faces a similar enemy in a vampire, like before. And their paths are literally, physically aligned for awhile."

"Not permanently," Dom insisted.

"Nothing's permanent," Lex agreed. "You made a choice to leave her. Why, again?"

"To get back here. Mal said I needed to get back here." And he rebooted another pattern when he left, because he'd basically told Vinny that his job was more important than her. That she was second place. And then he left. Yup, he torched any chance she'd want him now.

Lex was still talking. "He didn't say to abandon anyone."

"I didn't abandon anyone. Vinny is the most independent person I've ever met. You guys, though, need help."

"Yeah, but not instantly. The hellhole across the street isn't open now."

"It could open tomorrow."

"It won't," said Lily. "And there are other people we could call if needed. The whole Salem clan knows about this place."

"It's not the same," Dom insisted, his words sounding hollow to him. "At the end of the day, this is my house. My job. I can't let anything get in the way of that." *Not after I fucked everything up with Vin.*

"Being happy isn't going to get in the way of anything." Lex was looking at him with an intensity that was starting to make Dom really uncomfortable. Lex was far too good at sussing out things people would rather keep under wraps. "If this chica is so independent, she'll totally get that."

"I don't want her to get that. I have enough to worry about with you."

"Me?" Lex raised an eyebrow.

"Oh, boy," Lily muttered.

Dom clarified, "You and Mal."

"What about me?" Malachy walked up and stood next to Lex.

"Oh, Christ. Is this an intervention?"

"Yeah," Mal said. "We're intervening on you being a dumbass. You've been miserable and all stone-faced since Rachel. And while that was serious shit and worth being miserable about, it is time to move on. You found a girl who knows you hunt vampires and she stuck around. That's rare."

"Yeah, but…"

"And you love her," Lily said. "It's obvious."

"I barely know her."

Lex crossed his arms. "By definition, a person you discuss undead wereferrets with is a person you know well. That's just science."

"I've got too much going on to think about me," Dom said. "I need to be here for you guys."

"Dude," Lex said heatedly, "I don't actually need you to sign my permission slips any more. I'm a grown up. And so are you. Don't use *us* as an excuse for why you're afraid to live your own life."

"It's not up to me."

"What does that mean?"

"It means that if I do tell her that I want her in my life, she's the one who has to choose whether she wants to deal with the crazy that is our family."

Lex frowned. "Wait. You put it all on her? That's a dick move."

"I was trying to be mature."

"Fuck that. Did you even tell her what you want? That you're stupid in love with her?"

Dom's expression was enough to answer that.

"You didn't," Lex said. "Why the hell not?"

"Because that would…affect her decision?" Yeah, that sounded dumb out loud.

His brother looked like he wanted to throttle him. "News flash. You *want* to affect her decision. You *want* her to know you love her. Otherwise, she's going to think you don't and guess what. That will *affect her decision.*"

Dom looked sullenly over to Mal. "Is that what you were going to say, too?"

"Basically. Though Lex punched you less than I would have."

"It's too late now," Dom said. "I already messed it up." *God, and how.*

Lily held up his phone and wiggled it at him. "If only there were some sort of magical device that could allow you to reach out over thousands of miles to speak to her."

"Shut up. I get it." He took the phone, though he couldn't imagine what he could say to make it up to her.

"Don't recite a sonnet," Mal added. "Just talk to her."

"Dom can talk," Dom grunted.

"And don't go caveman."

"Dom not stupid."

Chapter 29

Since the morning Dom took off, Vinny put her mind to helping Emma as much as she could. Anything that distracted her from the hollow bit in her heart was good. Still, nearly every fifteen minutes, she thought of Dom. And she still couldn't hate him. Fuck.

They cleaned up the mess in the house that Jonas, and Jonas's demon, left behind. Emma took frequent breaks, blaming her recurring migraines. Vinny suspected that her friend just needed to curl up under a blanket, but didn't want to say so. Emma hated to be seen as anything less than tough. Just another reason why the two were best friends.

While Emma was sleeping, Vinny picked up her phone, having seen a familiar name.

"Hey, Brennan. It's Vinny."

Brennan sounded astonished. "Jesus, Vinny, how'd you get there so fast?"

"I just happened to be here when it happened," she said.

"Oh, no. I mean, I'm glad Emma wasn't on her own,

but I'm sorry you had to see it. Wow. Sounds like Jonas's inner demons finally caught up to him."

"Um." Metaphorical. Brennan's speaking metaphorically. Calm down. "You got it exactly right."

"You doing okay?"

"I'll survive, just like always," Vinny said. "Did you want to talk to Emma? She's taking a nap."

"Oh, don't wake her. I just wanted to call and let her know if there's anything I can do… just ask. Seriously. Anything."

"I'll let her know."

"And tell her don't worry about the article she's working on. I'll push the deadline back to the next issue, or whenever. She needs to think about herself now."

"Yeah. It'll take a while."

Brennan said, "It's really lucky you're there. I can't think of a better person to help Emma right now."

"Her family?" Vinny suggested.

"Sure, but there's nothing like a true friend. And that's you."

"You too," she said. "In fact, you should find a reason for Emma to come out to New York soon. It would be good for her."

"Oh. Um."

Vinny could practically hear him shuffling his feet. She grinned. "Just something to think about. I'll let her know you called."

Putting the phone down, she smiled. It would be nice for Emma to get a change of scenery. Even if it turned out to be just a fling.

Emma looked a little stronger every time Vinny saw her. They packed up Jonas's things for a moving company to pick up. They disconnected the surveillance cameras.

"I'll get a guard dog," Emma declared. They watched old movies and ate popcorn. Emma chose *The Philadelphia Story*, and Vinny chose *Dark Carnival*.

They sometimes talked, and sometimes not. Occasionally, Vinny heard Emma singing, so she figured Emma would be all right, eventually. Learning that your lying, cheating husband was willing to consort with the underworld to enable his lying and cheating would take a while to work through.

Vinny should be happy she was single.

She was not.

Two weeks ago, she'd been perfectly content to be single. Also, she had no idea vampires and demons and who the hell knew what else even existed. Also, she hadn't met Dominic Salem.

"I really, really, really should not have got on that bike," she muttered.

As if to stick the knife in farther, Vinny scrolled through the photos on her phone, stopping at the one she took of Dom when he first picked her up on the side of the road. The one she'd threatened to send to the cops if anything happened to her.

Dom was looking directly at the camera, not smiling. But the smoking hot image he presented was throughly photobombed by Piewicket, who was poking her little face out from behind his back, her eyes round and interested, her fur glowing from the sunlight.

Vinny laughed at the picture, then sighed. If only she'd known then just how tangled up she'd be by Dominic Salem. God damn.

"What're you looking at?" Emma asked, coming out onto the patio where Vinny was sitting.

Vinny showed her the picture. Emma smiled at it.

"They're both cute. When are you going to see them again?"

"On the twenty-first of never."

"What?" Emma asked. "You're kidding, right?"

"No. When he left, it was a permanent sort of thing."

"But…no." Emma seemed to be having trouble adjusting to the reality of Vin's situation. "That can't be right. Right?"

"It was good while it lasted, I have to admit," Vinny said. "I just wish it lasted a little longer."

"Wait. Did he really break it off with you cold?"

"Pretty much. He said it nicer, but he's got priorities, and a long-term relationship isn't one of them. Family first. And fighting evil second."

"Hard to argue with that, I guess," Emma said quietly. "But maybe he just needs some time to realize how amazing you are."

Vinny hung her head. "That's the worst part. He actually said that. I'm amazing. And it's still not enough." She leaned into Emma, feeling her friend's arm tighten over her shoulder. "This is nuts," she said. "I should be comforting you."

Emma said, "Eh. My soon-to-be-ex-husband nearly died because he was a selfish dumbass who let a demon talk him into making a really bad deal. I'd have negotiated way better perks per soul."

"Stop that," Vinny said, stifling a laugh.

"What else can I do besides joke? I'll lose my mind if I think about it too much. I just want to forget it. Don't you?"

"Yeah," Vinny said. But she didn't actually agree. She didn't want to forget any of it. It was like going back to black and white after seeing color for the first time. She wanted to know so much more.

But she also didn't want to worry Emma, who had plenty to worry about already, as she started to reassemble a life she'd put on hold for too long. So the two women just stayed there, huddled together while the sun set over the low mountain ridge to the west, the water in the bay turning as red and purple as the sky.

Hours later, Vinny's phone buzzed.

Emma, who was closer, picked it up. She frowned at the screen, then said, "*Undead wereferrets minimal threat. Also I miss you.* What is an undead wereferret?"

"Aw. He remembered." Vinny tried to stay cool, but a little shiver of hope ran through her body. He missed her?

"Explain."

Vinny shrugged. "It was just a thing we were talking about one time, and he said he'd look into it for me. It's not something we have to talk about now, because they're a minimal threat."

"He said he misses you," Emma pointed out. "Which is macho guy speak for he loves you."

"Don't make a text message into a declaration of love. If he meant that, he would have said it."

Emma snorted. "Like hell. He loves you but he's too afraid to say it."

"He fights vampires and demons. He's not scared of anything."

"Except being rejected by the woman he researched wereferret threat levels for. What are you going to reply?"

Vinny grabbed the phone. "Nothing!"

"Vin, you have to put yourself out there."

"That's exactly what I did! And he didn't want me."

"He made a mistake. You're about to make one too, if you don't give this thing with him another chance."

"He made himself really clear, Emma. You weren't there, but trust me. He very kindly told me that he had a great time, but I wasn't a long-term investment."

"Shut up with your one-percent speak. I know he didn't say those words. That's the sort of thing your parents would say."

That's exactly what her parents had said.

Emma was watching her intently. "Vin, not everyone is like your parents, seeing people as things. They messed up your childhood, but don't let their twisted mindset make your adult life miserable. You are worthy of love."

Vinny felt hot tears stinging her eyes. "I know."

"You agree, but I don't think you believe it yet. Say it."

"What are you, my therapist?"

"I'm your friend, which is like a therapist but with more wine. I love you. You came all the way out here to help me, and now I'm going to help you." Emma squeezed her tight. "Say it, bitch."

Vinny swallowed. "I'm worthy of love."

"Now say it like you believe it."

"I am worthy of love." The words felt odd to hear in her voice.

"He doesn't care if you're a musical prodigy," Emma told her. "He doesn't care about your last name or who you grew up with or how much money you've got in your Swiss bank account. Maybe a relationship with him won't work out, but you need to give it a shot. You listening?"

"Yes."

"So what are you going to do about it? Is there a ferret emoji?" Emma made a grab for the phone again.

"I'm not emoji-ing my way into a relationship!" Vinny held the phone out of reach. "Give me a minute to think."

She spent more than a minute, gazing at the night-blanketed valley scattered with tiny lights of other homes. Emma kept quiet.

Finally, Vinny took a deep breath. "Can I borrow a car? I have to do a thing."

"How long will it take?"

"If I'm lucky, the rest of my life."

Emma smiled. "Take the Benz, then. I never liked it."

She stood up. "Okay."

"Whoa. Not till tomorrow," Emma said quickly. "And not till after I make pancakes."

Vin laughed and sat back down. "In that case, I'll wait till tomorrow."

Epilogue

SHE DROVE THREE DAYS TO get to the small Ohio town that Salem Associates called their headquarters. Along the way, Vinny played old songs from all the bands she'd ever been in or played shows with, screaming at the top of her lungs, because she was in a Mercedes-Benz and no one could stop her.

But now, when she was at her destination, all the bravado melted away, leaving her shaking with nerves. Was she about to make a complete fool of herself?

Vinny parked the car on the road, just at the driveway of the address she knew was Dom's. A mailbox with the name Salem on it stood by the road. Well, *stood* was the wrong word. The mailbox leaned worse than the tower of Pisa, and the metal post looked like it had been whacked by a truck at least twice.

The house beyond didn't look that much better. It was one of those gigantic Victorian mansions that must have been gorgeous when it was new, but time had taken a toll. The rainbow of paint colors applied over the decades had all faded. Parts of the wooden siding were gone, and the roof sloped dangerously in places.

Still, someone was working on it, to judge by the pile of wooden beams to the side of the house. Scaffolding had been constructed along one wall where a huge bay window looked as if it was about to fall right out of the side of the house.

And yet there were flowers and plants growing in the front yard, obviously well cared for. Bright orange marigolds bloomed by the walkway, and there were white roses closer to the porch.

A guy in shorts and a tank top had been shooting hoops in the driveway when she pulled up. He stopped to watch her when she got out of the car and walked toward him.

He was like a younger, skinnier version of Dom. Same coloring, but definitely a later model. He tucked the basketball under his arm, giving her an inquisitive once-over.

"Afternoon," he said. His eyes were different than Dom's, she saw now. They were much lighter, almost a hazel. She got the sense that he was, and had always been, a good kid. "Sure you're not heading for the house across the street?"

Vinny looked over her shoulder. The house across the street looked popular. There were a bunch of workmen around and several cars in the drive. She turned back to the guy.

"I want the Salem house," she said.

"Oh. Then you're here." He paused, trying to guess *why* she was there. "You looking to hire us, or do you want to see a particular Salem?"

Maybe Dom hadn't even mentioned her to his brothers. Something in Vinny went cold. She made a mistake. She read way too much into a stupid text message. She should turn around and go.

The guy was still watching her. "You did want to see the Salems, right?"

"I want to see Dom."

The guy blinked at her use of the nickname. "He's inside. Or…actually." He pointed to the front porch.

Dom stood there, and Vinny's breath left her body. Lord, it had only been a few days, and she missed him so bad. Then he was joined by a slim, pretty Chinese woman, and Vinny hesitated. What else didn't she know about Dom's life?

Just as yet another guy walked out of the house—also a Salem brother, obviously—a meow reached her ear.

She turned her head in time to see a familiar shape. Piewicket streaked across the lawn toward her. Vinny crouched down to pick the cat up.

Pie nuzzled into her arms, purring madly.

"Well, at least someone's happy to see me." She glanced at Dom, and thus saw when the Chinese girl elbowed him sharply.

"Ow," Dom said. "I am happy to see you."

The girl rolled her eyes and stomped down the wooden steps. "Hi, I'm Lily," she said, offering a hand to shake.

"Vinny," said Vinny. Her arms were full of cat, but she extracted one hand to shake. Lily had been the one to help Dom on the phone. The researcher. Vinny felt better. "I don't know if Dom mentioned me, but I was there for the whole demon thing in Seattle."

"Oh, your name's come up." Lily threw a look over her shoulder. "Will one of you dorks invite Vinny in, please?"

"Does she know the secret handshake?" the youngest

guy asked, grinning. He was clearly enjoying the scene.

"Shut up, Lex," Dom said.

"Only if you invite her," Lex retorted. He nonchalantly rolled the basketball into the open garage, where it clattered against something in the dim back corner, followed by the sound of breaking glass. He winced. "Oops."

Dom walked toward Vinny, who still had Piewicket in her arms. He glanced back at everyone else standing around. "Don't you guys have anything better to do?" he asked crossly.

"Nope," said Lex.

"No way," the brother on the porch agreed. He was surveying Vinny with the air of a man who surveyed women very regularly.

Lily took pity. "Lex. Mal. Come inside and help me get dinner started."

"But the show's out here," Mal protested.

"You don't want to eat?" Lily asked. "Fine by me."

"Okay, okay, I'm coming."

Dom waited until the others filed inside. Then he said, "You didn't say you were stopping by."

"I'm very surprising sometimes."

"Agreed." He reached to take Piewicket out of her arms, and unceremoniously dumped the cat onto the lawn.

Pie yowled in protest.

"Tough," Dom said to the cat. To Vinny he said, "I really am happy to see you."

He proved it by catching her in his arms, holding her tight. She leaned forward to kiss him, and felt like she was spinning as Dom kissed her back. *This is how it's supposed to be when someone loves you*, she thought.

She was breathless when it was over, and the connection she felt to him practically crackled in the air.

"So. Miss me?" she said, as casually as she could. Her silly grin ruined it completely. She was so glad to see him, so electrified by his touch.

"Little bit. How long you thinking of staying?" he asked, trying to look cool and failing. He looked adorable when he was trying not to smile.

"Depends on you," she said. "How long you want me here?"

"We can talk about that." He looked her over, as if not quite believing she was there. "Assuming we can talk at all. Those monsters inside aren't going to shut up with all their questions."

"I'll risk it. What's this about an invite?"

Dom took her hands in his. "I need to invite you, or you can't come in. Even staying on the property would get difficult."

"Okay. So do it. Or is there some weird ritual?"

"Not usually. Otherwise getting pizza delivery would be super awkward. But I want to do this right."

He said, more formally, "Lavinia Rose Wellington Wake, I invite you into this house—"

"The house isn't enough," she interrupted.

"What?" he said, his face clouding.

"It's not good enough to invite me into the house. Maybe today it is," she amended. "But I want to be clear. If I stick around, if you want me to stick around, I'm not going to just stand by and be The Girlfriend. I'm going to learn what I have to do to fight like you. If you want me in your life, it's the whole life, or it's nothing. That's my offer."

Dom ran his hands over her shoulders and her arms, as if checking that she was real. "It's dangerous."

"I'm aware of that," she told him. "I've got a sneak

peek, and I'm still on board."

"There's a ton of stuff to learn, just the bare minimum to keep you safe. You need to know about spellcasting, which takes a long time to learn, and all the elements and signs. You need to know about how to use silver, and water..."

"Silver and water and love," she breathed. It all clicked. She remembered him saying that phrase, the iciness of the water, the relief she felt when she was released from the curse. The release that only worked because Dom loved her.

Dom looked surprised. "What?"

"That's what you said, in the river when you were holding me. When you were saving me. Silver and water and love."

"I had to say it. It was a sort of spell," he said, sounding shy.

"Was it a lie?" she asked.

"*No.*"

"So you love me. You loved me when you said it, and you love me now."

He nodded. "And I'll love you for a long time coming. The rest of our lives, if I'm lucky. For what that's worth."

"It's worth a lot."

"Be careful with your heart, Vin. Just because someone loves you doesn't mean you have to love them back. You said you had to think about it, and I believe you." He kissed her softly. "But yeah, I love you."

"Then you should know I love you too," she said. "I should have told you before, but...I'm not good at the whole love and relationship thing."

"Could have fooled me. Are you willing to give the whole love and relationship thing a go?"

"Are you willing to invite me in?"

He took her hands in his. "The handholding isn't necessary," he explained. "I just like to hold your hands. Ready?"

"Get on with it."

"Lavinia Rose Wellington Wake, I invite you into this house. You may rest in the beds here, eat food at the table here, feel the warmth at the hearth here. This place belongs to me and mine, and I open all doors to you. I, Dominic Benno Shelter Manuel North de Silva Salem, invite you."

"Wow." Vinny probably should respond with more decorum after that, but all she could do was smile. "That's your name?"

"Yup. Don't wear it out."

"I know all your secrets now, Dom."

"You don't know more than a sliver of my secrets, love."

Vinny laughed. "Okay, maybe not. But you still have to keep me close, right?"

"Definitely. Every day, every night." He smiled as he nudged the door open. "Now get in here. Welcome home."

* * * *

ABOUT THE AUTHOR

Elizabeth Cole is a romance writer with a penchant for history. Her stories draw upon her deep affection for the British Isles, action movies, medieval fantasies, and even science fiction. She now lives in a small house in a big city with a cat, a snake, and a rather charming gentleman. When not writing, she is usually curled in a corner reading...or watching costume dramas or things that explode. And yes, she believes in love at first sight.

www.ingramcontent.com/pod-product-compliance
Lightning Source LLC
Chambersburg PA
CBHW051644180726
48284CB00006B/1855